Landmark

Painter Place Saga 4

Pamela Poole
Inspiring Southern Ambiance
Published by Southern Sky Publishing

Dedication

For my Paw-Paw, who used to shake his head and mutter,
"Things sure have changed."
I can never thank you enough for all your prayers,
which Jesus faithfully continues to answer in my life
since you've gone on home to be with Him.

"One generation will declare Your works to the next
and will proclaim Your mighty acts."
Psalm 145:4

Author's Note

When I planned Landmark, Painter Place Saga 4, I was limited to working with characters, events, and places already established in the first three novels of the saga. This left me no freedom in my time frame. Characters had to meet and marry in the year 1960.

My research into the lives of teens and young adults in previous generations was thought-provoking due to their level of maturity. Education, morality, and community expectations for young people have changed dramatically.

The decade of the 1950s was the origin of modern dating and is iconic to American culture. Dating was an American phenomenon, practiced in few other countries and never on the level of freedom in this one. There were more intact family units to advise teens. Most people acknowledged standards of morality and church attendance was normal. Teens in the 1950's-1960 had more supervision and accountability. A chaperoned date was ideal and group dating was encouraged. Communities wrote up written agreements between parents and teens outlining what was and was not acceptable courtship behavior. Parents approved of "steadies," as these couples often got engaged and married.

The privacy of cars changed dating behavior. After spending $1.20 on a date, men expected women to be warm by "parking" with them. Yet, virtue was still considered ideal. One young lady wrote to a popular teen magazine that though she gave in to her past boyfriend and was no longer a virgin, she regretted it deeply and asked God to forgive her. She knew He would, yet she said she would always have the scar of what happened.

Considering the headlines today about the consequences of impropriety and the ridicule of the "Billy Graham Rule" for purity, perhaps readers will appreciate this look back in time.

Painter Place 1985
25 years after the prayers and hard work of the couples in this story.

Chapter One

Noble Painter missed his wife, daughter, and youngest son. His eldest son, Wyeth, would soon graduate college and come home to settle down as the future heir to Painter Place. If the Lord let the family continue to live on the island, Wyeth would be the one to hold on to it for another generation.

In a few weeks, Painter Place would be busy with summer guests. The Big House and cottages needed maintenance before the family hosted artists, writers, and musicians in need of a retreat or inspiration. College groups doing research would set up tents and study habitats and plants, and the northern side of the island would be busy with youth group camps.

All this waited for him back in America, in a South that was north of this wild jungle. Noble ached to get back to the challenges of life on a barrier island in South Carolina. He wiped off paint brushes that still had a few paintings left in them, but he tossed more than he kept into a trash can near his worktable. He would leave tomorrow, and after this private commission, he wouldn't have time to paint for a while.

The finality in the sound of the latches snapping on his biggest paint box made him sigh. Out of habit, he ran his finger over the engraved plate on the front that bore his father's name, Samuel Painter. Like his father, he closed the box that way only upon satisfaction with a job.

Noble was more than satisfied with this painting, however. He thought it marked the peak of his career, yet the public would never know about it. That was part of the agreement when he'd accepted a ludicrous amount of money for this commission.

He turned around to face weeks of constant work and met the chatoyant gaze of the wild animal in front of him. Nimble grace veiled the coiled energy which would translate into a terrifying spring, and silent paws rested on the peeling gray bark of a tree weathered by ruthless jungle elements. As he considered how he'd captured the phantom silence of this chilling predator, a powerful voice close by startled him.

"It's magnificent, Mr. Painter." With lithe movements like those of the giant cat, a man known to Noble only as Chavarria came near to stand shoulder to shoulder. The collector continued his assessment of the painting in an accent nuanced with Spanish. "You have far surpassed my imagination for this mission. It's hard to believe that the artist who created this masterpiece has never been in the Amazon jungle. I confess, I only agreed to this gift from my friend because he was adamant about it."

Another voice, in an American accent, hailed them from the doorway. It was the man Noble knew as Weaver. "And now, you can't imagine how you've lived without it."

Weaver came to stand with them, and his handshake was as straightforward as his manner and bearing. But his face was unforgettable, unsettling, and etched with a million stories he'd never tell.

These men lived secret lives; Noble was sure of that. He felt the same controlled energy in each of them that had inspired his depiction of the giant jaguar in the painting. Yet, they let him study their eyes as if they hoped he'd see their souls. They'd won his trust, and nothing else would have lured him into an untamed tangle of jungle that time had forgotten. Their unpredictable absences, helicopter landings, specialized vehicles, furtive meetings, and distant gunfire around the walled estate had all driven Noble to finish the private commission and get back home.

"Where did you place your signature?" asked Weaver, scanning over it with eyes trained to miss nothing.

Moving a step closer, Noble pointed at a stout tree trunk that lurked in the background. His signature crept up the textured bark like a chameleon. "It worked well here as part of the texture, and yet, once it's seen, you'll always be able to pick it out again."

Chavarria nudged Weaver as he gestured to the image. "See that edge on the jaguar's silky coat, just over there? It blurs, as if he's moved while we were looking at him!"

With a long forefinger pointed at the cat, Noble moved like a maestro. "You'll find that effect around the front paw, and the ear and whiskers. Blurred edges breathe life into a subject, so it isn't a cut-out image pasted against a background. Few people pick up the illusion. Unless you have a title for the painting, I simply named it *Jaguar*."

"It is incomparable!" exclaimed Chavarria. "I regret that such a prize must hang in this secluded jungle compound. I'm glad you approve of the commissioned frame from jungle hardwoods and hope you'll visit again someday to see it hanging on that wall. It will dominate this room."

The man named Weaver grunted. "It's fortunate for Mr. Painter that he had our photos to do all the planning and composition before arriving. He wears the unmistakable look of homesickness."

Noble locked eyes with him and sensed the reference to his home was opening a door. He waited in slow ticking Southern moments for Weaver to walk through it.

"Mr. Painter, I'm sure it's been lonely here. Chavarria and I aren't good company even when we're around, and there's little about a day in the compound that's normal. But we've enjoyed having you with us. We're reminded of the things in life we never had, and that there are still good people in the world."

"I didn't expect to come here for a vacation, Mr. Weaver, and being an artist can be a lonely profession. We all had a demanding job to do, and we did our best. I've enjoyed your company at dinner and appreciate the gracious hospitality. But as you say, I miss my home and family. My oldest son will soon graduate college and come home to stay. It's time to look toward what lies ahead."

Weaver smiled and exchanged a look with Chavarria. "Tonight, we'll celebrate your painting and Wyeth's accomplishment. Over dinner, I'd like to discuss a matter that concerns him and the future of Painter Place."

From the beginning, Noble sensed this painting commission wasn't only about his reputation as an artist. This was a test, and there was no use playing games with a man like Weaver. But the island and his heir? That could only mean one thing. How had he not seen this coming?

"You have a daughter," he stated.

Weaver held his eyes. "Yes. A remarkable one."

May 1960, Charleston, South Carolina

It was a sunny spring afternoon on the Charleston peninsula, and Phil Gregory hummed to himself. Things were great at Gregory Global, his family's company. It felt right again on the island of Painter Place since Noble Painter had returned home from South America, and their sons were home from college to settle down. It was a new era. There was a fresh wind blowing.

His wife Lucinda and the new housekeeper unpacked boxes in the historic property he'd purchased on Church Street. Someday, if the Lord was willing, he'd retire here. At least, that's what he'd promised Lucinda. Though he could hold his own, he was among the men in the Gregory lineage that didn't have the natural gift of financial genius to thrive at the family business. While trying to live up to the legends of ancestors in the past, they ran full throttle until they dropped dead. Lucinda didn't enjoy his jest that at least they left this earth doing what they loved.

This house in Charleston was the only way he'd keep from watching over his son Phillip's shoulder while he trained him to be the future head of Gregory Global. His oldest son oozed genius and confidence, and he was mature beyond his years. But he'd have to learn a few things the hard way. Phil couldn't spare him from lessons learned by failure, loss, and embarrassment.

He hummed the Glenn Miller tune he and Lucinda had danced to last night amid boxes in the living room. Stepping into a restaurant from the busy East Bay Street, he told the hostess he was meeting Mr. Montgomery Heyward for lunch. Her smile brightened, and she led him to a table far from other guests. Heyward rose from his chair and extended a warm handshake. He had striking features, but it was the man's magnetism that made Phil Gregory decide that he liked him on the spot.

After praying a blessing over the coming meal, their next conversation focused on Phil's recent purchase of the property on Church Street. As two waiters brought out steaming plates to the table, Montgomery stated, "I ordered for both of us. I hope I chose well."

Phil replied that he appreciated the kind gesture, and as he surveyed his plate, he appreciated the Low Country fare before him. His gracious host was treating this meeting as if he'd invited him to his own home, and Phil now realized this was more than business. Conversation between them was easy, and waiters came to clear away the table when he put down his fork. Over cups of steaming lemon tea, Montgomery told Phil that his daughter was a decorator whose team had worked in well-known historic homes.

Phil said he would need a decorator's advice soon and he would remember her. He enjoyed a sip of the tea in companionable silence, listening to the buzz of subdued conversation and the clink of flatware on dishes. He waited, sensing that his host would soon bring up the reason for this meeting.

Montgomery reached beside his chair, and for the first time, Phil realized he had a briefcase. He opened a clasp on a long envelope to remove photos and a paper, then he slid the information closer to his guest. "Phil, my daughter is the reason I asked you to meet with me. She's in the top photo."

"She's beautiful," Phil said. The young lady in the photo before him had enchanting eyes and an engaging smile.

His host's expression was soft. "She's so much more than that. When she walks into a room, she owns it. If she has an enemy, I've never heard of it. Look at the next two photos."

"What's her name?"

"Camellia Melody. She's named for the famous camellias at Magnolia Plantation that were blooming when she was born, and for the way she made her mom and me want to sing. We lost a baby before she was born and didn't think we'd have another one. You can imagine our joy at her safe arrival. It was a struggle not to spoil her."

With a lingering sigh, Phil said, "Yes. I understand. Lucinda and I—we had a miscarriage." It was always unexpected, that familiar ache, when he thought about the daughter waiting for him in heaven.

"I'm so sorry. It's something we must accept, but we never forget."

Montgomery took a pensive sip of the lemon tea, then he leaned back with an agitated set to his mouth. His eyes were stormy when he snorted, "The only eligible bachelors here in Charleston aren't even close to deserving Cami. Most of them are in those photos. See the guy who shoves his way to her side all the time?"

Phil nearly smiled at Montgomery's telltale opinion of the young man. He couldn't see the shoving in a still photo, but he thought he could tell which one it was. "The good-looking guy in the blazer, with dark hair and an arrogant smirk?"

Montgomery grunted and rubbed his face. "He's ready to propose to her. I have a friend at a local jewelry store, and he told me this young man had a family heirloom ring resized for her. He's from dwindling old Charleston money and his family wants him to make a smart match."

Phil looked across the table at the new friend who'd confessed a dilemma he could relate to. "Is he the one she wants?"

"She's never met a guy she wants. They are long-time friends, and he's been turning up the heat. I found out he's been an overnight guest with other women on his college campus. No one dares to tell her. But she grows lonelier and more bored every day. She's twenty years old, and she wants to start a family. Most of her closest friends are engaged, or married, with children."

Phil looked down at the photo in front of him again as he sipped the tea in his cup. His skin prickled with anticipation. Did Montgomery want advice about how to protect his daughter's inheritance in a prenuptial contract? "Why tell me this?"

Montgomery met his eyes. "I have a proposal. A smart match—between my Cami and your Phillip."

Phil coughed into the last sip of tea. How had he not seen this coming? His phone had rung at least a dozen times this spring with connections who knew his oldest son was out of college and ready to step into Gregory Global. The world seemed to be full of smart, beautiful, accomplished young heiresses who wanted a chance to become Phil's daughter-in-law.

He reached for the soft cloth napkin in his lap and tried to regain his composure. Montgomery sat up and pointed at the image of his daughter. "Cami must leave Charleston. I want my grandchildren to grow up at Painter Place. Your younger son is her age, but he will live in London, and I can't bear being that far away from her. The younger Painter brother is her age and he's next on my list if you don't think this will work out. But Phillip is far and away the best match. He's strong-willed and confident, and he likes a challenge. Cami needs someone who attracts people, so she doesn't outshine him. That would wear on a man."

Phil shook his head and rubbed his forehead with his hand. By the time he looked back at Montgomery, he was warming to his proposal. "I see you've discovered our guidelines for marriages at Painter Place. It's how we've survived, marrying well. Our children court a potential spouse under restrictions, for obvious legal and financial protection against false accusations, gossip, and for moral implications. Our families must approve a match. Many people view us as odd, and we don't dispute that."

In appeal to his position, Phil held out both palms. "A bad match would disrupt the way we live and work together on the island. We want the couples to choose each other and have what it takes to stay together when romance runs thin. For now, I don't want my son to know we had this conversation. Do you have a plan for Phillip to meet Camellia?"

Excitement flickered in Montgomery's eyes. "There is a concert in the gazebo at the Battery in White Point Gardens this Thursday evening. Camellia will attend, along with her single friends. Invent a reason for your son to come to Charleston, with both the Painter boys. I promise you, he will notice my daughter, but if not, Andy Painter will. And Phil—"

Montgomery leaned toward him. "Phillip places more value on things that don't come easy. He'll get the challenge he thrives on to win her."

Chapter Two

The wafting breeze from the Ashley River caressed concertgoers and teased towering palm trees in White Point Gardens. It was a lovely May evening in Charleston, South Carolina, a Thursday that felt like the weekend had already arrived. A scattering of tourists and other visitors of all ages filled the park at the tip of the peninsula, but it was the young adults from among local families that dominated the crowd. Clusters of friends gathered in semi-formal attire around lamp posts and park benches. Their laughter rose to mingle with the cry of gulls, the clopping sound of carriage horses pulling tourists, and passing motorboats in the river.

Four young men strolled leisurely from Church Street to the park as musicians tuned instruments in the gazebo bandstand. Phillip Gregory, Jr. had a list of things to do at the new property before returning to Painter Place on Saturday. His lifelong best friend, Wyeth Painter, had some business to take care of in a downtown Charleston gallery that carried his artwork. Wyeth's younger brother, Andy Painter, would take Phillip's younger brother, Justin, on a job with a fishing charter.

Phillip's dad had insisted that they have fun by attending the concert. The four young men reached White Point Gardens just as the colors of a coastal twilight dimmed and the stars came out. Justin Gregory gave a low whistle and drawled, "Charleston girls are easy on the eyes."

"You'd better let me know who you've scouted out, so I don't meet her first," quipped Andy Painter.

"Right, there's always that. I'll try to leave the one who looks most like a fish for you."

Wyeth scowled at them like a parent with unruly children, then glanced at Phillip. He did a double take at the look on his friend's face, then he followed his eyes. It wasn't hard to tell what had captured Phillip's attention. Wyeth watched her glide among her friends with a warm smile that had the effect of a candle to light each of them. They reacted by reaching out to touch her as if it was a special experience.

She didn't dress to be noticed like many other girls, but then, she didn't need to. Her simple, classy white sleeveless sweater sported a huge flat bow that lay front to back over her left shoulder, and a slender sage green skirt was modest while revealing a beautiful figure. Dangling earrings and a bracelet sparkled in the park lanterns overhead as she gracefully raised a hand to greet someone.

"Diamonds," Wyeth muttered, and he watched as several men arrived and walked straight up to her to greet her. She smiled and complimented them without committing to the dances they asked for.

Wyeth groaned. "Phillip, it's just like you to pick the only girl here that's impossible to get."

Then it happened. She looked over, noticed Phillip, and lost her train of thought in mid-conversation. Their eyes locked, and Wyeth would have sworn he saw a fateful flash. He knew he'd never forget it. She seemed bewildered, then recovered, turning her attention back to her friends. But she was distracted and ventured another look back to find Phillip. He hadn't moved or spoken. When she realized he'd caught her looking for him, she blushed and turned away.

Phillip kept his eyes on the young lady, but he turned his face toward Wyeth. "I didn't pick her. She picked me. And I'm not lettin' her down."

Wyeth turned to Andy and snarled, "Get ready. He might get us all in a fight."

Andy laughed in delight, watching a dark-haired guy beside the young lady reach out to touch her shoulder as if he couldn't help himself. She turned to smile at him even as she pulled away from his touch. "So much for our role as ambassadors. Look, the other girls all smile and try to be near Miss Congeniality."

Phillip's eyes never left the young woman when he responded. "That's because she's not a threat. They all want to be around so the guys will notice them."

The brothers all looked at one another, their expressions asking where in the world he'd gotten such an idea. The young woman laughed at something a friend said, and Phillip took an instinctive step forward, drawn to the sound like a siren call.

Wyeth scowled and stepped up to match him, growling to him under his breath that a woman dripping diamonds was a socialite who would never like Whitehaven and Painter Place. The rest of her friends laughed with her as if on cue. Another came up behind her to whisper something, and as she turned her head, her dangling diamond earring flashed against the creamy, flawless skin of her long neck.

As the friend pushed to position herself between the young blonde woman and the guy who had touched her, the blonde woman glanced back toward Phillip. Their eyes locked again, but she dragged hers away when the man who'd touched her shoulder earlier reached past her friend and pulled her arm.

The music had begun, and he acted like a dance was his privilege. She hesitated for a moment in which his expression grew annoyed. He leaned to say something in her ear as he pulled again, and she yielded.

Justin came to stand beside his brother and crossed his arms over his chest. "I don't know much about women, but this one doesn't want that guy to handle her, and she's curious about you."

"Don't encourage him, Justin—that guy's no wimp," warned Wyeth from his place on Phillip's other side. "Phillip would have his hands full, and we don't know yet how many friends he has."

Wyeth needed a breath and drew a deep one. His dad would be upset if they came to Charleston and got into trouble. They were the face of Painter Place.

"I want to watch them dance," Phillip announced. Wyeth noticed his best friend was looking the young lady over the same way he looked at a sports car he might invest in. As she danced, the slit in the slender skirt allowed the curves of her legs to peek through. In a park full of women tonight, some were prettier. But there was nothing to criticize about this jewel.

The blonde's partner caught her stealing a few glances at Phillip. He communicated his displeasure with a narrow stare at the object of her interest and a few sharp words to her face. Wyeth tried to read his lips. He seemed to ask what was so interesting about a stranger. She coolly ignored him, and his expression transformed into a possessive one.

Andy Painter positioned himself beside his brother, anticipating action. Wyeth glanced over at him and did a double take. "Put the beer can in the trash, Andy."

"A guy handed it to me so he could dance. It doesn't hurt to hold it."

"Then I'll make it hurt if you don't throw it away!" Wyeth barked. "If that doesn't work, I'll sic Phillip on you. You know what he'll do if he wakes from this trance and sees you with it. His tolerance level for alcohol is far into the negative side of a number line."

"He's playing peek-a-boo with the popular girl. He's oblivious to anyone else at the concert right now. I dare you to interrupt him."

Justin leaned forward and looked at Andy and Wyeth. He scowled at Andy. "If your own brother doesn't take you out, mine will. There's not supposed to be any alcohol on the premises."

Andy took a step backward with a hand up in surrender. "Okay, okay. When the guy comes back for it, I'll tell him to bring his problem to you."

The song ended, and the band's front man spoke to the audience, observing what a wonderful evening it was in the harbor. The blonde and the man she had been dancing with re-joined their circle of friends. She ignored his attitude as she talked to the other young ladies, and he started talking too loud to several other guys. They glanced over at Phillip, Justin, Wyeth, and Andy.

Some girls in another group waved frantically to get the blonde's attention. "Camellia!"

"Camellia," Wyeth heard Phillip say. He mouthed it, tasting it, and Wyeth knew his friend was thinking of how Camellia Gregory sounded.

He leaned behind Phillip's back to look over at Justin, who'd done the same on the other side. They raised their brows as they exchanged an alarmed look.

The young lady brightened when she saw another group of friends, and she waved. She touched the athletic arm of her former dance partner, the way a butterfly lights on a flower, and told him she'd be back soon. The dark-haired young man turned from his conversation with other guys and caught her hand, asking where she was going.

Camellia's smile was tight, and she nodded in the direction of the other group. He started to excuse himself from his friends, but she shook her head and pulled away, leaving the young man scowling after her. She greeted friends in the new group while Phillip watched them hug her. Then they giggled and directed her attention to the Painter and Gregory group. They sent all the right signals that they'd like to meet them.

Camellia's eyes found Phillip's, and this time, she didn't act embarrassed or look away.

Phillip commanded, "Let's go."

Phillip hoped he wouldn't stammer his introduction. "Like everyone else here tonight, I'm under your spell," he began, then hesitated. Camellia's eyes were like gemstones with facets cut to show off nuances of cool green. He blinked and cleared his throat. "I'm Phillip Gregory, and these are my brother and friends."

The Painters and Justin introduced themselves, and the eager group of young ladies responded with their names. The pairs seemed to sort themselves out according to mutual admiration just as the next song began with an instrumental solo. Phillip's mood soared. *Perfect*.

"Will you honor me with this dance?" he asked, extending his right hand. Camellia allowed him to take hers and lead her near the bandstand gazebo.

The poignant strains of the band's instruments tripped along in the soft breeze of the harbor. "I love this song," she murmured as the band leader smoothly cooed the words to "Stranger In Paradise."

"Did you know it's sung by a young Caliph to the woman he falls in love with at first sight, in the musical *Kismet*?" Phillip asked.

She turned to him in surprise. "Yes. Kismet means 'fate,' but I don't believe in fate for Christians. They pray to know when the right one comes along, and they meet their futures trusting that God is in charge."

Phillip's spirit soared, and he smiled with satisfaction. She was a Christian, and she knew how to defend what she believed. "Well said," he responded in a deep drawl.

"You're an expert dancer, Phillip Gregory."

"Every dance lesson and hours of practice culminated in this first dance with you—the only dance that ever mattered."

Camellia's lips parted in surprise at the boldness of the young man she was dancing with, and she couldn't think of an appropriate response. Then he did the most unexpected, romantic thing she had ever imagined. He softly sang the words of the song to her. "If I stand starry-eyed, that's the danger in paradise, for mortals who stand beside an angel like you."

She caught her breath. None of her male friends knew more than just the chorus to this song, and only a few had the confidence to sing a romantic song to a young lady.

"So, open your arms to the stranger in paradise," he sang near her ear, pulling her closer. She was so affected that she blinked back tears. She closed her eyes, escaping to another reality with this handsome, dark-haired stranger. Her heart insisted he was what she'd been waiting for, but how could it know so soon?

She blended her voice with Phillip Gregory's. Time seemed to have evaporated as she danced with this dreamy stranger, and she wished the moment would never end.

The next song began. She reset the respectable space between them. Her wits lay scattered in hopeless confusion around their feet in the trampled sand, and she chided herself for being in imminent danger of losing her heart to a suave stranger.

She blushed. A man who looked like this and exuded such power and confidence had to have a long trail of broken hearts behind him. She didn't plan to be the next one.

"No doubt a guy like you gets a lot of chances to dance and sing love songs," she ventured. "But I'm not one to swoon over a handsome face with a romantic pickup line."

Even as she spoke the last words, she wished she hadn't. Her delivery lacked any conviction at all, and she wondered if he guessed she was making a plea to know if he'd meant the song for her. His jaw clenched, and his eyes hardened as he looked over her head. He didn't correct her or respond, and they danced in awkward silence.

She looked around and noticed his friends were enjoying the company of hers.

"Your boyfriend is over there, with one of the other girls—the one who sends him all the signals she wants to be with him," Phillip said in a steely Southern drawl.

She looked at the band instead. "He's not my boyfriend, just a long-time friend. She knows she's welcome to him."

"He plans to be more than a friend. But that won't happen."

Startled, Camellia turned to search his face. Brian and his partner appeared alongside them, and she smiled at the other young lady. But Brian smirked at Phillip while he addressed her. "Camellia, it's late and your daddy expects me to get you back home soon. Just one more dance before your friend leaves town. Don't forget who's takin' you home."

He danced away as if he'd put a child in her place. Phillip remained relaxed. His brother and friends danced nearby with her friends, and she knew they had surrounded him.

The next song had a faster tempo, a good one for easing the tension between them. She was herself again, laughing and having fun.

When the music ended, he rushed to pull her by the hand to the side of the park nearest Church Street. He ducked them out of Brian's sight on the far side of a thick oak tree trunk, pausing a minute so they could catch their breath. They were reading one another's eyes in the filtered glow of the lantern light through the bent low-hanging branches.

"Cami Heyward, can I have your phone number? I won't undermine your dad's plan for you tonight, but I want to call him and ask if I can see you again. My dad bought a house on Church Street, and I'm only here for two days. But I live on an island not far up the coast and I can come back anytime you want me to."

Camellia nodded, hoping she wasn't betraying how star-struck she felt. Phillip had called her Cami, like her daddy did! He pulled two business cards from his pocket and pressed one into her hand. Then he picked up a burned wooden match and used the charred end to mark her number on the back of the other card.

When he looked back up, she was studying his face in the shadows as if she didn't think she'd ever see him again. Embarrassed, she turned her eyes away and gulped. He squeezed her hand and glanced around the tree trunk to find the self-appointed boyfriend searching for her.

He spoke in a breathy rush. "Cami, where I live, we have several public dances a year, and a ballroom for the New Year's Dance. We're brought up to dance to all kinds of music. I also need to interact in social situations with my dad's company. I can tell you're from an old Charleston family with the same expectations, so you'll understand."

He tucked a finger under her chin to make her meet his eyes. "Just so you know, I've never sung a love song to a girl before, and I'd never sing words like that to mislead you. From now on, when I hear that song, I'll remember how it felt to be with you. Like the song says, I hang suspended until I know there's a chance you feel the same about me. I'll call your dad so I won't be a stranger in paradise any longer than I can help it."

Then, with a resolute sigh, he said, "You should go. Brian and I can't meet right now." She nodded and tucked his card into her skirt waistband, then she turned to walk toward the crowd.

Chapter Three

On Friday, Phillip sat on a wicker chair on the upstairs piazza, enjoying the enveloping warmth of the morning sunshine in Charleston. Only a block away, the traffic noises on East Bay Street drifted up in the stirring breeze. Tourists enjoyed strolling toward the waterfront at the Battery, and neighbors jogged or walked their dogs. He looked to the southeast, toward Cami's home on Murray Boulevard. He'd found her last name in the phone book and there was only one listing closest to White Point Gardens. Montgomery Heyward had to be her father.

He was alone today with a list of chores in his dad's precise handwriting, but daydreaming would make it difficult to concentrate on his dad's expectations. What if he worked on the list until it was an acceptable time of day to call Cami's house? She might be home. But her dad was likely off at whatever his business was, and that meant Phillip was free to talk to her. If Montgomery Heyward was at home, he'd go back to the main plan, which was inevitable, anyway.

Humming tunes from the dance the night before, Phillip worked to check off items on his dad's list. At eleven thirty, he stopped where he was and picked up the phone receiver.

He set it back down. He stood staring at it, trying to calm his nerves in case Camellia's dad answered instead of her. With a quick but desperate prayer for the right words to express himself, he reached for the receiver again. This time, he dialed her number.

Perhaps if this went well, he could ask her to lunch. He mused over an impressive restaurant choice for their first date as he heard the phone ringing.

"Montgomery Heyward speaking."

Phillip felt a cold sweat. "Sir, my name is Phillip Gregory. I met your daughter Camellia at the concert last night. I'd like your permission to speak to her today and to see her again."

"Mr. Gregory, I'm not inclined to encourage male callers—on the phone or at my door—to speak to my daughter unless they live in Charleston. Will you be moving here with your family's business?"

Phillip changed the phone receiver to his other ear, raising his eyebrows. Camellia's father knew who he was and where he lived. She must have talked about him and shown him the business card he'd given her. Surely, being the heir of Gregory Global worked in Phillip's favor. He had not planned to disclose that information to Mr. Heyward right off the bat, but it was out there now. His confidence crept back up.

"No, sir. I'll stay at Painter Place and take over my father's company someday in Whitehaven. He'll retire in Charleston."

"My daughter has a good job here as a junior decorator for an established interior design company, and her friends are in Charleston's top social circles."

"Sir—"

"Our conversation is over, young man, unless you have a change of address in your future."

"What if I set her up in her own interior design company?"

Now it was Mr. Heyward's turn to pause, and it sounded to Phillip like he changed the receiver to the other ear. Heyward replied coldly, "Son, there were days in Charleston when I could have called you out to a duel!"

Phillip blinked, regrouping after realizing his blurted offer was misconstrued. A duel?

He stammered, "Sir, if you've checked on who I am, you know I don't collect women. I assure you I'd never dishonor Cami or her reputation in society. I just want an exceptional woman to become my wife."

This declaration echoed in his ears and he bit his lip. With an effort, he turned his attention again to Montgomery Heyward's voice informing him that if that were the case, Phillip might be too late. His daughter was heading to a certain café on King Street to meet a man for lunch, and he expected that this eligible Charleston bachelor was proposing today. "We'll also be traveling out of town next week, so Cami will not be available."

Phillip's mind raced. He needed to get off the phone. "In that case, will you please do the honorable thing and tell her I tried? I said I'd call and I'm a man of my word, not empty promises."

Mr. Heyward's intake of breath was so sharp that Phillip wondered if he'd crossed the line. But his resolve and confidence soared. Cami chose him last night.

Heyward's voice now took on that threatening edge he'd adopted when he mentioned a duel. "Mr. Gregory let's have a gentlemen's understanding. The sun rises and sets on my wife and my daughter in my life. Cami is my only child. It will take something epic to take her away from Charleston. But because you insist, I'll tell her that you followed through on your promise. Goodbye."

Phillip heard a firm click when Camellia's father hung up on him. He slammed the receiver into the cradle and gathered his wallet and a house key. He was going out to find her.

After that, he'd brainstorm something epic to get her out of Charleston.

Montgomery Heyward must be mistaken, Phillip thought. For a guy with a pedigree, Brian had chosen an unremarkable place to propose to the love of his life. And why had Camellia's father dropped the name of the cafe to him over the phone?

Cami was there with Brian, at a small table for two. Phillip would go unnoticed in the high-backed booths along the side of the room, and he slid into one that gave him earshot and glimpses of Cami from around another couple. With a glance at the menu, he considered what didn't have garlic or onions before he ordered.

As he waited for his lunch and took a sip of his iced tea, he watched Brian take Camellia's hand from across the table before their food arrived. He gave her what must be his most winsome approach as he made his appeal for a commitment, and Phillip fought a pang of nervous jealousy. Then Camellia told Brian he needed to focus on his last year of college.

Triumph blasted off in Phillip's heart. This was a gentle Southern way of refusing an ardent suitor. But it only made Brian more passionate. He pleaded his case by saying that her attraction to a total stranger last night had made him aware of how important she was to him and his future.

Nodding thanks to the waitress as she set his lunch on the table, Phillip considered Brian's cold blunder. She was "important to him and his future?" His own perspective on romance was limited. But the right words from Brian would convey his jealousy over her attention to another man, his devotion to her, and his heartbreak if he lost her.

What happened next made Phillip stop as he reached for another bite of his sandwich. Brian pulled out a ring box and reached across the table, pressing it into Camellia's hand.

Camellia stiffened in surprise and hid the box under her napkin as a waitress brought their lunch. She smiled and engaged in chit-chat with the waitress before she went back to work.

Brian scowled as he leaned forward on the little table and pulled the napkin away. Phillip absently chewed the delayed bite of his lunch, watching Camellia, who looked out the window and covered her mouth with her hand.

A young lady rushed into the door of the café. She found Camellia and hurried straight to her table, where she delivered news that jolted her. She reached for her sleek white clutch purse while her friend rushed back out the café door.

Brian shook his head and wiped his hand over his face, forgetting her lack of interest in his engagement ring. He snorted in disdain and said, "You can't get involved in this, Camellia. How did Tom let himself get caught? He knows better! We carry protection in our wallet so we're ready for every opportunity."

Phillip snapped his jaw closed, realizing he'd been gaping with food in his mouth. Brian withered at Camellia's expression. She held out her hand to him, asking for his wallet. Brian stammered something unintelligible from where Phillip sat. But he read Brian's stricken face, and his contrite tone as he reached to grasp her hand in both of his.

She evaded his touch and his expression turned to one of infinite, long-suffering patience. As if he was explaining something to a child, he said, "Sweetheart, you deserve better than a schoolboy."

Phillip flinched. This excuse always made him feel like he'd been slapped. He didn't appreciate Brian's insinuation that his own decision about purity put him in the category of an uninitiated schoolboy. Too often in college, he and Wyeth dealt with scorn from others when they didn't go to drinking parties or spend time alone with young ladies.

His anger flared, and he moved closer to the edge of the booth's bench seat. Camellia gathered her dignity and abruptly rose, almost upsetting her chair. She tossed the unopened ring box at Brian, who caught it before it fell into the floor.

"You're right!" she spat out, oblivious to the patrons who'd turned to watch the drama. "I deserve a godly Christian man, not an immature schoolboy who chases one escapade after another, brags to his friends, and justifies immorality by equating it with maturity! I deserve a man who doesn't hold my hand with hands he's had all over other women. It never occurred to me to think of my wedding night as a performance, you dolt! But then, that's none of your business, since it never occurred to me that you'd be there."

Brian shot to his feet with alarm and protested as she marched to the door. Phillip slapped a bill on the table to cover his half-eaten meal and a generous tip, then rushed out after her, dodging people on the sidewalk.

Reaching for her arm, he called, "Cami!" She jerked her arm away and turned on him. Surprise registered on her face, and he wondered if she'd been expecting Brian.

"I want to see your wallet," she announced. Her eyes were hard, but he saw the tremble of her lips as she held out her hand.

Recovering his presence of mind, he was glad he'd stuffed plenty of cash in his wallet before heading to King Street. He quipped, "My dad taught me to watch out for women who only want my money."

Her eyes flashed, and she continued to hold out a manicured hand. Phillip excused himself to a group of passers-by for being in the middle of the sidewalk, then he took her arm to lead her out of the way to the wall inset of a storefront. He reached into his pocket and handed her his wallet. "You need ID now? I thought Charleston was the most courteous city in America."

Shoppers and tourists passed as she glanced through his things. Handing it back to him, she ordered, "Your pockets."

"Excuse me?" Phillip's mind raced as she stood unmoved. He glanced around, then grasped her elbow to pull her to the corner of a tiny alley. He held up his hands. "I dare you."

"You know I can't do that, and I don't know how to explain this to you." When she looked out to the uneven cobblestones on the street, a haunting sadness crossed her face and squeezed his heart. He was only the wiser because of guy-talk and machines in men's restrooms.

This wasn't the same young lady he had danced with last night. She showed no sign of attraction to him.

He fished for his Swiss Army pocketknife and the key to the house. He held them out and pulled the lining of his pockets to prove they were empty. "This is everything I have on me. You sure have an unconventional way of gettin' to know a guy."

She flushed and looked away. He stood there drinking in her profile.

"Do you have to be anywhere?" she asked.

"Anywhere you are."

"You don't know what you're in for."

"And I don't care."

Her eyes were gauging whether he was serious. "You will," she answered, wearing that tragic expression he'd glimpsed earlier. Then she stepped out of the alley.

He caught up with her again and strode by her side, tucking his pocketknife and wallet back into his pants. He saw they weren't heading toward the tourist side of town. When they reached a shabby building with a sign advertising health services, she stopped and took a deep breath to collect herself.

Only Phillip's trust in her made him open the door, and she marched into an institutional-looking waiting room with a medicinal odor. At the front desk, she asked if her friend Jacqueline had arrived yet.

His heart sank. The receptionist said she'd just gone back with a nurse, and Camellia asked to see them. When she admitted that she wasn't a family member, the receptionist refused, and Camellia bolted through the door to the offices.

Calling her friend's name, she searched the hall. A nurse came to see what was going on, and Jacqueline ran into Camellia's arms. Both started bawling, and before he had time to think of what he was doing, Phillip motioned the nurses away in his best authoritative manner.

"They said it's only a mass of tissue, and they can make this go away so I can live life the way I planned," sobbed Jacqueline. "Tom—he doesn't want anyone to know what we've done, especially at church! Our dads are both deacons. I can't run off and have this baby alone, Camellia, you know I can't. And worse—this changed everything. Tom doesn't love me anymore!"

Camellia held her outside on the street, walking her away from the door with a disgusted last look at it. Phillip's head was spinning. She was not kidding when she said he didn't know what he was getting into.

Then he caught his breath. She had left the café on her way here to stop her friend from killing her baby—alone. She was crying, vulnerable, and she didn't know what to do next.

"Follow me," he ordered, considering the shortest route to his parents' new property on Church Street.

Chapter Four

Camellia thanked Phillip for the hospitality as she settled Jacqueline onto a sofa and phoned Tom. Then she asked to use the powder room, and when she came back, she had repaired makeup ravaged by tears. She asked if she could make tea.

Phillip led her to the kitchen and pointed out the tea service and other things she would need. But he restrained a smile at how Cami was playing the memorized part of the well-bred Southern belle. She would confront and survive any unpleasantness she could not ignore, but she would face it in her makeup with style and grace.

Pacing the rug while he waited, Phillip prayed. He could not reach his dad for advice today, for he was in Myrtle Beach with an important client. Noble Painter, his godfather, was in Columbia on business.

But Wyeth was here. He took the stairs to a private phone in his parents' room, flipped the thin pages of the phone directory for the name of a local gallery, then dialed and waited for someone to bring his best friend to the phone.

Back downstairs, Camellia had set his mom's silver tray on a low table. She poured from a fancy teapot and handed a steaming cup to him and Jacqueline.

"If you and Tom were married, you'd be ecstatic you're havin' his baby," she said. "You'd never think of it as a mass of tissue. Instead, you'd stand on the scriptures that say God planned us before we were in our mother's womb. The people at the clinic lied to you, Jackie. They profit from young women like you with an unplanned pregnancy, but you're the one who lives with the aftermath. Every Mother's Day, you'd wonder what might have been. Every year on your due date, you'd cry over your empty arms. And even with Jesus' forgiveness, you'll never be able to forget. Once you confess to your parents, we'll decide what comes next."

"Everyone will know what we did!" wailed Jacqueline, ignoring her tea and putting her hands over her face. "We've let so many people down, Camellia! My daddy will have to resign his position at the church. Momma and Daddy don't deserve this humiliation."

Camellia sighed. "Our actions are never private, Jackie. Everyone who loves us is collateral damage when we don't live by the rules. I hear people say what they do is nobody else's business, but they are mistaken. Everyone around them pays a price."

She sipped her tea and pointed to Phillip's mother's dainty teacup. "Drink that, Jackie. It's herbal, no caffeine. There are two of you now."

Jackie sniffed and wiped her nose with a handkerchief. When she raised her teacup to her mouth, Camellia said matter-of-factly, "There's nothing to do but face this. Tell your parents how sorry you are. Tom may fail you, but Jesus never will. You didn't pray about what to do today, Jacqueline—surely you understand that He never led you to the place I found you. That's dangerous and illegal, both in His law and man's."

This brought a fresh outburst of sobs from Jacqueline, which unnerved Phillip. He set his tea cup on the table and rose from his seat to pace, arms crossed over his chest.

"From the night it happened, I've begged God for forgiveness," Jacqueline cried. "I promised Him I'd wait until we married before it happened again, and I asked Him not to let me be pregnant. He's punishing me. I only went to the clinic the first time for a pregnancy test, but after Tom's reaction, I panicked, Camellia. He said he had to go back and finish school, and this would ruin our lives. I begged him not to stop lovin' me."

Jacqueline's voice caught, and she squeezed her eyes tight. "The way he looked at me—how can I forget it? He acted as if I was trapping him, and he wanted me out of his life. I asked if he remembered what he'd promised that night, and he got angry. He said this changed everything, and he didn't feel the same."

She covered her face with her hands, and Camellia moved closer to put her arm around her friend. "Jackie, God knows your heart. He forgave you. You know the Bible promises that. But He doesn't always protect us from the consequences. He's not punishing you for something you're forgiven for. A spark of life ignited the night you and Tom were together. It was a miracle, despite the circumstances. God placed the responsibility for your decision and for that new life into your hands."

Jacqueline became calmer, and Camellia pushed a warm cup to her. "Tell me how this happened."

Phillip looked away as Jacqueline spilled her heart about an evening when she and Tom went over to Wild Dunes with another couple, and they found a secluded spot just off the beach. They had blankets, picnic baskets with dessert, and transistor radios. When the other couple left for more privacy, Jacqueline pointed out to Tom that being alone was against the dating rules they had made with their parents. But his mood changed, and he waved off her protest. They laid on the blanket, looking at the stars and listening to soft music. Then he became insistent on pushing their boundaries.

"I told him to stop, but he didn't," Jacqueline blurted. "He reminded me how many years we've loved one another, and that we'd get married when he graduated college. One time was enough until then. He kept kissing me and whispering how much he loved and respected me, and I—I didn't want to say no anymore."

The front door opened. Phillip's taunt nerves made him jump, and Wyeth's solemn expression softened when he came in. He nodded at the ladies during Phillip's introductions, then he asked Phillip to follow him out to the piazza.

An agitated young man waited on the steps. Tom introduced himself and said Camellia and Jacqueline were expecting him. Phillip invited him to sit and talk for a few minutes until the girls came out, but Tom refused. He leaned against the railing.

"Why should I talk to you? Who are you—to Camellia?"

"We only want to help. This isn't about me and Camellia. You're the one in trouble."

Tom pursed his lips and looked out into the garden. "I grew up in a private Christian school with Camellia and Jacqueline. Our dads and granddads—maybe our great-granddads—they're deacons, Sunday School teachers, Bible Study leaders. Our moms lead mission groups and women's groups at church. Jacqueline and I, we're the couple in Youth Group that everyone thought was a model of well-brought up behavior before marriage."

His voice grew thick and he cleared his throat. "I guess you think I should man up and marry her."

"No, I don't think you should marry if you know it won't work. But you can't murder your own flesh and blood, a defenseless child, to save yourself."

Tom flinched, then ran his hands over his face. After an awkward silence, Phillip said, "Provide for Jacqueline to have your baby. Another man will marry her."

Tom grimaced. Phillip added, "It's easy to forget that in a romantic relationship between believers, the man is the spiritual leader. She's supposed to trust you, Tom. You're supposed to look after her best interests, not your own. If I understand what happened that night, you forgot that she was your sister in Christ first."

"She should've stopped me!" Tom burst out. Tears were standing in his eyes and he gestured his helplessness. "We agreed not to do this. What kinda girl falls for that and gives out free samples? Not the kind I thought she was."

Wyeth shot up from his rocking chair. "If you want God's help, you'd better admit that you're to blame and ask Him what to do next!"

Tom reigned in a sob. Then he looked back over to the garden, his jaw clenched in defiance.

"There's nothing new under the sun, Tom," Wyeth continued. "Have you heard the Bible's account of King David's eldest son Amnon? He was crazy with love for his half-sister Tamar until he raped her. Then, she was disgusting to him. After he disgraced her, she begged him to keep her, because in that culture, she had no hope for marriage. But he was cruel. He had her kicked out and he bolted the door. Tamar's brother Absalom waited two years until the right moment to murder Amnon for what he'd done to his sister."

The look of defiance was wiped from Tom's face. When he didn't reply, Phillip said, "Tom, it sounds as if you've turned Jacqueline into a symbol of moral failure on both your parts. Maybe that's too much to overcome. Maybe you think you don't want to see your baby when it's born, because you'll be ashamed. If Jacqueline feels the same way, there's someone, somewhere who wants a baby to adopt. But Camellia saved you today from the worst possible failure for a man. As a Christian, you've got to ask yourself what you can do now that will make this a mistake you can live with, one that reconciles you with the people you've hurt. Unless you marry Jaqueline, your child will want an explanation someday. Any other woman you might love and want to marry will need to know why she should trust you despite your earlier failure to someone you claimed to love."

Camellia opened the door and took a few steps to stand in front of Tom. But he looked away. As quick as lightning, she slapped him. Stunned, Phillip and Wyeth took a step forward in case Tom struck back.

"How dare you!" she seethed as Tom's hand shot up to his stinging face. "I can understand when feelings run away with you. But to abandon your long-time friend and love when she needs you most, when she's desperate to protect both of you—I'll never in a million years be able to grasp that, Tom. And I never dreamed you were capable of it!"

Tom sobbed and reached out for her, pulling her to him in a desperate hug. "I'm so sorry, please, please forgive me," he repeated several times. She cried and assured him she did.

When he was calm, she reached for a handkerchief in her pocket to wipe her face. He pulled out his shirt tail and dried the wet trails on his own. Then he reached out to take her hand and said hoarsely, "Brian's foolin' around back at USC, Camellia. He talks to the guys about his exploits and my mind followed a trail I got lost on. I should have obeyed the Bible verses about bad company corrupting good character."

"I want to see your wallet." She held out her other hand, and Phillip bit his lip and glanced at Wyeth.

"I'll pay for Jacqueline's expenses, I promise," Tom said, fishing in his pocket and handing a well-worn square of folded leather to her. "Take everything in it and I'll come up with the rest, even if I have to borrow it."

Dubiously, she opened the wallet, and sudden understanding dawned in his eyes. "You won't find that, Camellia. I tossed the package in the nearest public trash can the night the guys got them. Brian handed me one and I didn't want to argue with him in front of the others. I never planned to need it. I guess I did."

Camellia handed the wallet back to him and sighed, squeezing her eyes tight and rubbing her fingertips into her temples. "Brian blurted out the truth today at lunch when he said he couldn't believe you'd gotten caught, 'cause you carry something. I assume I'll know it when I see it."

She dropped her hands to her hips. "Can you imagine? He'd tried to give me an engagement ring without even proposing. He announced that I'm important to his future. Rumors are that his family's old money is dwindling. The other things he said—"

Camellia crossed her arms and rubbed them. "Oh, Tom, it makes me shudder."

He hissed through clenched teeth and pulled her into another hug, patting her back. "Good, it's over. This way, he has no one to blame but himself, and none of the guys can take sides against you."

Jacqueline came to stand in the open doorway, her eyes red-rimmed from crying. Tom went to face her.

"I'm sorry, Jackie. This is my fault. I see it now. When I asked you to forgive me that night, you did. But I haven't asked you to forgive me for what I said yesterday. Honestly, I don't understand who I am anymore, or what to do. We'll get through this, one step at a time, beginning with telling our parents."

Jacqueline swallowed, sniffed, and nodded. "When I panicked yesterday, I threw myself at you, and I should have had more dignity than that. I wish I'd waited for the right man, the one Mama, Daddy, and I have prayed for."

She sniffed and crossed her arms. "Camellia just called her parents, and they're inviting ours over to their house. It's best if we break the news with another couple from church. They'll need their friends to get through this."

Tom was taken aback. "Camellia's always right. It's better this way." He reached for her hand, but she put her own behind her back and met his eyes with a firm look and a tilt of her chin.

"Jackie, we can work this out."

Phillip and Wyeth exchanged a meaningful look. The tables had turned.

"I'm sorry, Tom, but it will be hard to forget how you looked at me yesterday, and what you said. My heart broke into a million pieces, and I've never felt so abandoned. You're not the man I want, and I'm glad I found out before we married. My baby and I need security."

Tom rallied a protest, but Camellia took his arm to pull him toward the driveway. "We'll settle this later. Thank our hosts for their patience and hospitality."

Tom turned to Phillip and Wyeth. Jacqueline reached out to take Phillip's hand.

"Mr. Gregory, I'm humiliated that our first meeting must have been utterly shocking for you. I will always think of you as the knight in shining armor that Camellia and I needed today. Thank you for the invitation to your lovely home while I picked up the shattered pieces of myself. I'll never forget your kindness. If my baby is a boy, I'll name him after you."

With a sad smile, he replied, "The honor is mine. I'm sure I was hopelessly inadequate. Keep up your courage and resolve."

Beside her, Tom reached to shake the other two men's hands. "Thanks for talking sense into my hard head, and for savin' my baby."

Wyeth said, "Look, you don't know us, and you'll have much better counselors. But can we pray with you?" They joined hands to form a circle, and Wyeth began. Tom tried to pray, but he became too emotional. Jacqueline couldn't talk without crying, and there were no dry eyes when Camellia finished. Then Phillip closed with a brief prayer, and Tom thanked them and led Jacqueline to his car to wait for Camellia.

"I can drive you, so they can be alone to discuss things," Phillip offered as Camellia wiped her eyes. He sniffed and reached for her hand. Her skin was soft as he ran his fingers over her knuckles.

With a shy smile, she shook her head. "Call me the next time you're in town. Now you know why I demanded your wallet, and I don't know what to say."

"Cami, I knew why you asked. Your dad told me where you were, so I went to the café and ordered lunch. I couldn't hear everything Brian said, but I know he insulted you. You'll never think of a guy's wallet the same way. I'm glad you gave me a chance to prove you can trust me."

Phillip and Camellia studied one another's eyes and said a quick goodbye before she left the piazza for Tom's car. "She's the one," remarked Wyeth. "I'll be jealous and lonely."

"No way. We're a dynamic duo, Wyeth—remember, 'best friends forever, blood brothers to the end, and so on and so forth'. Aren't you glad that part of our duty to Painter Place is to love a good woman?"

With a wistful sigh, Wyeth stood with his hands in his pockets, watching the tourists in the street. "Other people, they don't want a baby because it will mess up their lives. My life feels messed up without the chance to have one. I'll do what I can to preserve Painter Place for the next generation, but I expect to remain a bachelor. A good woman wants kids, Phillip. You'll have 'em, Andy and Justin, they'll have 'em, and so will Juliette. That's the future of Painter Place."

Chapter Five

In clear weather, Main Street in downtown Whitehaven, South Carolina came alive on weekend evenings. The small town had been slow to adopt flashy trends of the past decade, but by the summer of 1960, there were new neon signs sprinkled around the historic buildings. The most cheerful one blinked about the ice cream and soda treats at the Blue Skies Sundae Shoppe. Next door, a pulsing sign designed to look like a record was the main feature in the front window of the Five and Dime Variety Store. A bold poster of Elvis announced that he was back, and fans must be quick to collect his records while they were in stock.

A theater marquee tempted the crowds to see the latest movie in town, *Wild River*. Bright neon script over the front window of the Coastal Corner Pharmacy lured townsfolk into the Soda Shop. The rhythmic flashes of the popular jukebox promised access to the latest favorite tunes.

The eerie glow of a neon slice of pepperoni pie advertised a pizza parlor, but it was the Sand Dollar Drive-In that drew the hungry crowds. The irresistible smell of grilled hamburgers, barbeque, and onion rings wafted down Main Street. Patrons in cars ordered curb service through the metallic static of speakers while radios throbbed and conversation buzzed.

Both sides of Main Street were busy, and Andy Painter draped his suntanned left arm over the door of his Corvette convertible. He scanned the crowds for something interesting. By the time he could ease the sparkling black sports car forward, he couldn't help exaggerating a heavy sigh. He was bored.

In the passenger seat beside him, Justin Gregory chuckled. Andy slowed again to make a left turn where the row of businesses ended and the road darkened, just before the Gregory Global building. Manhandling the wheel at the turn, he growled, "Go ahead, laugh, world traveler. In a few days, you'll go back to the withering wit of girls with British accents."

"It's my only option, Andy, short of putting Global London in the hands of hired help over there. That's never goin' to happen while Global has an address on Threadneedle Street. My Grandpa poured his heart into it and was proud to leave me that legacy. Dad doesn't need me here yet, but someday, with new technology, maybe we can operate out of a central location."

Andy waited at a traffic light and glanced over at Justin, who'd taken on the brooding demeanor of his older brother. When he did that, he could almost pass as Phillip's twin, and Andy tensed.

He looked straight ahead. "You still miss your grandparents."

At first, Justin only stared up at the traffic light. It changed to green, and Andy eased the car forward. "Yeah," he answered. "The house is mine now, but it feels lonely, you know? I'm surrounded by the things that remind me of them. They were happy as long as they had one another, even when life brought them challenges that would give other people nightmares. Grandpa didn't want to remain here without her. It hurts, but I'm glad he went so soon after she did. When I finish at the university, I hope I'll marry someone who will make the place come alive again."

The next intersection brought them back around to the lights and sounds of Main Street on Saturday night, and Andy waited behind two other cruising drivers in hot rod cars. He tapped the steering wheel. "Is it me?" he growled. "We bring horsepower to town and flex our muscle cars at the girls, but we creep down the street."

A guy in front of them had graduated with Wyeth and Phillip. He dangled an arm out his window, with his tee shirt sleeve rolled up to show his beefy arm to its best advantage. He waved at someone that Andy knew was still only in high school. She was in a car packed with giggling girls, leaning out and waving. Her dark hair was curled and pulled it into a flirtatious ponytail that bobbed as she smiled in poppy red lipstick.

A song about a dream lover ended on Andy's car radio, then one of his favorites came on. "Dance with me," flowed the harmony from the speakers.

He shrugged against the unwelcome stab of loneliness, then followed other cars through the intersection. "Wish I could get to Charleston more often. The girls we met Thursday night were classy. I got a phone number."

Justin drummed his leg to the beat of the music with one hand and pointed to a coveted empty parking spot with the other. Andy slid his Corvette in front of the ice cream shop. "Hold me closer, closer and closer," poured the music from his radio.

Reluctant to cut the song short, he turned the engine off while leaving the music on. Then he looked up into the loveliest, most vulnerable green eyes he'd ever seen. Those eyes and the song were all that mattered, and he wasn't sure for how long.

But it could only have been for a few moments because Justin was handling first-name only introductions to four girls he'd never met in town before. The willowy, dark-haired one with the beautiful eyes flashed him the most spontaneous, engaging smile he'd ever seen.

Andy nodded hello to them before three former classmates rushed over to mob the Corvette. A pretty blonde named Ruby came to the driver's side, leaning into the convertible. She purred, "Andrew, you rascal, where've you been? Come join us at the jukebox to dance and have a soda float."

A brunette leaned into the passenger side and gushed, "Justin, it's so good to see you in town. We miss you! Will you be here for a while? Let's get together."

Andy flipped off the radio, and both he and Justin volleyed their practiced, good-natured rejections with their admirers. Grinning at the blonde, but pulling back away from her, Andy quipped, "Ruby, I told you I could never dance with a lady who would put her feet into those torture chambers you call stiletto heels. I'm a big chicken about my foot being stabbed. You never seem to take my advice to find the courageous man who deserves you."

She looked down her shapely legs to the red high heels she was wearing, then reached to pull them off. Dangling them in one hand, she wheedled, "Andy, I'd take 'em off to dance!" With an alluring pout, she pleaded, "Come on, get out and hang around with us."

The third former classmate came to join Ruby, eyeing the four other young ladies on the sidewalk. She pulled the blonde's arm. "Come on, girls, we interrupted him and Justin. Andy, look for us when you're through, okay?"

The blonde grumbled and put her shoes back on. As the three of them stepped away from the convertible, she turned to wink and blow a kiss at Andy.

If the four young ladies in front of the Blue Skies Sundae Shoppe considered those gathered around the convertible to be rivals, they didn't show it. They chatted and laughed together before two other young men on the street walked up and invited them to go inside for ice cream. The one that had captivated Andy shook her head at a young man who didn't hide his disappointment while her friend explained that they'd already enjoyed a sundae and could not eat another bite. The young men asked if they'd be around town to meet up later.

When the potential suitors went inside the shop, Justin greeted the four young ladies again and asked where they were from. Three of them were outgoing and came forward to stand close to the Corvette to talk, but the green-eyed one quietly stood behind them. They said they were from Georgetown. An aunt lived in Whitehaven and they were staying the weekend with her. "Right, Valerie?" asked her friend, and they parted to make space.

Valerie blushed when she realized Andy had caught her admiring the Corvette. Before he thought about the implications, he had invited her to go for a ride.

Her demeanor changed in an instant, and she recovered her poise by glancing at her friends. Then she rolled her eyes and quipped with a rich Southern accent, "Oh, sure. Then we end up in a dark corner of a park somewhere, right? At least you don't have a back seat."

Two friends gasped, the other one giggled, and Justin threw back his head and laughed in delight. Andy blinked and swallowed hard while his mind raced for an acceptable comeback. "Ma'am, I admit you've got me thinkin' about things I wouldn't want my preacher to guess when he's eloquently expounding in front of my pew tomorrow in church. But rest assured, I'd never put either of us in a situation that makes anyone suspect us of actin' like we're married before we are. If you have any experience in the back seat of a parked car, I'd like to know about it now, before things go any further."

Indignant, Valerie sputtered, "I haven't!"

One of her friends asked another, "Did he say they might get married?"

Still chuckling, Justin opened his door and took a jaunty step onto the sidewalk. "You're safe with Andy," he drawled in his deep voice. "He may take you around the block to cruise, but you keep those pretty hands to yourself, and don't lose your heart to him like all the other girls in town."

Andy sprang from the driver's side and went around, holding the passenger door open gallantly. Flashing what he hoped was his most disarming grin, he added, "To be fair, when Justin is in London, there aren't many other guys in town to compete with."

Valerie's friends pushed her to the car, assuring her it was all right, and they'd wait with Justin. "It's just a few minutes," one of them urged.

Gathering her dignity, Valerie sat gracefully in the low seat of the car. She turned a lingering look at her friends.

Andy closed her door and checked for oncoming traffic before going to the driver's side. Justin waved and winked, and Andy felt a surge of adrenaline. Something interesting had happened to him in Whitehaven. This young lady from Georgetown would be glad she came to town tonight.

Reflected signs and lights lived in other dimensions in the gleaming metal of the car bodies in downtown Whitehaven. A friend stopped, honked, and waved at Andy, giving him space to pull out of the popular parking spot he occupied. Another acquaintance shouted a greeting from across the street.

"You must know everyone," Valerie commented.

"Yeah, maybe. I can't get by with anything 'cause everyone's watchin'. They know my dad, and they like him better than me."

He stopped at an intersection and glanced at her while he waited on two cars. "Sometimes, I get to Georgetown, on business. I rarely get past the harbor though."

As he eased through the intersection, he felt her studying him. "I live in a historic home near the waterfront. It was my grandfather's, and my mom inherited it."

"Really? I live in a historic old house, too, so we have something in common. I'm glad you came to town with your friends tonight. You saved me from another boring weekend."

Now she smiled, but it wasn't the smile that rocked him the first time he saw her. Politely, she said she was glad she'd come to Whitehaven, and that it was a nice little town. She kept conversation going by adding, "Your car suits you. I mean, I don't know you, but how a person handles himself says a lot more than words. You seem to be grounded, but fun-loving."

Surprised, Andy glanced at her. "That's a deep thing to say. You could learn more about me on a boat, I think. But I hope this means you like the Corvette."

"I do, it's an exciting car, but you're rather tall to fit inside, if the top was up."

He laughed. "I'm learning about you, too, and so far, that's exciting. Has anyone ever said you remind them of Audrey Hepburn? Different eye color and height, but there's a resemblance. When you smile, it's like a promise that somethin' fun is about to happen."

Pleased, Valerie relaxed back into her seat. "Yes, sometimes people mention it. Thank you. And my mom's name is Audrey. I've always thought it sounded mysterious and sultry, and I wish I was like that."

With a tilt of her pretty chin, she gazed up at a bright moon that had been full two days ago. "What happens in your life when you aren't being the most popular guy in Whitehaven?"

They were almost to a church parking lot, and a quick jerk on the steering wheel pulled the Corvette into it. With a decisive move of his hand, Andy put the car in park and left the engine running. "What does that mean?"

"Well, the girls in town go out of their way to get your attention, and everyone else seems to want you to notice them. You're good-looking, in a rugged, outdoorsy sort of way, you're outgoing, smart, and your manners come from a well-bred background. Either your father is rich, or you're successful, because you drive this car and wear tailor-quality clothes."

When his look didn't soften, she sighed and looked out at the street. "OK, maybe that was derogatory. At least you mentioned church, so maybe you're a Christian." Then she turned to meet his eyes. "I apologize if I insulted you with my assumption that you're a guy who gets around. But I'm honestly curious about who you are, how you spend your time, and what you dream of."

Andy looked away with a grimace and lightly slapped the steering wheel. When he looked back at her, he said, "I don't know why you hold men in such disdain, but when we spend time together, you have to lose the attitude."

"See! There you go again. You said 'hold men in such disdain,' and a regular guy just doesn't talk like that. You're educated and—"

She blinked, and the look of triumph in her eyes vanished. The vulnerable, shy Valerie was back. "Wait. Did you say, 'when we spend time together'?"

The star-struck sensation he'd felt the first time he'd seen her was back, too. Andy sighed and ran one hand through his hair. "Yes. Can I call you soon?"

Chapter Six

Wyeth Painter licked his lips and jammed his hands into the pockets of his khakis. He tried to hide the unsophisticated country bumpkin he felt like since arriving in London and meeting Dante Kent. Now, he found himself as far off the map of his plans as he could imagine. Flexibility was the rule when teaching art workshops though it was easier to handle situations when he was not travel-weary, halfway around the globe. He needed a replacement model for a portrait painting session in two hours. The only alternative was to capture the commanding presence and wolfish appearance of his new British friend.

A woman dressed in a navy business skirt and blazer entered the room where he and Dante Kent waited, and for the third time since they'd passed the front door security, Dante explained their presence. She scrutinized them, narrowed her eyes, and cleared her throat. "It's not uncommon for artists and photographers to come here seeking a model on short notice, but it's unheard of for me to get an order to allow a particular one to work with two artists who had not made the arrangements themselves. I can only envy your connections."

Wyeth swallowed his surprise. His artist associate didn't confirm or deny their interrogator's insinuation, but he flashed a charming smile and bowed slightly. Wyeth knew he was bluffing. Neither of them had any idea what connections she was referring to.

They were led into a huge room filled with models, photographers, and assistants. A coiffed young lady whose face was shining with perspiration brushed past them in an elaborate evening gown. She gulped down the contents of a paper cup. A frantic aide followed, directing her to a makeup station.

Wyeth was taller than most others in the room. His eyes scanned over people's heads to analyze the props and stages set for the models, looking for ideas to use in his work.

He stopped when he saw a setting that captured the look of a romantic European evening, and he caught his breath when he thought he saw the famous American model and actress Sandra Dee. But this model was tall and had more curves in her figure. She cast a playful expression over her shoulder and wore a satin cape against the imaginary chill of the darkened sky. Moving through poses as she was being directed, Wyeth wondered how anyone would choose between the pictures to select just one.

"Now, open the evening wrap and pull it back to show us your gown, as if you're getting ready to leave it at the coat check desk," someone commanded from the sidelines. The model pulled back the cape and poised her opera-gloved hand on one hip. After one more pose with the wrap open and deliciously draping down her arm, an aide came to take it away.

The young model now wore a simple evening gown with a plunging neckline that managed not to be immodest. It rose to her creamy shoulders with a crisp step-up inset and created more drama that she'd have encountered in the imaginary theater she pretended to be attending.

She put a gloved arm out at a right angle to an architectural column. She turned her profile the other way while cameras flashed.

Wyeth did not know, nor could he describe, what happened inside him in those moments while the model held the pose. He memorized her profile, her figure in the dress, and the backdrop. He never wanted to forget it.

The woman with the all-business attitude came back for the two artists and led them into a hallway, asking them to wait a few minutes while the model changed to street clothes. People kept a hectic pace on their way to check something off their schedules, and Wyeth frowned at the face of his watch.

"We'll make it," Dante assured him.

"I haven't looked over my notes or unpacked my supplies. I'm not accomplished at presentations like my father is, and I still can't believe he arranged this. He should be here, not me."

"Ah, but you're accomplished at painting, and you've memorized what your father teaches. It will come to you, and our students won't know any better. He has confidence in you, my friend."

Dante reached out to pat his shoulder. The little gesture had the intended effect, and Wyeth was grateful for it. His new friend's accent and clear enunciation of his words was like a polished aristocrat in a black and white British horror movie. Wyeth appreciated that Dante refrained from using the slang so common among Brits, and they had no trouble communicating.

But the next voice he heard was American, and his heart jumped at the sound of his own country. It had the lacy edging of an almost-Southern accent. Virginia, maybe?

The model who'd captivated Wyeth's imagination was coming down the hall, escorted by the woman in the navy suit who told him and Dante to wait. She wore a lovely white summer dress with pearls and carried a chic straw handbag. Wyeth stared.

The photographer for the dramatic evening theater stage walked beside her, and he laughed as he reached for her hand. He asked her to join him for dinner, but then a man called for him to get to the next session. The model disengaged her hand from his while he took backward steps toward the door and promised he would discuss dinner plans with her later.

The manager retrieved her fountain pen from over her ear and handed Dante a clipboard. "This says you hired our model for a classroom event in a hotel facility, in this case, the Mayfair. She has a security team and transportation. Check the box I've highlighted, and both of you must sign and date at the bottom. Are there any questions?"

"Uh, yeah, I'd like to ask the model a few questions to see if she's what I need for the job. What shall I call you, ma'am?"

Wyeth wondered if he'd made a clumsy social blunder when the manager raised her brows in surprise. The model held out her hand. "I'm Chrissy Carnet. Please call me Chrissy."

"Enchanted, I'm sure, Chrissy. I'm Wyeth Painter. Call me Wyeth." He held on to her hand until Dante handed him the clipboard for a signature.

"I'm Dante Kent, at your service, Chrissy."

"Gentlemen," the manager interrupted. "I assumed you were familiar with Miss Carnet's work and had paid her fee in advance because she was the model you wanted."

Wyeth studied the model's name to be sure how her last name was spelled. As he expected, the pronunciation was French, with 'net' sounding like 'nay.' Then he saw her fee, which was double what he would earn from the painting class.

He scowled and handed the clipboard back. When he turned a questioning look at Dante, the artist shook his head. Wyeth told the manager, "No, ma'am. We expected to pay the fee today. The agency we work with called to tell us our scheduled model had an emergency, and they gave us directions here to sign for her replacement. Chrissy is far and away too professional for our job. A three-hour painting workshop is nothing like an advertisement for a designer gown."

"I've done artist modeling before, Wyeth," Chrissy rushed to say. "I understand about sitting still for stretches of time. How long will you expect me to hold a pose?"

"About 20 minutes if possible, then you can take a break. While a model relaxes, I talk to students about our progress and show them how to fill in areas I didn't finish."

"I don't do nudes."

"I don't either."

Dante cleared his throat and explained the job in more detail. "We want a shoulder or three-quarter pose, and you will have a comfortable chair. We may ask you to wear a prop such as a fur wrap, scarf, or hat."

Chrissy Carnet nodded at the manager, then turned to Wyeth. "Please, Wyeth. I want to do this job, and someone's already paid for it. What have you got to lose?"

"I'm famished, Wyeth. Can we go get something to eat?"

Chrissy came to stand by the blue artist's apron draped on a chair near Wyeth's easel. She stood barefoot and stretched gracefully from side to side, the way a ballerina would warm up before a performance.

Startled, Wyeth looked up from organizing the paint tubes strewn across the table during his portrait demonstration. He had braced himself for the moment she would walk out the door and out of his life forever. Now, he wasn't sure what to make of the familiar way she'd just inserted herself into his evening.

She smiled at his expression. Flushing, he busied himself with wiping his paint brushes. "I assumed—what about your dinner plans?"

Chrissy's laugh was easy and warm. "I don't have any dinner plans. Do you?"

Dante Kent returned from seeing students out to the door, and Wyeth looked up at him. "Dante, do you mind if Chrissy joins us for dinner?"

He got a perverse sense of satisfaction at seeing surprise almost register on his suave friend's face. But Dante composed it into delight. "You must join us, Chrissy! I've arranged a special menu here in the hotel. Only a few years ago, we were still under a food rationing system in my country, and I know from my travels that Americans expect much more flavorful food."

"Dante, you think of everything!" Chrissy exclaimed. "I'm looking forward to spending more time with you and Wyeth."

She turned and gestured to her portrait. "Wyeth's work is so painterly, isn't it? I wasn't sure if I might end up like a Picasso today, with several faces and arms akimbo. But this is my idea of what art is, what real talent is."

Wyeth's heart soared to hear Chrissy's praise, and he chuckled at her speculation of his vision of her in a portrait. She smiled at him and glanced back at Dante. "I'll never forget what he told the students today, about how the canvas becomes a place where an artist reacts to his subject, and that his hands, heart, and head are engaged in a challenge of his skill and emotions. That's different from a photo. I never realized that an artist can never capture the same painting in the same way again because the experience changed him."

Turning a beaming look at Wyeth, she added, "This portrait takes my breath away. I hope you will allow me to purchase it."

He swallowed hard. How could he explain why he didn't want to sell the painting? "I haven't signed it yet. I want to look at it again later, to see if it needs any adjustments."

Dante stroked his short goatee and continued to study the artwork on the easel, pointing out what elements contributed to its success. "He created the touch of magic with the watery blue tones in the silk scarf. The colors and free-flowing movement are the dynamite that amplifies your eyes and makes you appear confident and free-spirited."

"Oh," Chrissy breathed, staring at the painting. "Wyeth, is that the outcome you planned from the beginning?"

Wyeth stepped back for a view from another angle. "The blues lean toward lavender, which sets off your hazel eyes. I could've used the fur wrap Dante supplied and a dramatic dark neutral background. It was predictable, but sophisticated, a great composition considering your career. I chose the scarf. It reminds me of home."

"And where is that?"

"I live on an island, across from a tiny coastal town in South Carolina. It's called Painter Place."

Chapter Seven

At Chrissy's invitation, Wyeth joined her for an afternoon of sightseeing on Thursday when his workshop was over. Her driver took them to some casual art exhibits and a sculpture garden in a park. He discovered that photography was one of her hobbies, so they talked about views that would make great compositions and paintings. Several times, he was her subject, with an interesting background. He agreed to be in the photos if he could take some of her, and if she would send them to Painter Place after she had them developed.

Phillip was negotiating an important business deal for Gregory Global, one that would seat him securely in his father's role. Wyeth waited until he thought Phillip would be home before he found a pay phone and called the Gregory mansion. When Lucinda found out he was sightseeing with his portrait model and that Dante had no dinner plans, she insisted that he bring them to eat with the Gregory family that evening.

The house in London was the same as Wyeth remembered, but it was difficult not to see Alton and Diana Gregory come into a room at any moment. Their absence made him feel pensive despite the thrill of getting to spend more time with Chrissy.

Conversation in the dining room was engaging, but Wyeth was quiet. Missing Phillip's grandparents here set him back to feeling chaotic and clumsy. The special dinner gathering was slipping by with the measured tick of the grandfather clock in the mansion, yet he dreaded the inevitable instead of enjoying the moment. He still didn't understand how the portrait model he'd hired had upended his life, but he was sure that saying goodbye would hurt when he boarded a plane home.

While a butler replaced his empty plate with dessert, Chrissy said, "When Wyeth explained why he'd chosen the scarf for my portrait, it ignited my imagination. I'm sure I was forward when I invited myself to join him for dinner, but I had to know more about what evoked such devotion in his eyes. Painter Place sounds enchanting!"

At the head of the table, Phil set down his glass. "I live there too, and I think you're interested enough for me to brag. When his ancestor settled the island way back in 1685, he wrote that he'd raised an Ebenezer, which is a landmark, or a stone of help. He based it on Bible verses like 1 Samuel 7:12 and the words in his favorite hymn, 'Come Thou Fount of Every Blessing.' He dedicated the island to God and charged his descendants not to dishonor Painter Place."

Dante paused with his dessert spoon in midair. "Where did Patrick Painter live before he settled the island in America?"

"Here, in your country, Dante. They confiscated all Gregory holdings here in a time of religious persecution, and my middle name is the same as the sole survivor, Chadwick Gregory. He was older than Patrick Painter, and a shrewd financial genius. Patrick's father hid him in exchange for liquidating their wealth before they suffered the same fate. Chadwick found passage to the colonies for himself, Patrick, and Patrick's mother and grandmother. They never heard from Patrick's father and older brother again. Chadwick became a mentor for young Patrick."

Justin dabbed his mouth with a napkin. "The generations have been faithful to Patrick Painter's vision. Every Painter generation has produced an artist to inherit the island. Every Gregory generation has produced a financial watchman to look after the Painter interests. Phillip and Wyeth will tackle holding on to Painter Place in a modern culture. If they mismanage it or disaster strikes, the island will be sold or turned into a historical state park."

Lucinda reached to clasp her husband's hand, and they smiled at each other. "We can only survive the stress if we love and follow Christ. Young adults in both families have left the island to pursue other dreams or callings. Painter Place isn't for everyone. But if the heir ever drops the ball, everything changes."

"Wyeth, I am heir to the stewardship of a similar place!" Dante said with excitement. "Remember yesterday when we met and had a sense of destiny in our friendship? I can relate to Painter Place."

"Oh!" Lucinda exclaimed. "You and Chrissy should visit. I'm sure your schedules are busy, but—"

"I'm not," Chrissy blurted. "Tomorrow morning is my last modeling commitment for a while. Would it be an imposition if I make plans to arrive after your return?"

Lucinda was delighted. "We'd love for you to come to the island! Why not plan to attend the Island Summer Dance on the first Saturday in June?"

Dante wished a gallant good night to Chrissy in the hotel lobby and dismissed himself to supervise arrangements for the art sessions the following morning. Wyeth dared to put his hand on the small of her back to lead her to an ornate sofa. He glanced around as they sat together.

Chrissy smiled. "The reason you sense you're being watched is because you are."

"It's not just the bodyguard and chauffeur," he muttered.

"Right. It's my father or someone who works for him."

Startled, Wyeth stared at her, and she reached for his hand. "Wyeth, you live the life of my dreams. Your family misses you and you're homesick. Only the housekeeper and some friends miss me. My mother died last year because of her job, or because of my father's job. I've grown up with security in the background. But sometimes I sense a different presence, and I believe it's my dad. I hope that doesn't make you feel creepy."

"Okay." Wyeth rubbed the nape of his neck. "How do you want me to feel about it?"

"Well, honestly, I hope you will try to understand, after what happened to my mother."

"I know how to be mindful of sticky situations and of how I might influence people, but I can't imagine guards around. If you were my daughter, though, I'd station guards everywhere."

Chrissy smiled and ran her fingers over his tanned hand. "Wyeth, is there someone special waiting to marry you and become a part of Painter Place?"

Wyeth looked up in surprise. "No."

"If you were searching for someone special, you'd be better at it."

He chuckled. "Ouch!"

"I've loved spending time together the past two days, and I'm certain you've had fun, too. It's so easy to be with you, and your perspective on things is remarkable when you share your thoughts. You're trying not to encourage me to think of us as a couple, but it's keeping a distance between us I want to cross. Can I be honest? I'm eighteen and haven't been on a real date. I'm unsure how to break past your reservations, and my forward behavior may scare you away."

Wyeth stared at her, off-kilter, both elated and alarmed. She'd just placed herself at his mercy, and frankness was the only honorable response.

"Look, it's true, I'm dismal at romance. As you said—I'm not looking for it. Until a few weeks ago, my focus was on graduating from college. I want—love, and a wife. But women want children, and I'm not likely to have any because of a childhood illness. The Lord knew what was ahead for me then, and in the Bible, Paul says singleness is a good thing, so I'll trust that."

He had expected it to be a traumatic experience the first time he explained this to a potential girlfriend. Instead, he was relieved. He wasn't sure what came next, and they shared silence while a group of guests entered the lobby. When their voices faded in the hallway, Chrissy said, "I've never dreamed of children. There are other men who don't want them, but it's often because they're divorced or they're pursuing careers instead of a family. I want more."

Wyeth ventured, "I guess childbirth ruins a model's figure."

She laughed. "True enough! But unless she models swimsuits, she recovers to model other clothing styles. I don't want to raise children around security guards, who may end up with a murdered mother and no answers for comfort. I'm less of a liability to my father if I am childless. Besides, anticipating a husband's attention all to myself makes me happy. Is that a healthy perspective? I'm not sure. But I am sure that Christ will move my heart if He plans a child for me."

"I assumed you were a Christian from things you said yesterday. Then tonight at dinner, you didn't scoff at the bedrock beliefs at Painter Place."

"And I suspected you were a Christian from the things you said when you hired me to model. Then, I noticed a well-traveled Bible tucked in your bag when you unpacked supplies, while you and Dante set up the workshop."

Chrissy leaned closer. "Wyeth, my faith is simple, based on scripture, not on theories, conjecture, compromise, and traditions. I believe a true moment of being born again isn't just an emotional experience, it's when someone encounters Christ."

She smiled and met his eyes. "My mother's dating advice for me was that He is here, with us, right now. I accepted Jesus as the Savior of my soul in Vacation Bible School at the Baptist church where I was raised. My mother insisted that I only align my closest relationships with fellow believers because darkness has no fellowship with light."

Wyeth exhaled and took a few moments to digest her profession. "Wow. You are—refreshing and straightforward. My beliefs are the same, and I accepted Christ in my mama's lap, looking at the constellations out over the Atlantic Ocean."

They sat together in the afterglow of a special like-mindedness. A few smiling moments later, Chrissy said, "Wyeth, you're thoughtful, quiet, and mysterious. I'm not the first woman who's chased you, I'm sure of that. But the moment I saw you at the agency, I had a sense of destiny, as Dante mentioned tonight."

Wyeth glanced away at a couple who'd come into the lobby doors from the street, then met her eyes again. "Chrissy, do you have something formal to wear to a reception? I'm going to one with the Gregory family tomorrow night, and I'd like to take you as my date. My painting workshop ends by noon. If you finish your job, we could do more sightseeing in the afternoon, then eat a quick dinner and get dressed for the event."

She rose, pulling his hands, so they would stand facing each other. "It's a date! I don't fly back to the States until Saturday."

"Will the guards be there?"

"Only as our transportation. They'll be lurking around somewhere, but they specialize in making sure no one else will notice. I've never tested their dating protocol, whatever it may be."

He hesitated, unwilling to part. She sighed. "It's just a goodnight, Wyeth, not a goodbye. I'm already looking forward to seeing you again tomorrow."

Without waiting for his response, she leaned closer to hug him, the way a butterfly touches a bloom without settling on it. But his reflexes were quick as she drew back. A gentle pull brought her to his heart.

Chapter Eight

Phillip Gregory admired the ample decks of the *Dominator,* a sparkling new super yacht at a private wharf on the Thames. It was his last evening in London and the end of a nerve-frazzling week. He was comfortable in a tailored tuxedo, but uncomfortable with being resigned to navigating meaningless conversations.

Beside him, his brother Justin said, "News travels fast when you follow the money." He nodded into a dining area of the yacht where Phillip saw their parents sampling food with other couples, and a hired photographer was getting snapshots of them all. "Dad was congratulated several times about your success in landing the King's Road project today. It's every bit as huge as we predicted, and they're saying it couldn't be more appropriate that you're aboard the *Dominator* tonight. You've picked up a nickname."

Phillip snorted mildly. "You know Dad had that all set for me to seal and deliver. It was in the works before I got home from college. All I had to do was sell it."

Justin sighed and chided him. "Phillip, this kind of respect launches you to fill Dad's shoes someday. Nobody sees you as some kid fresh out of college anymore. They believe in you, and you saved those investors. The only ones making any money through Wilfred Rothchild are the local pubs."

"But this is his city, his stakes," growled Phillip. "He needed this deal. I didn't. Ask around and see if he's interested in comin' in to Global to talk. I can find a commission he can oversee here as an independent contractor."

Justin hissed and leaned in closer, keeping his voice low. "You have stakes in this, too, Phillip! Uncle Perry was a British soldier and we don't even know where the pieces of him are. He wasn't just fighting for his own ideals or his country, he was protecting Dad's sister and Global London. The office was bombed, and his wife died from the gases she inhaled. Our grandparents never got over losin' Karen Anne, and then they had to leave Painter Place to build Global's office back again. They were retirement age, comin' here to struggle with food rationing and shortages. Dad was concerned and rarely able to reach them. Our family has every right to profit from rebuilding here!"

Phillip grimaced. "Maybe I just wasn't ready for this big launch so soon."

"You're ready, you're just tired. The jet lag kicks you every time you visit here. Stay close to me or Wyeth. We'll try to make you look more approachable."

Phillip took a sip of sparkling fruit punch in a fluted crystal glass, which he'd taken from a tray to serve as a buffer between himself and other people. "Yeah, well, Wyeth has an understandable distraction tonight. It will be impossible to avoid Victoria unless you help me by askin' her for a few dances."

A middle-aged British couple who recognized Justin came to offer kind condolences about his grandfather's death. Justin agreed that his grandparents had lived long lives and were together again in a better place. Then he introduced Phillip, who wore an obligatory smile. But his heart ached at the mention of his grandparents, and he hated vague references to a "better place." Heaven was so much more than that.

Wyeth escorted Chrissy back to an open deck to join Phillip under the stars, and he gently nudged his friend's sleeve. "I need to talk to you."

From his place against the ship's railing, Phillip tensed and looked out over the black water. In a voice for his friend's ears only, Wyeth said, "Two ladies were in the waiting area for the powder room, and Chrissy and I overheard them. At first, I could only see

Victoria. I don't know how the conversation got started, but she told someone her father owned this yacht and promised her he'd schedule Charleston as a port of call soon. She told her your fathers had been discussing a marriage arrangement between you two."

Chrissy leaned toward Phillip and added, "She said you are the most eligible bachelor in the whole world. The woman she was talking to asked Victoria why you two weren't a couple already."

She and Wyeth exchanged glances, and Phillip growled, "Go ahead. Why aren't we a couple?"

Wyeth drawled, "Because her dad prefers Malcolm Richards, since he lives here in London and doesn't have a problem with social drinking and other things your family is backwards about. She said your father claims you two are incompatible, and that anyone you marry will have to move to Painter Place."

Chrissy narrowed her eyes and said, "Then, Victoria laughed and claimed she'd rather die than live on a desolate island so far from civilized life, but Charleston might be acceptable for a few months out of a year. She claims she could become what it takes to make you happy, so you'll fall in love with her. Once you're married, you'd be the one doing whatever it takes to make her happy, because the Gregory family doesn't believe in divorce unless it's a Biblical exception."

Wyeth added, "Then, guess who walked out beside her, the one she was confiding in?"

"Phillip, there you are, darling! It's wonderful to see you!"

Wyeth grimaced at Victoria's voice calling for Phillip, but he pasted on a lame smile and turned around when she came up to his friend's side. Phillip was stiff as she linked her arm through his.

"Good evening, Victoria."

"Isn't it a lovely night for this reception? I'm thrilled that you are here!" She looked past him to Wyeth and Chrissy. "Is this Wyeth?

Oh, my, it's been a while, and you grow more dashing every time I see you! Introduce me to your beautiful date."

Wyeth touched Chrissy's arm. "Victoria, this is Chrissy Carnet. Thank you for adding her to the invitation list."

Victoria waved a bejeweled hand and insisted that it was nothing. "We lived in New York for years before moving here, so I believe we may have more Americans on board tonight than locals. I've asked the musicians to play popular Broadway tunes for the occasion. Chrissy, I heard that you're a professional model who met Wyeth while posing for an art demonstration. How incredibly romantic! It's easy to see why he simply couldn't let you go."

Chrissy thanked Victoria and smiled up at Wyeth. Victoria twisted to look back over the guests, and she tugged on Phillip's arm. "Come with me, there's another American I want to introduce you to. Oh, Malcolm," she called, waving across the deck. "Bring your date over to meet Phillip and Wyeth."

Phillip blinked in surprise, but otherwise remained composed as Victoria led him across the deck. "Phillip, meet Camellia, Malcolm's date tonight. I believe the last name is Heyward, is that right? Like the guy who signed the Declaration of Independence, or something patriotic like that, back when America was a bunch of troublesome colonies. Camellia and her parents are guests at the Richards' home in London for a few days, isn't that lovely? I found out she's from Charleston, and thought it was fun we have two families—no, wait, Wyeth makes three families from South Carolina here on daddy's boat tonight!"

Phillip hoped he looked unfazed while he considered his options. It would be awkward for Camellia if Victoria discovered she had confided in the woman he was trying to date back in Charleston. It was safer to act as if they'd never met and let her be the one to reveal whether they had.

With a slight nod and a smile, Camellia stayed silent. Beside her, Malcolm took a step forward to shake his hand. "Congratulations, Phillip, you're the man of the hour! Everyone's talking about your epic deal today, and some are anointing you as the Dominator, since you're celebrating victory here on the yacht tonight."

Phillip avoided Camellia's eyes as he shook Malcolm's hand and mumbled the obligatory thank you. Victoria purred as she wrapped both her arms around his. "Daddy doesn't mind letting Phillip share the spotlight with the yacht tonight. But we hope that the Rothschild fellow doesn't show up. How awkward! We invited him because we didn't know who would get the contract, and we had to have the day's big winner on board. Daddy says it's just good business, but I find it uncivilized."

She didn't seem to notice how Phillip stiffened again. As she introduced Wyeth and Chrissy to Malcolm and Camellia, the band played a song from the musical *The King and I*.

Phillip extended his hand to Camellia. "Let's celebrate an unexpected meeting in London with a dance."

She handed Malcolm her water glass and Phillip led her over to join two other dancing couples on deck. "I'm dreaming," Phillip said close to her ear.

"Then we're in the same dream," she murmured back. "I can't even imagine how this happened."

"Until you showed up, my dream was fast becoming a nightmare. In fact, it still might be, if Rothschild shows up."

She squeezed his hand. "You look like a thunderstorm, Phillip. Where's the tall, dark stranger in paradise I can't get out of my mind?"

Startled, he looked down to search her face. "Ah, there you are, stranger," she teased. Then she looked past him to smile at the other dancers. "Do you mind if we don't mention how we know one another? We can admit that we've met before in Charleston, if I can handle it with finesse."

Victoria and Malcolm came to dance nearby, and Phillip whispered, "The secrets we share are mounting up. Soon, you'll have to marry me to keep me quiet."

Wyeth hadn't come down to earth since meeting Chrissy, so it wasn't surprising that he was dancing on air. She seemed to float in the sweeping wisps of a formal dress that was the dusky purple of an unfolding evening sky over Painter Place. His heart soared. The yacht, the velvety night sky spangled with stars, the dreamy music, and the beautiful young woman in his arms were all real, and yet a dream. Romance had waltzed into his life.

The musicians played a song from Broadway's *Music Man*. The hopeful notes of "Til There Was You" trilled and encouraged Wyeth's mood. "I can't believe I'm dancin' with the most beautiful woman I've ever seen."

The words had flown from his mouth. He gulped.

Chrissy's eyes were shining when he got up the nerve to look down and meet them. She said, "And I'm with the most handsome man I've ever laid eyes on." She rested her hand around the collar of his tuxedo and ran her fingers lightly through the ends of his hair. "I love the rebellious edge that the length of your hair gives you. Is it a personal statement, or do you like it longer?"

With a boyish grin, he quipped, "People expect artists to have something eccentric about their appearance. It authenticates us, and that impression sells paintings. It doesn't occur to them that I simply like how the sea breezes toss it around."

She exaggerated a sigh, and he searched her face. What he found there sent his heart racing, so he pulled her a little closer to slow dance. He basked in her sincere admiration, and it felt so right to hold her. Wyeth dared to let himself wonder if they were made to be together.

As they turned to the music, his adrenaline surged again. From another boat nearby in the private wharf, a man stood watching them. He wore dark, unremarkable clothing and a cap that covered his hair color.

How long had he been there? Unfazed at being discovered, the man held Wyeth's startled stare for seconds and frantic heartbeats. Then he dissolved into the shadows.

"Wyeth, what is it?"

Shaken, he tried to resume dancing, but it was no use. The man's eyes, his expression—the message he was conveying kept unfolding, deeper and wider.

"Can we take a break?" Wyeth croaked.

"Of course. What happened?"

Wyeth saw Phillip and tilted his head over to the refreshments. The two couples met in the yacht's spacious dining area, and Camellia suggested that she and Chrissy go freshen up.

Phillip had to ask Wyeth twice what had happened. With a furtive glance around, Wyeth lifted his chin and tugged at his blue bow tie. "It's ridiculous, bein' with her. Someone's always around and I don't mean a chaperone. I could never catch him. Now I know why."

"Was he out there?"

"You bet he was, close enough for me to read his eyes, eyes like the fearless confidence I see in hers. It's her father. He has the face of a man with a million secrets, Phillip, a man who takes care of things the rest of us don't want to hear about. Little wonder he decided not to be part of her life."

With a nervous tug at a button on his white tuxedo jacket, he glanced out the panoramic span of windows into the darkness. "Her mother was murdered last year, and somehow, I'm sure that's why he let me see a flash of the deepest grief I can imagine. He was letting me know he didn't do it and he hunted down the one who did. The killer won't come after Chrissy. A man like that has friends and enemies in the lowest places."

Once he'd blurted all this out, Wyeth wondered that he'd read so much in so little time. He must sound like he was over-reacting, or maybe he watched one too many detective and spy shows on television. But this was not half what he saw in the man's face.

Phillip caught his mood as he glanced around. Their dates were at the table, selecting elegant appetizer samples to fill small crystal plates. "Wyeth, I believe you, but this isn't the place to turn away from Chrissy. Shake it off and we'll deal with it later."

Chapter Nine

The waning crescent moon overhead reminded Phillip of his home state's flag. There were no palmetto trees in London, yet he still had the prize of South Carolina here by his side. He didn't know how long he and Camellia had together before Malcom and Victoria injected themselves back into their evening, but it would be tricky to hide his attraction to her.

Only last week in Charleston, he explained to her that part of the reason he learned to dance well was because he attended social functions with his family's business. Tonight, she understood. The reception wasn't the familiar crowd with which she was so popular, but sometimes, people who met her reached out to touch her arm during introductions. She was beautiful in a navy taffeta evening gown and sparkling sapphires.

He checked on Wyeth, unnerved at how his friend's enchantment with Chrissy had evaporated. He'd never thought of his best friend as a guy who could fall in and out of love, as the cliché's implied. He wished he'd seen the man who had disturbed Wyeth so much.

Then he groaned out loud into the crystal goblet he'd just raised to his lips. Victoria was greeting a late arrival to the party—Wilfred Rothschild.

Justin touched his arm from behind and came to stand beside him. "Wilfred's arrived, Phillip. As usual, he drowned his disappointment in a pub. Dad sent me to tell you to give Wilfred space to blow off steam and insult us. Ignore him."

"Noted."

"Dad and mom will begin the next dance, and they suggest we get on the floor and do likewise. I'll find a wallflower."

Camellia handed her empty plate to an attendant while Phillip set his glass on the same tray. He'd already taken Camellia's hand to dance when Victoria's voice called to him. He stiffened and Justin hissed under his breath.

"Phillip, darling, Wilfred would like to meet our guests from Charleston." She glided up to them with Wilfred at her side, yet she avoided touching him. Her upswept black hair shone under the lights overhead, and her false eyelashes were flirtatious against her creamy skin. Phillip knew he was in trouble the second he met her dark eyes.

"Wilfred, this lovely young lady is Camellia Heyward from Charleston, South Carolina. She and her parents came all this way for business her father had with our Malcolm's father, so they've been touring our fair city this week. Can you believe it? You're a gambling man, what are the odds of us having three families from the Charleston area represented on Daddy's boat tonight?"

The two men nodded stiffly at each other, and Camellia tightened her grip on Phillip's hand. Victoria waved at someone over Camellia's shoulder. "That's Mr. and Mrs. Heyward, over there. You must forgive me, I can't recall their names."

Phillip turned to acknowledge Camellia's parents while she filled in the blanks for their hostess. "My father's name is Montgomery Heyward, and my mother is Charlyn."

Disconcerted at how much Camellia was like her father, Phillip tried not to stare at the tall, striking man who had been so rough with him over the phone in Charleston. Wilfred reached out his hand for Camellia's and asked her to favor him with a dance.

"What a lovely gesture, Wilfred!" Victoria exclaimed disingenuously, and Phillip knew she had suggested to his rival to ask to spend time with Camellia. It would be rude to refuse. And once Victoria had her arms around him on the dance floor, it would be awkward to get out of her cage.

His spirits sank as Camellia let go of his hand and allowed Victoria to separate them. On cue, Wilfred reached for Camellia. With so many eyes on them, the only polite thing to do was follow.

A song from the Broadway musical *My Fair Lady* entertained guests on board the *Dominator*. Malcom danced near the yacht railing with a petite young woman whose father was a Gregory Global client. Victoria smiled at Phillip and said, "I told Wilfred you didn't talk business with anyone tonight. Daddy wouldn't have allowed him on board in his condition, but he was on the top deck with someone to see the helicopter landing pad. Under the circumstances, I couldn't bring myself to humiliate the poor guy further. He looks dashing in a tuxedo, don't you think? But he'll ruin his good looks if he keeps drinking."

Phillip grunted. Wilfred and Camellia had come close enough to speak to, and Victoria's cultured voice lilted to hostess mode. "Camellia, dear, I couldn't help noticing that you seem to have met Phillip before. It's such a small world. Do you know one another?"

Wilfred eyed Phillip and pressed his hand into the small of Camellia's back. "When we talked earlier, I wasn't sure you were referring to the same man I'd met in Charleston," Camellia responded. "As you asked Wilfred, what are the odds of that? But once you introduced us, I knew he was the one who recently came to my rescue to help a friend in desperate circumstances. You're right, he's a remarkable man, and not easily forgotten after you've seen his caring heart."

With a turn, Wilfred swept her around to dance away from Phillip. Speechless, Victoria searched his face for a reaction, so he glanced away under the pretense of not bumping her into Justin's partner. Then he turned toward the sound of his own name.

"Phillip Chadwick Gregory, Jr., is a lot different man when he's working to get a woman in a bedroom than when he's working to destroy a competitor in a boardroom."

He flinched at the sound of a sharp slap, then he heard Camellia's indignant retort. "How dare you touch me that way and publicly insinuate that I have no virtue! You're the one who has no honor."

Victoria gasped, and Phillip abandoned her to take a menacing step toward his rival.

Camellia's handprint grew redder by the moment on Wilfred's face. "You've been duped, sweetie. I've seen Phillip's heart, too, and yours is on your sleeve. You'll be used, trampled under his ambition. No one will ever be more important to him than Gregory Global."

Victoria rushed to Phillip's side and tried to rein in Wilfred's behavior. "Really, Wilfred, you need coffee and a cold shower," she exclaimed, snapping her fingers to get the attention of an attendant to bring coffee. "Trust me, you'll regret this tomorrow when you're sober. Apologize to my guests right this minute!"

Wilfred smirked hatefully at Phillip, who growled, "He's not sorry, and what he did to Camellia is inexcusable. He needs more than a cold shower. He's goin' for a swim."

His next step closer was checked by a strong grip on his arm. He almost jerked away before he realized it was his dad, and no level of fury would override that authority. Justin wedged himself into Victoria's former position, placing a firm warning hand on his brother's shoulder. Now, three tuxedoed Gregory men stood united before Wilfred.

Camellia's parents pushed guests away to rush to her side. Her mother wrapped an arm around her, and her father's eyes snapped with rage as he waited for an apology that would never come.

Wilfred swayed on his feet and raked smoldering eyes over Camellia. Then he turned to Phillip. "So, that's your weakness, Dominator. A woman! How predictable. I won't forget it."

Phillip snarled and leaned forward on the leash of his dad's hand. "Better a woman than a bottle, Rothschild. And you'll wish I'd forget what you've done tonight!"

The musicians stopped playing to rush out and watch the scandalous confrontation on the deck, and Victoria's father boomed a command to remove Wilfred Rothschild from the yacht.

The Heyward and Gregory families accepted the gracious efforts of their unfortunate host to smooth over the incident on board the *Dominator*. Victoria's father abandoned his role as a tour guide on his yacht and took charge of the reception, promising that any publicity would edit out the confrontation and any photos would be destroyed.

Montgomery and his wife had gathered Camellia to themselves, saying they were too shaken to remain. As they readied to disembark the yacht, Phil and Lucinda Gregory pressed for an opportunity to take the Heyward family to their home in London. Phillip's eyes pleaded with Camellia to influence her parents, and she touched her dad's arm. He leaned down to let her whisper into his ear, then he straightened and accepted their invitation.

Victoria was distraught at their departure. While the Gregory family said their farewells to guests and prepared to leave with the Heywards, Victoria took Phillip aside and reached for the back of his neck. Pulling his face closer and standing on her tiptoes, she kissed his cheek with warm lips. He melted into the comfort of an affectionate gesture after an emotionally draining incident.

"I'm devastated about what happened, darling, and I beg you for a chance to meet again under better circumstances," she murmured next to his ear. "Other people don't understand the family loyalty and social propriety we live by. The *Dominator* should be coming into port in Charleston this summer. Meet me there to tour the city and then take me to see your island."

She pulled back to search his reaction with lovely, luminous, desperate eyes. He swallowed and smiled wanly. "I'm sorry for losing my temper. You've been a stellar hostess tonight, and you'd be a wonderful guest if you ever visit South Carolina."

The light in her gaze and a seductive smile on those warm lips told him she was appeased. He felt a stab of guilt at misleading her. Then he recalled what Wyeth had overheard earlier about her true intentions in their relationship.

Wyeth sat behind Chrissy's beefy chauffeur, staring out into the night at the passing lights along the streets of London. Not so long ago, the city was dark during bombing raids, and no one knew who would be alive to see what the next morning would bring. That was true hardship. Compared to what had turned his life upside down, there were much bigger issues in the world.

The rows of buildings, encroaching signs, and odors always made him feel claustrophobic when he traveled to cities. His nerves were ragged, and every dark window, doorway, or alley might hold watchful eyes that observed him. He tugged at his bow tie as if he needed fresh air.

Beside him, Chrissy said, "We'll be there in a few minutes. Would you like a ride back to the hotel later?"

He did not need coaching in romance to pick up the translation. She was waiting for an invitation to come inside where maybe the vaporized magic would return.

"If you'd like to come in, you'll be welcome. Camellia seemed to draw comfort from you. But I don't have to return to the hotel tonight if you need to go on. The Gregorys can take me to check out on the way to the airport in the morning."

He was not sure if he had been clever or not. He had extended an invitation on behalf of the Gregory and Heyward families without committing himself. The door was open if she wanted to walk through it.

Beside him, she only sighed. He waited for her decision, but she stared through the windows. By the time they arrived at the mansion, he was feeling antsy. The chauffeur parked behind the empty limo in which the Heyward family had left the wharf.

Wyeth didn't yet know whether he was saying goodbye to Chrissy forever, but her chauffeur jumped out of the car and briskly rounded it to open her door. Wyeth linked her arm in his before ringing the doorbell to announce their arrival. The chauffeur posted himself at the foot of the stairs, and Wyeth glanced around in the deep shadows of the neighborhood.

A butler opened the door and greeted them. Wyeth led Chrissy to the sound of voices in the drawing room, where Lucinda came to touch his shoulder and take Chrissy's hand as if they hadn't seen one another in ages. "Wyeth, Chrissy, we're so glad to see you. Here, come, sit," she commanded, leading them to the comfort of a cozy upholstered love seat. "Let me get you something. Lemon tea? Chrissy, would you like honey in yours?"

Chrissy thanked her and Wyeth nodded. His mind strayed to a bizarre place that tried to reconcile the irony of a loveseat, lemon, and honey in their relationship.

Then his intuition went wild at the veiled tension in the room juxtaposed with an added nuance. Somebody was faking it.

The butler served refreshments while they exchanged the expected Southern pleasantries about the residence and any notable furnishings. It was no matter that this house sat on London's soil. Phil Gregory's parents built it, so it was sanctioned South Carolina territory.

A large painting of the English countryside that hung over a sofa charmed Charlyn Heyward. Lucinda told her the story behind the setting, then she pointed out the artist's signature. It was the name of Wyeth's ancestor.

Then Montgomery's attention went to an antique grandfather clock that had chimed, and Phil told him about an ancestor who commissioned it. As Wyeth watched the two older men, he saw something passing between them. Whether they'd met before or simply understood one another, these men were in a different place than anyone else in the room.

Camellia seemed interested in a design on the Persian rug and Phillip was silent as a tomb. Wyeth felt a surge of protectiveness. He knew his best friend was calmly corrected on the way here about losing his temper in public and threatening a man everyone knew was out of control. But he was also complimented for his gallantry in defending a woman's honor. Contradictions in Southern manners were memorized, not understood.

This made him remember his own manners. He whispered to ask Chrissy how she was doing, and when she met his eyes, something in his stomach flipped over to see the unspeakable loneliness there. But she put on a one-sided smile and whispered that she was fine.

Wyeth's impulse was to reach for her hand, but she had them both on her cup of tea. Then, they turned their attention to Phil, who had steered conversation to the reason his guests gathered at the house so late. He used the soothing, businesslike tone that Wyeth knew well. He was negotiating and closing a deal.

It was hard to watch Phillip's tension, so Wyeth looked down to the cup of warm tea in his hands, decorated with a beautiful pattern he remembered from other visits to this house. An unexpected wave of sadness swept his heart. The original owners had passed into another existence, yet something so fragile as the china remained and served their descendants. When he left this life, he'd have been the steward of the things that remained. If he could have children of his own, they might appreciate them, for his sake. But would his future nieces and nephews understand his sacrificial stewardship? Like the verse in Ecclesiastes, who knew if the next man was a good one or bad?

Montgomery Heyward's voice jolted him. "Young man, if my daughter can't escape your enemies all the way across the Atlantic Ocean, what else must she endure? In front of most of the guests on board tonight, someone suggested she was your mistress, a naïve young lady who should be pitied for being seduced by you, and she was humiliated by the groping hands of a drunk man who thought he could have your leftovers. Do you expect me and my wife to want this kind of life for Camellia?"

Camellia and Chrissy gasped, and all eyes went to Phillip, whose face blanched. But his knuckles whitened in a death grip in his clasped hands, and Wyeth saw the rally going on in his mind. He braced himself, and sure enough, Phillip slowly stood to look down on Montgomery.

For an instant, Wyeth saw the thunderstorm he'd witnessed on his best friend's face when he'd challenged Wilfred, and he knew Phil Gregory was holding his breath. The ticking grandfather clock was the only other sound.

"With all due respect, Mr. Heyward, I expected more insight from you," Phillip said evenly. "It wasn't me who escorted your daughter across the Atlantic Ocean to London, or to that reception. It was you, and Malcolm Richards. Yet neither you nor Malcolm came to her defense. I didn't want to attend tonight. I struggled about that deal for Global because Wilfred's deceased father left him his company. Now he's destroying it in the local pubs."

He paused and glanced at Justin. "The investors entrusted me with their money because of my vision and family values. In return, they know I'll respect their hard-earned money. Global and

Rothschild both have a reputation, and Global won. The King's Road rebuilding project is mine today because God gave it to me. I'll thank Him and do my best, for His glory, not mine. I don't want praise and I don't need the money. Why is it that so many investors and other guests on the yacht respect me, yet you show me none?"

Then he looked at Camellia. "Cami, if I've mishandled anything at all since the moment we met, I am deeply sorry. I'm better at business than love at first sight."

He turned on his heel to walk out of the room. Wyeth jumped up to follow him, but he froze when Camellia shot up and called Phillip's name. She turned a pleading look to her father.

Her parents rose from the sofa and Montgomery cleared his throat. "Please accept my apology. I'm grappling with my shock at the appalling public insult to my daughter. But as you've pointed out, I'm the one responsible for her attendance in the first place, and I should have challenged Rothschild myself. No one could have foreseen what happened. Please, for Camellia's sake, bear with me for a few minutes longer."

Slowly, Phillip turned, and the grandfather clock measured the time he and Heyward looked at each other. The older man held out his hand and took a step forward. "I'm among the investors for the project, with Malcolm Richard's father. That's why my family is in London."

Phillip blinked, then he stepped over to shake his hand. "I want your approval to date Cami."

Heyward sighed, as if cornered. But Wyeth was certain this was the end he'd been working toward. With a tone of finality, he replied, "Granted."

At the hotel entrance, Wyeth asked the chauffeur to wait a few minutes. He dreaded saying goodbye to Chrissy, but he'd rather be able to do it in private. He turned to her and said, "I know it's late, but will you join me in the hotel lobby?"

Inside, where the plush décor awaited hotel guests, Wyeth led her over to the same spot where he'd been so happy with her. Was it only last night? He cleared his throat as they sat down. But when he opened his mouth, he had no idea what he should say first.

"I'll be okay, Wyeth. But it's sad that you don't respect me enough to explain."

"I do!" he blurted, then wiped his hands over his face. "I do. But I believe what happened will hurt you."

"It hurts anyway."

"I saw him."

Her head shot up. "He let you see him?"

"Well, a man like that isn't easily surprised, so maybe it was his way of meeting his daughter's date. I looked out over your shoulder and there he was, observing us from another yacht. I can't shake it."

"Shake what?"

Wyeth's exaggerated sigh bought him seconds to grasp for words, but none were right, so he waved a helpless hand in the air. "The whole—encounter. It was like he was unpacking his life and I felt—challenged."

Chrissy became disconcerted and covered trembling lips with one hand. She squeezed her eyes shut.

"I've upset you. I couldn't bring myself to do that on the yacht."

"You did that on the yacht, anyway!" she retorted. "The way you shut me out was much worse."

He shook his head in exasperation. "I'm deeply sorry about how I've mishandled this situation. Surely you know in your heart I didn't mean to be cruel. I'm a man out of his element, Chrissy. I can't think straight about you and now he's come along. I'm shipwrecked!"

"If I believed you meant to hurt me, I'd have left. We were great together, Wyeth. Then like a switch went off, I lost you. I suspected that you might have seen a guard and had decided you couldn't be yourself. But it was wrong not to warn me he was there. I've never seen him!"

Abruptly, she stood up and swiped the back of her hand over her cheek. Wyeth rose and kept his voice calm when he told her, "I won't deny I'm wrong about how I handled this situation, but he wouldn't have let you see him, I'm sure of that. The message was for me. I knew who he was by his eyes. I'm not certain what color they are from that distance, but there's a strong likeness to you, both in physical structure and a confident manner. Only—"

She sniffed, hanging on his description and anticipating what came next. His hand trembled when he passed it over his brow, then he sent a furtive glance around. "Chrissy, I don't know what to say."

Chrissy's voice choked. "He revealed himself to you, knowing you'd tell me. Do it."

Wyeth reached for her hand and kept his voice low. "He was almost in the dark, ready to melt into it, on a nearby yacht at the wharf. He wore a cap and dark clothing, nothing remarkable. But his eyes—he had the eyes of a man who lives a secret life, trained to do whatever it takes to do whatever his job is. He was grieving, Chrissy. He loved your mother, and he made sure her killer came to justice."

Silent tears wandered down her face, and she swallowed before trying to speak. "Thank you," she said hoarsely. She pulled her hand from his and brushed it across her face to dry the tears. Backing up, she rasped, "I should go now, it's after midnight and I have an early flight."

Wyeth stood awkward and off kilter again. "Of course. I'm sorry about upsetting you, about how things turned out."

She nodded and took another step away, out of his reach. His heart ached, wishing for yesterday, when he thought his dreams might come true after all. "Goodbye, Chrissy Carnet," he uttered, taking a hesitant step toward her.

"No, Wyeth. Not goodbye. Goodnight. Have you forgotten? Lucinda Gregory invited me to visit for the Island Summer Dance. My dad just told me he wants me to be there."

In the sumptuous formal gown he'd admired all evening, Chrissy walked out alone into the middle of the night with the same dignity and poise she modeled the first time he saw her.

Wyeth stared at the door. He had no chance to tell her not to come to Painter Place because he was protecting it from her.

Chapter Ten

Phil Gregory had promised his son a car for his college graduation gift. After winning the King's Road rebuilding project in London, he told Phillip to pick out anything he wanted. When their plane landed in Charleston, they took Wyeth along with them to get the one Phillip had dreamed of: a brand new 1960 Maserati 3500 GT Spyder Vignale.

Sitting in his new car now, Phillip still found it hard to believe it was his. But Camellia wasn't. She felt she belonged in Charleston, and it was difficult to leave after spending several days with her there.

He already missed her as he drove his new sports car home with his best friend in the passenger seat. Beside him, Wyeth's sun-streaked brown hair blew in disarray in the convertible, and he stared out at the passing views. He was distant and distracted since leaving London a few days ago.

Phillip hadn't pressed him to share his feelings and didn't know how to help. Over the years, their troubles with young ladies were limited to who to take to the Prom and how to discourage potential girlfriends. This was the first time either had a serious interest in any particular young lady.

But he had never needed Wyeth's advice more than he did now, and with a pang, he realized how much he missed the days before Camellia and Chrissy entered their lives. He prayed the saltwater and fresh air of Painter Place would heal Wyeth so they could get back on track.

"Thanks for helpin' me pick out my car, Wyeth. Have you decided on the one you want yet?"

Wyeth was startled back into reality. "Sure thing. It was fun. This style looks good in silver, and it suits you. I don't know what I want yet, maybe the 300 SL. But it's not practical. I should get something with trunk space for carrying painting supplies."

He looked back out the window, done with the conversation. Phillip knew his friend was in no mood to discuss the pros and cons of the Mercedes-Benz roadster.

"Come back, buddy," he pleaded. "I miss the good old days, and I need you."

Wyeth turned and threw him a half-hearted grin. "I'm still here, I'm just homesick. Get me there in one piece."

Phillip guffawed. "You're lovesick, not homesick. Help me sell Cami on Painter Place. Currently, she has no intentions of leavin' Charleston."

Wyeth scowled. "What, you're thinkin' of a weekend-only marriage, or movin' Global away from Whitehaven?"

Phillip shrugged, then realized his mistake and shook his head. The dread he kept pushing behind a door leaked under it, and he felt his jaw clench.

Wyeth twisted a little toward him, his hair blowing to the other side of his head now. He shot a narrowed look over at Phillip. "No! Don't you ever shrug about leavin' the island! It won't happen, and it's not up for discussion. Hear me?"

Groaning, Wyeth tapped his palm on the console. "Is this what happens when I take the luxury of my own rare crisis instead of babysittin' you? We said we'd never let a pretty face confuse us about our future. What about our bond to protect Painter Place, 'blood brothers forever' and all that? Will you let a woman undermine your future and destroy all your most foundational relationships?"

It was no good pretending those things hadn't crossed his mind. Wyeth had a gift, or maybe it was a curse, of insight, and now he'd be like a radar.

Phillip shook his head again. "I won't."

"That's right, Phillip, you won't. This isn't complicated. I'll listen to your meltdown if things don't work out, but make no mistake, your life is at Painter Place. If she chooses Charleston, this wasn't mean to be. And don't forget, the seed is planted in her mind with Victoria's tactic about how to manipulate you."

"You said she was the one, the day she came to the house on Church Street!"

"Don't pull that one on me, Phillip. I'm no genie or prophet. Sometimes I sense things, know things, but it's just some kind of intuition or discernment. It's God-given for a purpose I can't see."

"But you've never been wrong, either."

Wyeth exploded. "Well, there's always a first time!"

Brooding and abashed, Phillip eased the silver convertible onto the bridge to the island. Wyeth made the situation sound so simple. But if Cami wasn't convinced to leave Charleston, he couldn't fathom letting her go.

He turned into the parking area behind the French Colonial mansion affectionately called the Big House. As they both combed back their hair with their fingers, Wyeth said, "She'll be here for the Island Summer Dance. There's no better time to fall in love with the island. This comes down to how much she wants you, so be irresistible."

Phillip retorted, "Oh, so Wilfred was right when he warned her that no one is more important than Global?"

"That's exactly right, Phillip!" Wyeth shouted. "Anyone who doesn't understand will destroy you! I don't pretend to be an expert about love, but that's not what it looks like."

Huffing, he got out of the car. Andy Painter trotted over to welcome his brother, opening his arms for a bear hug, and Wyeth snapped, "Don't even think about it!" With a withering look over his brother's grimy tee shirt, he asked in a more normal tone, "What are you workin' on?"

Andy dropped his arms. "Some improvements to let more northern light in your studio. We've got huge picture windows installed that take up the back wall to see the marsh. You can stay in the air conditioning and paint the views on steamy hot days this summer."

"Oh," Wyeth said lamely, and he ran a hand over his brow. "I'm sorry, Andy, I didn't mean to sound so rough. You always do a great job and I've wanted those windows a long time. It is good to see you, and to be back home."

With a nonchalant shrug, Andy whistled at the Maserati. Phillip tipped his hand and smiled. "Good to be home, Andy." He dangled the keys in front of him. "Get cleaned up. You can test drive it for me. Shake it down and give me a critique."

Andy pointed a work-roughened finger at him. "Later. My dad has me on the clock right now. Congratulations, Hotshot, nice wheels!" Then he turned to jog back into the studio buildings.

In the days when there were a pair of horses on the island, the studios served as a carriage house and sturdy stables. After the last world war, when people started buying cars and traveling on interstates, Painter Place became a destination along the coast. Collectors wanted to purchase art on the island and learn from the artists. So Noble and Phil expanded by converting the building into studio space and a gallery. Phillip, Wyeth, Andy, and Justin had all worked alongside their dads and hired contractors to make the dream come true.

Sitting in his Maserati now, Phillip stared at the structure. He could almost smell the pungent cedar wood they'd been hammering, mixed with the musk of sweating adolescents. He'd been happy back then, working with his best friend toward the future, when they'd be the formidable team that led Painter Place.

The nostalgic, possessive pang that struck his heart almost took his breath away. He filled his lungs and looked around. But Wyeth had disappeared into the house without saying goodbye.

Battery View at Sunset, Two Meeting Street Inn, Charleston SC
by Pamela Poole

Leaning against the railing of a veranda that cuddled up to most of the outside of the Big House, Wyeth watched the restless sea and wondered how to describe it to someone like Chrissy. Behind him, the front door opened softly, and his mother came to his side.

"Try Maggie Jane's magic lemonade. She wants to cheer you up."

He smiled and took the glass from her hand, sampling a sip to see if it was too tart, too sweet, or just right. It was a game he played to tease Maggie Jane about her recipe.

"Just right," he muttered, and took another sip. "I'm lookin' forward to a Painter Place breakfast again. How's she doin' Mama?"

They gazed at the last glow of light on the horizon, thinking of Maggie Jane's fiancé, who was killed by the Vietnamese he was training to fight Communism. "I've never seen such a heartache," his mother said. "She insists she'll never love again. It makes me sad to think such a wonderful young lady has decided her chances of love and marriage are over. She says she'll spend her life here, dedicated to Painter Place instead of a family. I hope you'll encourage her not to give up on love yet."

Juliette shattered their gloomy mood by bursting through the door and wrapping her thin arms around his waist. "There you are!" Wyeth exclaimed to his ten-year-old sister. He bent down for a butterfly kiss as she did a pixie dance of joy, her bare tiptoes on the boards of the veranda.

"I was at camp," she sang out. "And I missed you. Did you bring me anything?"

He laughed. "Oh, I see how it is. You just want your present. Well, it's up in your room, so I guess I'll see you later."

She hugged him. "No, I don't. I mean, yes, I want a present, but I want to be with you more. Who's the beautiful lady in your painting?"

Wyeth froze. "What painting?"

Juliette clucked at him. "Silly, the one in your studio! I went out to find you when we drove up, but you weren't there. A few paintings from your trip were on some easels. Daddy said Phil had brought them with your luggage a while ago."

Noble Painter stood in the open doorway. "Hope you don't mind me unpackin' your supplies to be sure nothin' was leaking. Phil tells me the model in your portrait is an American, and she came with you to dinner one night and a reception the next. She's quite stunning."

Wyeth did in fact mind that Chrissy's portrait had been seen before he was ready. He was not ready to talk about her. Guardedly, he said, "Thank you for your help. Yes, she's stunning. Juliette, the first time I saw her, she was modeling for a magazine."

Juliette bounced on her toes again. "What did she wear, an evening gown?"

"You guessed it! The most dramatic evening gown I've ever seen, with opera gloves and a silk formal evening wrap. She posed with an outstanding background that looked like a night out at the theater in a big city. Her expressions were innocent, sophisticated, and confident all at once, and she glided through the photographer's instructions like she was doin' him a favor."

He glanced up from Juliette's sparkling eyes to find his parents looking at him in astonishment. An incriminating flush crept up his neck.

"Oh, Wyeth!" Juliette breathed. "Did she just happen to look over at you, and it was love at first sight?"

"No, little pixie, she had to follow instructions carefully. I was in the back of the room. But after that, we met in the hallway to sign a contract, because the model we'd hired had an emergency and couldn't show up. The agency already had her assigned to us and—"

He blinked and stood open-mouthed. Now he knew who paid for Chrissy to model for them.

"So, when you saw each other, did you know you were meant to be together?"

"Uh—no, honey. Well—at least, I didn't, anyway." But his heart wrung at the memory of Chrissy's voice saying she had a sense of destiny upon meeting him. He could not manage a forced smile to his face, so he cleared his throat. "She is too professional for my talent and I told her so."

He tweaked Juliette's freckled nose. "You know what I mean, right? Like all the times you've modeled for me or dad, and you had to sit still for a long time. Then you'd ask us questions about why we painted you the way we did, and we taught you some of our secrets."

She nodded and let him swing her back and forth in his arms. "Sure, but she didn't let that stop her."

"Stop her? From what?"

"From bein' with you, silly."

Wyeth sighed. Juliette wanted a fairy tale story. He wished he had a real one to tell her.

"Well, maybe. She did some art modeling before and pleaded for the job. Can I tell you a secret? I think she just wanted an adventure that day. Everyone knows how much fun artists are."

Juliette turned a surprised grin up to him. "Yes, you are fun! What happened next?"

He pretended to strain to remember. "Well, she said the fee was already paid, so I had nothing to lose by letting her try. But neither Dante nor I paid for a model yet. Like I told you, Juliette, all things considered, she probably expected an adventure."

"How romantic!" his mother exclaimed, and Wyeth caught her exchanging a look with his dad. "What's her name?"

"Chrissy Michelle Carnet, spelled like 'net' but pronounced 'nay.' She asked me to call her Chrissy."

"Oh," Juliette breathed. "Even her name is marvelous, just like a super model, or a movie star! They should name a fashion doll for her. So, Chrissy sat for you, listened to you teach, and she fell in love. Is she heartbroken that you had to part?"

Wyeth hoped his chuckle didn't sound forced. "You're doubly endowed with the Painter imagination, my shimmery little jewel. But you may get to meet her. Lucinda invited her to visit Painter Place in time for the Island Summer Dance."

Juliette beamed. "Oh! I hope she'll bring one of those fancy designer dresses. Did she wear one around you?"

"Yes, she did. She didn't get enough adventure on the first day and went with me to a formal party on one of those new super yachts. She wore a gown the color of twilight at Painter Place."

"Are you in love, Wyeth?"

He bent down to kiss the top of her white-blonde head. "Life isn't a magic story, honey, but if you'll go get ready for bed, I'll read one with you. You pick it out and I'll show up. Deal?"

Juliette studied his face in the shadows created by lamps coming on in the house. "Deal! But Wyeth, this isn't like the other portraits you've done. You painted as if you were in love."

Andy peeked into his brother's studio the morning after he'd arrived back from London. He found Wyeth sitting on a tall stool, hands clasped between his knees, staring at a painting on one of several easels.

He tapped on the door frame, and Wyeth jerked to attention. When he walked in and reached his brother's side, he blinked in surprise. "Who's that?"

Wyeth shrugged and turned to put a worn denim work apron on. "A model we hired in London for the workshop. Dad arranged for me to work with a British artist named Dante Kent. He lives on an estate with castle ruins on it, called Seamure. You'd like him. He looks like a wolf hybrid and has a goatee. Imagining him around the castle ruins under a full moon makes me want to write a book, like Mama."

Andy chuckled at the wolf imagery but didn't take his eyes off the portrait. Juliette burst through the door, singing a nonsensical song she'd learned at camp. She came over to stand with her brother Andy and informed him airily, "They're in love, you know."

Andy turned in surprise. "What?"

"See the soft blur there, on her lips? He likes her mouth. She looks like she's just said something for *his ears only*."

Her emphasis on the last words had the intended dramatic impact on Andy, so she pointed at the painting again. "And look here, her eyes—that sparkle is private, even though they were in a room full of artists. It's as if they created their own special space apart from the real world. Maybe she just knew how to pose that way since she's a professional. Or, maybe he could've just imagined her like that, since he's so creative."

Then, she pointed to an earring that peeked out from under Chrissy's hair. "See that reflection? That's Wyeth, 'cause it's the color of his work apron. He put himself into the painting with her. And the scarf, it's about Painter Place. I know, because he told me when he packed it. He imagined her here."

Dumbfounded, Andy stared at his little sister, then turned to Wyeth, who had stopped what he was doing. The expression on his brother's face made Andy have that sensation he hated when an elevator jerked before descending.

Juliette stood back to study the painting again. "He never signed it. He doesn't want it to be over, and he doesn't want to sell it."

"Juliette, are you helpin' in the studios today?" Andy asked. "Dad said you were goin' to clean up for him before he got out here. I need to talk to Wyeth."

With an adorable pout, Juliette's eyes pleaded with Wyeth to overrule their brother, but he smiled and nodded his head to the open door.

Andy asked her to pull the door closed behind her, then he went to stand by the window he'd installed while his brother was in London. He stared at the view of the marsh. "Is it true?"

"I met an American model for the workshop. We saw each other a couple more times. Juliette is ten years old, Andy, and she's been at camp, where the girls exaggerate about their big sisters' romances. She spends too much time with me and dad, talkin' about painting techniques. Dad still hopes she'll be a second artist in the family instead of leaving for Hollywood someday."

Andy turned around. "No, Wyeth. She's always been mature for her age and she spends most of her life around adults. She has a vivid imagination, and she's insightful. Since she pointed it all out, it's obvious and I don't know how I missed it. Are you okay?"

"Sure. I need some art therapy today, that's all. Maybe after I paint the marsh from the new windows you built into my studio, I'll tell you what happened. I appreciate what you did. It's a fresh start."

"Wyeth, I don't like bein' the one to say this, but the odds of someone like that fittin' in here aren't good."

Wyeth shrugged and busied himself with setting up a palette to paint. Andy knew it was pointless to keep after him, so he changed the subject. "Can you help me out with somethin'?"

Now his big brother looked up sharply. "Sure. Fire away."

"I've met someone."

Wyeth set down a paint tube. "Someone?"

"A young lady."

"There's no one in Whitehaven for you, Andy. Is this one of Camellia's friends in Charleston, the one you danced with?"

"No, I haven't called her yet. I met this one two days later, and she lives in Georgetown. She came with friends to visit Whitehaven that Saturday when Justin and I went cruisin.'"

He took a few steps closer, then picked up a towel and toyed with it. "I can't stop thinkin' about her. I've called her a couple times."

He could feel Wyeth's eyes boring holes through him. "I wondered, if she and her friends come back up this weekend, will you go to town with me and meet her? Just me and you, not Phillip."

Now he looked up to see Wyeth's reaction. His brother nodded. "Does anybody else know?"

Andy shook his head. "No, I want you to meet her, maybe tell me if I'm actin' stupid."

Wyeth looked back down to select a handful of brushes. "Sure, I'll go to town to meet her. I hope this works out for you."

When Andy left his brother's studio, he knew Juliette was right. Wyeth's heart had taken a turn that had changed him. But if this was love, it hadn't brought him happiness.

Wyeth tried painting the marsh view from the new windows in his studio, but the portrait of Chrissy lurked behind him as surely as her father had on the yacht last Friday night. Finally, he stood and stretched, satisfied with the blocking-in stage of the landscape he was working on.

I can put the portrait in storage for now, he thought. But he didn't. Ignoring it, he went to get his outdoor painting gear ready.

His dad came to the open studio door. "I wondered why I heard you packin' up instead of painting. Can't get the view through the windows?"

Wyeth glanced up. "Oh, yeah, I got a great start on a large landscape. I need to get outside that's all."

He felt his dad watching him. "Want a tag-a-long?"

"Oh, thanks, but I know you're tryin' to finish up the painting for the show in Charlotte. I may go out to the chapel. We sold the last painting in inventory. Can I use your truck?"

His dad stepped back from the door to let him pass into the hall, commenting that they couldn't seem to keep paintings of the chapel in stock. Then he dug into his pocket for keys. When he put them in Wyeth's hand, he held on to it.

Wyeth had to look away from the searching scrutiny in his father's wise, sea-blue eyes, but he didn't pull his hand away. Quietly, he told him, "I can't talk about it now, Dad."

With a nod and a firm pat on Wyeth's hand, his dad said brightly, "You're twenty-two years old, son. It's time you stopped borrowin' my truck. Let's go look for a car soon."

Relieved, Wyeth answered, "Yeah, I need to decide on one. We'll go drive a few on your next day off."

A guest was in the Painter chapel when Wyeth pulled the truck into a sandy parking area nearby. A bicycle leaned on its kickstand near a short column where a weathered verdigris sundial rested, and he recognized the sea-glass green paint color as the code belonging to one of the island cottages. He tried not to disturb anyone inside while he selected a view of the building and set up his easel under a shady grove of palm trees.

He pulled out a small canvas hoping he could finish in one session, making sure the back was stamped with the Painter Gallery branding. The new acrylic paints made it easy to have a day's work dry and ready to hang in the island gallery.

There was a new technique he wanted to experiment with, using transparent layering to achieve a sunlit glow on the side of the building. But it was a slower process than he expected. After several times when he caught himself clenching his jaw in impatience, he stepped away to the truck and grabbed a thermos of cold water.

He leaned back against the door and stared at the chapel, searching for some key he missed that would help the painting. After several gulps of water, he looked away, into the garden.

Why was he so frustrated with a painting? If it didn't work out, he'd paint over it. It was no big deal. Yet he made a big deal out of everything these days as if he wore a "Do Not Disturb" sign to warn life to leave him alone. He was unsure which was worse, to grapple with life's challenges in fear of making a mistake or to have nothing special ever happen to him.

He put the thermos back on the front seat of his dad's truck and shut the door. With a purpose in his stride, he went to stand in front of the easel, refreshed his palette, and painted again. As he painted, he poured out his heart in prayer, as the person in the chapel was doing. By the time he finished, the guest came out the double front doors.

Upon noticing Wyeth, a young lady wiped her eyes and re-did her auburn ponytail. She went to the bicycle but didn't get on to ride. Instead, she looked back at him and then at the chapel.

Wyeth stopped short of a groan under his breath and waved back at her politely. Now, he was stuck talking about the painting, and maybe about the whole island once she asked him who he was. His stomach was growling for the late lunch he knew Maggie Jane was keeping for him.

The young lady walked the bike over to his easel. "Excuse me, sir, but are you painting the chapel?"

"Yes, ma'am. Nice day for a bike ride. Hope you're enjoyin' the island."

"Oh, yes, it is, and I am. I'm here with my aunt, as a companion to help her this summer. She's a writer. We leave tomorrow, so I asked for the afternoon to roam around. May I see your painting?"

Wyeth stepped back. "Sure."

The young lady pushed down the kickstand on the bike and came over to look at the picture. Then, she brought her hands to her mouth. After a few moments she asked, "Is that what it looked like out here while I was praying?"

"I'll never be able to capture it the way it really was."

"I knew it! At first, I pleaded for what I want, for a sign, or something Jesus could do to help me make the right decision. After so long in the chapel, feeling like my prayers were only hanging out around me, I told Him I'd go His way, if I could only see it. After a while, I didn't know what else to say to Him except that I love and trust Him, whatever the outcome. He hears us, I know that by faith. But it didn't feel like He was there."

Her ponytail swished as she turned to Wyeth. "He was out here, with you!"

Wyeth stared at the painting to see how she'd come up with that idea, then he looked up at the building. The light had already changed. "Ma'am, Christ is omniscient and omnipresent. He's with you and me at the same time."

"Were you praying, too?"

His expression was her answer. "Yes, you were. What did you pray for?"

Wyeth shifted his weight to the other leg. "The same thing. It's a universal condition, what we're seeking. In the end, even if we don't get what we want, we trust in the right outcome. Some of the most solid people I know are the ones who had bad outcomes and grew from the experience."

She looked back at the painting and whispered, "He was here. His presence is so clear in this painting."

"Would you like to have it?"

"Oh, yes! Is it for sale?"

"No, ma'am, but I'll give it to you. In dark times, maybe it will help you remember that Christ is always with those who love and follow Him."

Chapter Eleven

It was Friday night, and the weather couldn't have been better if Andy had ordered it. Yet now that the time was here to take his brother to meet Valerie, his stomach was in knots. He wondered if he'd worn the right clothes and if he would remember to say all the smooth things he'd been practicing.

He glanced over at Wyeth in the passenger seat. Never one to be talkative, his brother was even more subdued since coming home from London. The unusual revelation in Wyeth's studio two days before still rocked Andy when he recalled it. Sometimes there was truth to the adage that a picture spoke a thousand words, and with some help from his little sister, the portrait Wyeth had come home with revealed things about his brother that made Andy wonder if he knew him at all.

He still hadn't confided in Andy about the portrait model, which meant he hadn't gotten over her. And since he was annoyed with Phillip, Andy was sure he hadn't discussed her with his best friend, either.

Unnerved at being ignored by Wyeth, Phillip had gone back to Charleston for the weekend to see Camellia. Good riddance, as far as Andy was concerned. Tonight, he had high hopes for a camaraderie between true blood brothers—not the kind Phillip and Wyeth had become years ago, when they went up to Dog's Head, made a small scratch on their right hands and mixed their blood, promising to always be friends and work together for the good of Painter Place.

It was only a drive across the Intracoastal Waterway bridge and a right turn to be on Main Street in Whitehaven and join the weekend parade of chrome and metal. Wyeth grinned and shook his head when Andy slid his Corvette behind a long, low '57 Chevrolet Bel Air in sparkling two-tone red and white.

Andy ventured, "What, you too old for this now?"

"I still have the full-page ad in the Whitehaven Register burned into my memory when the Bel Air came out."

Now Andy laughed outright. "You mean, the one dad and Phil frowned at because of the sexual overtones? 'Sweet, Smooth, and Sassy,' and 'the saucy new slant of its High-Fashion rear fenders'?"

"That's exactly the one."

"I struggled for weeks, tryin' to prove they were wrong and old-fashioned, but my imagination kept goin' where they predicted it would take us."

Wyeth smirked. "You can give up on provin' Dad wrong. It'll never happen. Even the Whitehaven Register refused to print that ad after they heard Dad's opinion. But I thought I was above it and could name the guys he was talkin' about. It was a humbling experience to fight my imagination."

"You? Na. You're kidding! Not you."

"I can have a relationship, Andy, I just can't get any kids out of it."

"Yeah, I know that, I didn't mean it that way," Andy sputtered. "But—you? You're perfect. I'm the Painter family's risky business."

"You think I'm perfect because I keep my mouth shut and try to stay out of trouble. Besides, guys are curious about women and we have imaginations. We want a wife someday and we wonder about what it'll be like. We crave a woman's respect, and we want to act like we know what we're doing even if we don't. God understands that. Temptation isn't a sin, it's where we take it afterwards that can let God down. Those ads sell cars, but they lead us to a place in our minds that demeans a woman."

Andy kept one hand on the wheel and dragged the other one through his sun-bleached blonde hair. This was precisely why he'd often longed for time alone with his brother, but Phillip always seemed to be around. Little wonder Wyeth never got into trouble. Phillip was the iceman, always doing and saying the right things.

Wyeth nodded ahead at the saucy fenders on the Bel Air. "Who's drivin' that thing, anyway?"

"William Park, now eighteen years old, better known around these parts as 'Willie Park.' And we all know he will. Girls fight over him. He spends every paycheck on his car and runs it up to the Grand Strand to shag and drag on Saturdays."

"You mean the kid who works for his dad, the mechanic with the garage just outside of town?"

"That's the one. He grew up."

The expansive stretch of metal on the sleek Bel Air mirrored lights and blinking neon signs. Wille Park tapped the horn at two girls eating homemade strawberry ice cream cones from the Blue Skies Sundae Shoppe. They waved frantically and trotted over to the car. Traffic waited while they opened the doors and jumped in.

Wyeth whistled at a 1956 convertible Mercury Montclair that was crawling along in the other lane, sporting a blue and white paint scheme. The car's radio blared hopeful words to a song promising that life could be a dream. "Wonder how long it took to bleach off those white walls so he could take 'em out tonight?"

Andy smirked. "Last week you were dancin' on a super yacht. This week you're gawkin' at land yachts. You really need to get out more."

He craned his neck toward the Five and Dime Variety Store to see if Valerie and her friends were standing outside yet. The tricky part about cruising was the timing. He didn't want to waste the precious minutes with her by circling around the slow-moving traffic. A blue '55 Ford Crown Victoria was pulling out of a parking space right up front, so he held up a Chevy Skyline while he waited to parallel park in the coveted spot behind the monstrous wings of a green '58 Buick.

"If you don't mind waitin' a few minutes, I'm supposed to meet Valerie here. Her friend saved enough for an Elvis record."

Wyeth stared at the neon sign urging music lovers to buy Elvis records while they lasted. Then he twisted enough in his seat to look along the length of the sidewalk. "Things look different at night when the neon comes on in little bitty Whitehaven."

Andy flipped off his radio during a song about faraway places with strange-sounding names. "Things have changed here, Wyeth. You, me, and Phillip, we're facin' a different time than Dad and Phil did. Dad says the culture will be turned on its head in the next few years. Any day, I could get drafted. I want to get married and have kids before that, kids that will be the next generation at Painter Place, even if you're the one who has to step in to be like their dad if I'm gone. This will be their town someday."

Another long convertible cruised by with the Peter Gunn theme pulsing from the car speakers. Andy drummed his steering wheel to the beat. "There are good jobs around here now, drawing people in. A former pro ball player named Wallace built an athletic apparel manufacturing place not far up the highway as you head out to Myrtle Beach, and he built a big house in Whitehaven across the water. He has a view of Painter Place at Dog's Head from his new pier. A few others came and set up some decent businesses, too, like an ex-military guy named Grayson. Whitehaven is stretchin' out like a sleepy cat in a sunbeam."

The first movie showing ended and a stream of people poured from under the running lights of the theater's marquee. When a group of young ladies spotted Andy, they waved wildly for him to wait as they crossed the street.

"You're jaywalkin'!" he teased as they surrounded his Corvette.

"Oh, nobody will run us down," retorted a brunette with startling pink lipstick.

Another girl came to Wyeth's door and smiled at him. She smelled like the mouthful of bubblegum she was chewing. "Hi, Andy's friend. Y'all wanna go over to get some pizza with us?"

As if on cue, Valerie and her group filed out the door of the Five and Dime. Andy said, "I heard the pizza is good, but we already have dates tonight. There they are now. Be more careful crossin' the street."

"Aw, Andy, no, they're from off!" protested one of the girls. Her friend pulled her arm, and they waved reluctant goodbyes to the Painter brothers while Valerie and two friends stood waiting in front of the store window.

Considering Wyeth's recent whirlwind romance in London and his brooding existence since returning, Andy wasn't sure how to spark social exchanges between him and Valerie's group. A cruise around the block with her in the Corvette was out of the question unless his brother was enjoying the company of her friends. Which he wasn't.

As the evening wore on, it would become clear that nothing would bloom between either of them and his handsome older brother. But upon meeting him for the first time, they reacted as Andy had seen all his life. They found his gentle brown eyes, strong jawline and brow, aristocratic bearing, and aloof personality to be irresistible. In fact, they barely stopped short of gushing over him as they parted to make a path so he could get out of the car. Then they sandwiched him between themselves and asked him about his favorite things to do in town.

They all strolled together down to the Coastal Corner, stopping to chat along the way with the locals. There were only two stools available at the long counter in the crowded soda shop, so Andy told Valerie's friends to sit in them and order what they wanted.

He led Valerie to go dance by the throbbing jukebox to the instrumental "Walk, Don't Run" by the Ventures. One of her friends asked Wyeth to dance while the other friend designated herself to watch over their orders. She beamed when Wyeth smiled politely and told her his next dance was hers.

The following song was a beach music tune, and Andy asked Valerie if the Carolina shag was okay. She turned a dubious look to other couples shagging nearby, swinging her dark hair. It picked up the neon colors of the surrounding lights while she replied, "I'm not good at the turns."

"Then you need plenty of practice. Stay close, there's not much room. I'll teach you turns if you'll come to the Island Summer Dance next Saturday at Painter Place and be my date."

"You're invited to Painter Place? Do you know them?

"Ok, now—watch." He guided her slowly through a turn. She bumped awkwardly into him, which he thought was a bonus. Andy pulled her firmly to his chest to steady her before he caught his brother's smirk. He winked at Wyeth and let Valerie go.

"It's a good start, Valerie. You'll get the hang of it. Come on, loosen up, you're too self-conscious. Now I know what's happening, and I can adjust. We might create our own moves."

A second beach song came on and Wyeth switched between Valerie's friends to dance. Andy saw him helping her with the first turn and two moves, but she did well for the rest of the song. He smiled to see the young lady leaning into his brother every chance she could. How many times had he seen this over the years at the Island Summer Dance, where all the single girls expected to dance with Wyeth because he never had a date?

By the end of the song, Andy had created a new turn that Valerie could do well. She wore the irresistible smile he loved. "What song do you want me to play next?"

"My favorite song is the one you had on in your car the night we met."

"Really? That's my favorite, too. Come on." He pulled her over to the jukebox and fished for change in his pocket. She searched the colorful tags and found the song, then placed her finger on it the same moment he told her to play P3. She pushed the right buttons, and he pulled her back to the floor.

Andy softly sang along, then led her through his adaption of a shag turn. He experimented with a new flair, and she handled it well. "See, you're good at this."

"Do you dance to this song much on weekends? You knew which number the song was."

He gritted his teeth. There was always something that came up to make her wonder if he was spending time with other women. He tried to ignore it and hoped she'd stop altogether when she knew him better. "No, I don't come to town much on weekends. But I eat lunch in here sometimes. Do you dance much on weekends in Georgetown?

He felt a thrill of victory at the look on her face. He'd turned the tables on her. If she wanted to corner him about how he spent his weekends, well, he wouldn't mind knowing how she spent hers.

"Must be convenient, the master comin' home again to find Maggie Jane's man dead and outta the way," jeered a voice that Andy recognized as a troublemaker in town. Ralph was surly when sober and out of control when he was drinking.

Andy jerked his head around to find Wyeth, who calmly told Valerie's friend to go back to the counter and get her purse. Andy nudged Valerie to follow her.

"What, is this about us?" she whispered. He nodded impatiently and pointed to the counter before turning back to his brother.

"They better not start nothin' here in our town, like they did in Greensboro and Charleston," added another man with Ralph.

Some patrons started leaving quietly or backing away from the dance floor where Wyeth stood. African American patrons in the store and soda shop walked out, and two who worked there went behind the counter to get the owner.

Startled confusion was all over Valerie's face when she glanced back at Andy from the counter, where she and her friends gathered their things. He beckoned with his hand for them to hurry. But before he could get his group to the door, the troublemaker made another insinuation about Maggie Jane and Wyeth, calling her names that sent gasps through the soda shop.

Wyeth bolted toward them, but he'd only taken two steps before the owner rushed out in his kitchen apron to get between them. Red-faced, he spread his beefy arms to keep them apart. "I don't want any trouble in here tonight, boys. Ralph, the cops are on the way to sober you up. If I were you, I'd wait on them rather than face the mercy of the crowd outside. Wyeth, you and Andy get your friends back to the sidewalk 'til he's gone. You got cause, that's for certain, but I'll handle this now. Tell Ida Mae and Maggie Jane I'm awfully sorry. Yes, sir, I'm awfully sorry. Nobody believes a word he said, I promise you that. That kind of talk makes me want to wash the place down."

Ralph and his companion leered at Wyeth. His friend's voice slurred in a taunt. "Looks like Wyeth Painter ain't the master 'round here, anyways."

The owner told him to shut his mouth or he'd shut it for him. Wyeth took a few steps backward as Andy tugged his arm, but he kept a smoldering glare on Ralph. It took a lot to rattle Wyeth, but Andy feared the repercussions when his brother reached his limit. He wasn't surprised when Wyeth played a trump card.

"Never come lookin' for extra work on the island again."

Ralph's smirk faded. "Your daddy's the one who does the hirin' out there."

"Not since the master came home, as you say. That's my job now and I'll be the one in charge of it all someday. I have a long memory."

This scathing warning had the intended effect. As Andy pushed Wyeth and Valerie's friends out the door, he shot a look over his shoulder to see the panic in Ralph's eyes.

On the sidewalk, groups had gathered upon hearing there was trouble inside. They stood waiting for the outcome, and when Wyeth came through the door, they rushed toward him in support. He was the reluctant man of the hour.

The last thing Whitehaven needed was a mild racial clash. Once a rare incident reached the newspapers, the town would be tagged with a reputation it didn't have. He and his brother encouraged everyone to get back to their plans for the evening, then they ushered Valerie and her friends to the Five and Dime.

"Where are you parked? We'll walk you to your car, but we need to leave, in case there's any more trouble. I'd feel better if you called it an evening, too."

Valerie's friends rushed to assure him they were just a few parking spaces up the sidewalk. One friend's aunt was expecting them, so they would leave when Andy did.

"Andy, what just happened?" Valerie asked. "It sounds like racial tension. That guy, he was referring to the sit-in in Greensboro, and the one it inspired in Charleston. Who's Maggie Jane?"

Wyeth blurted, "Maggie Jane is the daughter of the head cook and housekeeping manager at Painter Place. Her fiancé was killed in Vietnam last January, by imposters, as he trained Vietnamese to fight Communism. Maggie Jane is like my sister, and there haven't been any slave masters on the island. Ever!"

Valerie and her friends stared wide-eyed while he jerked the passenger door of the Corvette open and sat down. Andy turned a regretful look to Valerie and reached for her hand to ask if he could call her soon.

She swallowed and said, "You're Andy Painter. You and Wyeth—you're the brothers who live at Painter Place."

"Yes. Does that matter?"

She pulled her hand from his and took a few steps back. "I am afraid it will." Then she turned away and ran to catch up with her friends.

"I can never thank you enough for offering Jacqueline a temporary position working for Gregory Global," Camellia told Phillip. "You've been amazing about that whole situation. If I didn't know you better, I'd wonder if you were just trying to impress me."

She elbowed his rib playfully. He took advantage of her closeness to link his arm through hers while their shoes tapped the ballast stones from long ago ships in the port of Charleston, South Carolina.

"The help I offered is heartfelt, but she is torn, I think. She'll give me an answer soon."

"She's still prayin' about it. I expected more condemnation from folks here, but most in our church home are reaching out with support. Some have handled similar situations with family members. No one, except their parents and mine, know about the abortion plan. That's a step too far for many to accept. Tom seems to be takin' the worst of it, as he expected, because of his leadership as we grew up. He was the role model among us."

Phillip scowled and grunted as they crossed an intersection to King Street, and they strolled in silence for a few moments. The sidewalks were crowded with shoppers, and wonderful scents wafted through some of the open doorways.

"Does Tom have any plans?"

"His parents figured out how he can finish his last year at college and get his degree, with a part time job. They're past the shock and lookin' forward to being grandparents. He asked Jackie to marry him in a civil ceremony, then move with him into an apartment. He has a summer job lined up there now, and she could help with making ends meet if she finds temporary work."

"So, she's holding out."

Camellia sighed. "She's always dreamed of her engagement ring, her wedding dress, her honeymoon, and her new life as an adored wife with a romantic husband who is well respected. Now, she'll have a simple wedding band, no wedding or honeymoon, she'll gain weight and wear maternity clothes, and struggle financially with medical bills to have the baby. Her life won't be the fantasy she planned, but that's not the worst part. Something inside her heart shattered, Phillip, when Tom wanted her to abort their baby. The fairy-tale prince in her dreams slipped off his throne, and she doesn't see him the same way anymore. She doesn't trust him."

Phillip reached out for her hand to make sure she was steady on her feet over a huge tree root that upended the paving stones. "Even a friendship can be like that," he said. "Everyone will let you down sometime, that's what Savanna Painter says. She tells us at Painter Place that we should spend our lives with the people who are worth the pain when they disappoint us. It's only a matter of time before everyone will."

"You know, I never thought of it that way. But there's also a point when the damage is beyond mending. Your whole reality changes once a spotlight illuminates a reality that's not acceptable. You can forgive, but you move on. We must ground any deep relationship in trust."

"Can trust, on its own merit, be enough, without romance?"

Camellia turned to glance at him. "Well, sure, I suppose. Like, satisfaction in successful arranged marriages, or the settled relationships of couples who are married a long time and seem to just be friends. What does that—"

"Do you trust me?"

She carefully stepped over a manhole cover. "I met you once before I took you with me on a mission to rescue a good friend and her baby, didn't I?"

"Yes, and I followed. So, we have a relationship built on trust."

She laughed, and a lady carrying several shopping bags glanced over to look at them. The woman smiled knowingly, and Phillip grinned and winked. Then, to Camellia's surprise, he steered her by her elbow through a door opened wide to welcome shoppers.

"You said Jacqueline had dreams of her wedding and engagement ring, and the life she'd live with an adoring husband. And you agreed that we have a relationship grounded in trust. So, tell me about your wedding and engagement ring dreams."

Camellia gasped before exclaiming, "Phillip!"

"Is there anything I can help you with today?" asked a clerk. Then she recognized Camellia. "Camellia, how wonderful to see you!"

"Oh—yes," Camellia said, holding out her hand. "It's wonderful to see you, Loretta. How are Larry and the kids?"

The clerk took her hand in greeting, then released it. "Well, thank you! It's so kind of you to ask. You remembered Larry's name!"

"Yes, but I can't recall the children's names. I only know they are adorable!"

"No matter, sweetheart, you made my day," laughed the clerk. She turned to Phillip. "Any friend of Camellia's is a friend of mine."

Phillip grinned and stuck out his hand to shake hers. "It's a pleasure to meet you, Loretta. I'm Phillip Gregory. I'm visiting your fair city for the weekend and tricked Camellia into strolling King Street on such a beautiful day. We discussed a friend's wedding dreams. I thought it would be fun if Camellia trusted me enough to share her engagement and wedding dreams, and this looked like a store where a woman would get grand ideas."

Loretta touched his arm. "Oh, honey, you came to the right place. She and her friends drop by here sometimes to try things on. More than once, her mama and daddy have been in here askin' what she likes. But she never seems to decide on engagement and wedding rings, like the other girls. She said she wants her fiancé to pick one out."

She turned to Camellia. "Do you mind if I show this young gent what other things you like?"

"I don't suppose it would do any harm."

Loretta led Phillip on a tour around sparkling glass display cases. "Just two weeks ago, Camellia and her friends were excited about this." Keys jingled in her hands as she opened a display case, then she reached for a silver bracelet. "It's a bangle style, which is a big trend coming for the next few years. This one has a hinge and safety latch."

Loretta demonstrated how to wear the bracelet, then asked Camellia to extend her arm. She snapped the clasp on Camellia's wrist.

Camellia's eyes lit up as she held her arm out to Phillip. "See the carvings on it? They are palmetto roses and palm fronds, and tiny diamonds here and there in the design are like the sparkle of the sea and the stars. I love this because it feels like home."

Phillip captured her wrist in his hand and studied the workmanship. "It's beautiful, and it suits you. It reminds me of my home, too."

He looked at Loretta. "We want it. Don't worry about putting it back in the box, she'll wear it."

Camellia protested and Loretta beamed. "Don't worry," Phillip told Camellia as he made his way to the cash register. "We can share. If you tire of it, just give it back. My mom would love it."

"But—no! I won't tire of it, that's the thing."

"Great! You won't get tired of me, either."

Chapter Twelve

Wyeth stood on the veranda on Sunday afternoon, enjoying a quiet view of the Atlantic over a warm cup of tea. It had been a stressful weekend since the confrontation at the Coastal Corner on Friday night. In a rare role reversal, it was his brother who was praised by their father for his actions to remove them both from trouble. Wyeth hated disappointing his father and knew he should have handled the incident better. He had a lot to learn before he'd be the man his dad was.

The incident sparked an undercurrent of electric tension in the small town of Whitehaven, an outcome Wyeth was sure Ralph had aimed for. But he had not figured it would inspire sermons in churches around town today, like the one Wyeth's pastor preached from Genesis about how the word "race" is not in the Bible. The pastor reminded his congregation that humanity is one blood, and he traced facts to show them how it had been modern theories of evolution that planted ideas of superiority.

None of this was news to Wyeth. But a good portion of Whitehaven attended his church, and for some in the congregation, their faith was mostly a Sunday-only event in their week. They rarely picked up their Bibles to read for themselves. This had been an eye-opening reminder for them, and no doubt had been the topic around many tables after church today. Some had the pastor for lunch, but Wyeth prayed that most would find the truth to be a healing salve on their hearts. They could influence others in town.

He turned when the door opened behind him. Phillip was back from a weekend trip to see Camellia in Charleston, and Andy was giving him his perspective on what happened on Friday night.

Phillip's brow was furrowed as he came up to stand beside Wyeth and peer into his eyes. Wyeth looked away and asked, "Did you accomplish what you hoped to?"

Phillip snorted, then rubbed his hands over his face. Andy grinned. "What's wrong, did you drive that new Maserati down a one-way alley in Charleston?"

Phillip's striking blue eyes narrowed. "At least it was a two-seater, not a bus."

Andy reddened and sputtered, "What's that supposed to mean?"

"Do you know Valerie's last name?"

"No. I wasn't ready for her to know who I was. She found out from Ralph on Friday night. What difference does it make?"

"An introduction is first thing, straight up, for a Painter who lets a girl ride alone with him in a car. Justin was there, too, and he knows better. You should've identified who you were settin' your sites on before you started aimin'."

Andy's eyes flashed, and he took a menacing step forward. He hissed, "You're goin' too far, you jerk! Exactly what's your problem with Valerie?"

"I've got no problem with Valerie, Andy. But her dad's a huge problem for Painter Place. If your dad was pickin' a bride for you from an approved list, she wouldn't be on it."

Abashed, Andy stood rooted in place on the veranda. Wyeth growled, "Just spit it out, Phillip! Who is she?"

"Her father is a notable heart surgeon in Charleston named Dr. Anthony Rush, whose romantic exploits often turn up in the society pages of the local papers. He and her mother separated when Valerie was a little girl, but they've never divorced. He makes sure it's better financially for her mother not to divorce him, since marriage is a convenient excuse for not committing to any of the other women."

Wyeth turned to watch Andy's reaction. Shock and dismay filled his brother's eyes. Wyeth's heart sank, for there was no question of Valerie's resemblance to Tony Rush in the grainy black and white photos in the society pages of the Whitehaven Register.

Andy spun on his heel and stormed through the front door into the Big House. Wyeth whirled to turn on Phillip. "What's wrong with you?"

Phillip's eyes were full of regret, and he set his mouth in a grim line. He looked out to where the earth split between Carolina blue sky and an ultramarine Atlantic. "I'll go apologize."

Wyeth put his hands on his hips and seethed. "Misery loves company, I get it. You're stressed out, I'm stressed out, and now Andy is, too. The only thing keepin' me glued together is lookin' to the future, Phillip!"

With a broad sweep of his arm, he said, "I can't do this alone, but your heart isn't here anymore. Is this the day you're tellin' me you're leavin' and goin' to Charleston?"

The door opened again, and his mother announced that Wyeth had a phone call. Phillip followed him.

"This is Wyeth," he said gruffly into the receiver.

"Wyeth, this is Chrissy. Did I catch you at a bad time?"

He drew a sharp breath and glanced around, but Phillip wasn't in the living room. In fact, no one was. "No, I just came in from outside. I hope you're doing well back in the States."

"I am, thank you. It's busy, since I'm getting my house ready for the market here in the Washington area."

"You're—you're selling your home?"

Chrissy sighed into the receiver, and it made an intimate breathy sound. "Yes, I had the process started before the trip to London. It's difficult to move on with my life here after what happened to my mother right outside our door. Most of my friends are off at college, or busy with a career, or getting married. I have no ties here anymore."

"Oh. Where's your new place?"

"I've been too busy to look for one. The real estate agent warns me this one won't stay on the market long, so I'm praying about where to go next."

Wyeth rubbed his forehead and shifted his weight to his other leg. She said, "The reason I'm calling is because I didn't get Lucinda's phone number to follow up on her invitation to visit Painter Place this week. Can you share it?"

"No. I mean, yes, I could, if you want to talk to her. But there's no reason you and I can't work things out. About your visit, I mean."

He flushed. Years of training to be socially graceful seemed to drip down the drain when he was with Chrissy. But she always had the savvy to smooth his awkwardness into a meaningful conversation. "Oh, that is terrific, as long as I'm no trouble to your family. I'm not sure what Lucinda was planning for accommodations, or what to bring to wear to the Island Summer Dance."

"You can stay here at the Big House. There's a guest room with its own bath that will be available, just down from—" He paused and swallowed. "Camellia's family will stay in the guest house on the Gregory estate. But Lucinda has other rooms if you'd prefer to stay there, near Camellia. It's up to you."

"If I have a choice, I'd rather be where you are."

He picked up the base of the phone and stretched the coiled cord, so he could sit down in a nearby wing chair.

"Wyeth?"

"I'm here—I just needed to sit down. I mean—you can bring something semi-formal to the dance. Keep in mind that there's a lot of sand. We have a big covered pavilion deck to dance on, but a lot of guests like to be barefoot in the sand. Most will walk out on the pier or the beach. Don't wear something that will be ruined by salt water."

"I think I have just the thing. I'll call Camellia and see what she's wearing."

Wyeth sighed and glanced around, but he was still alone. "Have you been in touch with her since London?"

"Once. I called to see if she was okay after that humiliating encounter on the yacht, and if she was planning to attend the dance. She was still indignant about Rothschild, and she hopes never to meet him again in her entire life. She said you and Phillip had just left that day in Phillip's new Maserati. Sounds like a hot car."

Wyeth's attention split in two directions now. "Yeah? Oh, yeah, it sure is. A very expensive one. You like hot cars?"

She laughed. "Most young ladies like sports cars, Wyeth, because they like the men who can pay for them. If they can afford impractical things like expensive cars, they can buy dresses and diamonds. In my case, I appreciate the exciting designs of the cars, but I'm relieved not to have a self-destruct button for men who collect them."

He chuckled. "I see where you're comin' from. And I assume that you don't include Phillip in that category."

"Hmmm, how do I respond to that? His looks put him squarely into the stereotyped playboy role, but he's proven to be trustworthy and his parents are good people. I'm intrigued by his hedge of protection around you, and I'm certain that any young lady who wants to get close to you will have to meet his approval."

"You're insightful."

"I cut my baby teeth on observation skills."

The man he presumed to be her father flashed into his mind, and he swiped his hand across his eyes. "So, what kind of car do you drive?"

She laughed again, and Wyeth wished it would go on and on. Her laughter was like a homing beacon.

"My mother said people often identify with their vehicles, and in that light, I must drive an American car. She worked for the government and was patriotic almost to an extreme. I got a new white Thunderbird on my seventeenth birthday, and that's what I'll be driving to Painter Place tomorrow."

"Tomorrow?" Wyeth shot to his feet.

"Yes. The real estate agent wants to invite other agents to meet here at the house tomorrow, and then schedule showings this week. I need to be out so it will remain clean."

"Right. Of course. What time should we expect you?"

"If my mapping and directions are accurate, I'd say around three in the afternoon. I can delay somewhere along the way, if the timing is better later in the day."

"No! I mean, three is fine. Three o'clock. Sure, yeah, that's good." He joggled the phone cord up and down. "I'll take care of things on this end. Chrissy—be careful driving and call me if you have any trouble."

"I will. And Wyeth?"

Wyeth gulped. "Yes?"

"I will be alone. Completely."

The mansion was quiet. Wyeth walked past the massive staircase in the heart of the house on his way to the library, where his parents spent Sunday afternoons together. The double doors were always open as an invitation for anyone who wanted to join them.

His mother sat with a relaxed but perfect posture in her favorite wing chair by the glass paned French doors that lined the wall and opened to the veranda. A book was in her hands, but she was staring out at the sea.

His dad was sitting on a generous leather sofa in front of the fireplace mantle, his feet propped on a ottoman. The book in his hands was oversized, yet he held an antique magnifying glass to it, studying a detail on a painting.

Often, classical music played faintly in the library on Sundays, but today, it was quiet. Wyeth wondered if his parents expected him. Without turning around, his dad drawled a warm welcome to come in, but it was his mother's smile that drew him closer. She'd been far away in her imagination, writing another book, and he recognized the look of re-orienting herself to the reality of the moment. He was a frequent traveler to those imaginary places where he composed paintings that may or may not make it to a canvas.

He wandered over to his mother's chair and clasped her outstretched hand in a gesture of welcome and love, then he sighed and turned to look at the Atlantic through the French doors. "I have a guest who will be here tomorrow. Is the Sunflower Room still available?"

His father twisted with an arm over the back of the sofa. Wyeth could feel his stare. His mother rose from her chair. "Yes, it is. It's time someone was in that charming suite."

"Chrissy Carnet will be here around three in the afternoon. She just put her house on the market, so she wants to stay away and keep it clean for showing."

He didn't need to turn around to know his parents were looking at one another, and his mother came to stand by his side. "The Sunflower Room will be ready. Why don't you tie up loose ends in the studio so you can be free while she visits?"

"I don't know how long she'll be here. At least until after the dance next weekend."

He could hear the worn leather creak as his dad rose from the sofa. "She can stay as long as she likes. I don't want to be nosy, son, but it would help me avoid social blunders if I knew what she means to you."

Wyeth clasped both hands behind his neck. "I told you on the veranda how we met, in London. As I was cleaning up after the class she modeled for, she asked to be invited into our dinner plans.

I'd expected her to leave with her chauffeur, since it was a business arrangement, and I'd overheard a pushy photographer promise her a dinner date that night. But she claimed she didn't have plans. So, Dante and I invited her to eat with us at the hotel dining room."

"A pushy photographer?" asked his mother, and he knew he'd given himself away. He turned around and stuffed one hand into his pocket. He wandered over to the mantle and absently traced a finger over the rich wood carving designs.

"When she wanted to know about why I chose the scarf, I told her it reminded me of home. That was the first time I'd mentioned Painter Place. We did some sightseeing the next day and had dinner with the Gregorys, where she learned a lot more about the island. We kept spending time together until the night of the reception. In the hotel lobby those nights, we talked about our lives. She doesn't know her father, but he supports her and keeps tabs on her. Her parents planned to tell her who he was on her eighteenth birthday. But her mother died right before that, in front of their house, and Chrissy realized how dangerous their lives had been. Until then, she didn't appreciate growing up with security systems or a guard. Sometimes, she thinks one of her guards is her father, and she's resentful that he's not communicating with her. He didn't even comfort her in her grief."

He turned to walk toward a view of the sea and told them about his discussions with Chrissy about children and their faith. "I invited her to go to the reception with me, and we had a great time until I glanced over her shoulder while we were dancing."

Wyeth rubbed the first signs of stubble growing on his chin since shaving that morning. He went to stand in front of a painting displayed on an ornate easel. His father had painted the busy European evening street scene on his honeymoon with his mother. Lamps lined the sidewalks and cast fascinating shadows. There were so many places someone could hide, unobserved, or blend in.

His father stood beside him. "Wyeth?"

"Everywhere we went, there was a chauffeur, a bodyguard. And sometimes, there was someone else." With a sidelong look at the library door, he shrugged, shaking off a ghost. "Things felt good with her, and I hoped she could be the one for me. Then I saw someone in the shadows of a nearby yacht, in a hat and dark clothing, and his eyes—"

Wyeth grimaced and bit his lip.

"Did he threaten you?" His dad kept his voice low.

"No. No, not at all. That's the thing. He didn't hide, either. When I look back on it, I wonder if it's my imagination. Something about his face, his eyes, reminded me of Chrissy. In that instant, I believed it was her father. But in those moments while we locked eyes—I don't know how long—I saw, or sensed, profound grief and loss, and revenge. Maybe not revenge, but more like justice."

Agitated, he wrung his hands together. "I'm certain he does things we don't want to know about. What I saw in those eyes shook me to the core, and I'll never forget it. I saw deep love. And I saw something like—like resignation. Or trust. Or the passing of a torch."

He wiped his hands over his face. If only he could forget that meeting across the mooring of yachts in the darkness of the Thames River!

His mother came to stand beside him. "Phil and Lucinda said you acted as if someone flipped a switch in your demeanor, and that Chrissy was hurt. Did you talk to her to explain?"

"Yes, but not right away. I couldn't think straight. We went by the house in London after what happened with Camellia, then her chauffeur took me back to the hotel. In the lobby, I tried to explain, but she became upset. She said the incident is a message. Her dad wants her to be here, at Painter Place, and she's determined to find out why."

He raised his palms in a helpless gesture. "She walked out before I could explain that I have to protect Painter Place from her, from the surveillance and darkness she might attract to the island. But she knows it's a problem for me, because she told me she will be alone when she comes tomorrow."

His dad cleared his throat. "So, she's driving by herself, no chauffeur or guards, unless they are tailing her?"

"That's right. I told her to call me if she had any trouble. But Dad, that man—I can't explain how I know this, but he must have connections and enemies in the highest and lowest of places. I want you to understand whose daughter will be on the island this week. And maybe he took care of the man who killed her mother, but what if more come after her? She'll lead them here and put us all in danger."

His mother rested her hand on his arm. "Wyeth, is Juliette right about your feelings for Chrissy?"

"I betrayed myself in the portrait. I'm naïve. It was foolish to lose my head over someone I knew for three days. It sounds melodramatic, I know, but now I think she's the daughter of a fearsome international spy, or maybe an assassin."

"Wait a minute, hold on here," his dad sputtered, waving a hand in the air. "Hold on, now, son. Even if you're spot on about her father, you don't know for certain that trouble will follow this young lady to Painter Place. You've got a vivid imagination, and that comes in handy for painting. But stop lettin' it run wild. You don't know that the island will become a stage for espionage while she's here. I'm told she's a beautiful, well-brought up young lady with a can-do attitude. She's poised, smart, kind, and assertive, like your mother. We want to give Chrissy a chance, and I hope you will, too."

Wyeth's pulse shot up and he tried to normalize his breathing. Had his father so easily swept away caution about such a woman? He'd been raised to have reservations about anyone who might bring trouble to the island. Even if his dad was right about Chrissy's attributes, Andy had a point, too. She was too much for Painter Place.

"But Dad, Painter Place will get boring for someone like her. Then what? And she might change her mind about a family."

His mother took his hand. The quiet voice that could command the attention of a crowded room said, "Wyeth, you said Chrissy talked about her faith. I assume she's a Christian?"

"Yeah. Yeah, she's very outspoken and serious about her faith." A tight grin won its fight for a place on his face.

"Then, do you trust Jesus to work out all these problems you're predicting, if she's the woman you've been prayin' for all your life? Could you be the man in a safe place she's been prayin' for?"

Wyeth swallowed. He knew the answer he should give. But he struggled before he could utter, "Yes."

Dinner at the Big House was always a casual affair on Sunday evenings. Everything in town was closed except for church services, which didn't meet in the summer except for revivals and events. The housekeeping staff was off, and the Painters could eat leftovers, sandwiches, or try out their cooking skills.

Often, the Gregory family joined them. Lucinda and Savanna cooked well, and Noble and Phil were handy in the kitchen. Juliette learned to cook while Wyeth, Andy, and Phillip did anything that was asked of them. They all looked forward to time spent talking together about current events in Whitehaven and the world.

On the Sunday before the Island Summer Dance, they made an easy spaghetti dinner with a light sauce and salad, then went out to the beach to set up a game of horseshoes. Phillip asked Wyeth to walk with him before the games got started, and they waded in the surf up toward the north side of the island.

"I'm sorry about the way I dropped a bomb on Andy today," Phillip began. "I talked to him after Chrissy called you. You're right, I'm stressed out. And I admit, the possibilities of establishing an office of Global in Charleston crossed my mind more than once. If Camellia doesn't come around to the reality of living here, there's no point in our relationship anymore. But I've gotten my mind straight about it now. I'm not leavin' Painter Place, Wyeth. I'm not. So, stop waitin' on me to betray you. I don't deserve this, and I miss you."

Wyeth was quiet as they walked further up the beach, kicking foam from the surf. Then he replied, "You're right, and I'm sorry, too. I'm not myself—or worse, I've been faking it and this is who I really am. You don't know how much I needed to hear that you're not leavin' the island. And Andy, he's handling his bad news all right tonight."

After a glance back at the family, Phillip said, "He went to talk to your dad about it, after you left the library. He got a caution light to move forward since he'd already committed himself to a date for the dance. It would be rude to withdraw an invitation to a lady. Your dad told him to brace for reactions when people around town figure out who she is."

With a wince, Wyeth replied, "Only fools rush in, they say. Andy and I stand guilty. Lesson learned."

Phillip stopped to let a group of small fish slide over his foot. "You weren't foolish, Wyeth. The way I see it, you were smart enough to walk through an open door. Can you talk about it yet?"

Shading his eyes with his hand, Wyeth studied a small watercraft bouncing in the waves. "Can you tell if that's someone local?"

Squinting, Phillip identified the sparkling boat. "It's a new couple in town, older than us. He's a former pro athlete named Wallace, and he opened a sports apparel business that brought jobs to Whitehaven." Then he slapped Wyeth on the back. "It's not Chrissy's father."

Wyeth blew out a breath and looked relieved. "It would be great to talk to someone who was there, in London. Andy won't understand."

"I was there. Let me help."

Wyeth picked up a shell and threw it out as far as he could into the waves. "Was it a dream?"

Phillip searched for a shell like the one Wyeth had thrown, and with all his might, he threw it farther into the water. "No. Chrissy is real, and she was genuine about her interest in you. She knows what she wants, and she'll be here tomorrow to get you to see things her way. It won't be much of a challenge."

Wyeth found another shell and threw it. "What about when she discovers I'm boring? If I let myself fall for her, how could I ever get over it when she rejects me and Painter Place?"

Phillip had been scouring the sand to find a similar shell. When he found one, he grunted as he swiped it up into his palm. "You've already fallen for her, Wyeth. I've heard women look for security, not excitement. You're messed up after turning her away. Why not go all in?"

He threw the shell, and again he covered more distance than Wyeth. His friend didn't pick up another shell, but he stood staring out over the ocean. "Because I'll lose my objectivity and my willpower. She's dangerous, Phillip."

Phillip guffawed as he scooped up two more shells and tapped Wyeth's arm to hand him one. "You couldn't be more right about that! And her dad's face haunts you like a nightmare." He threw the shell as hard as he could. "But I like her, and I like him. I want her here, and I want her dad to know she's here. A world of threats is out there for Painter Place, but Chrissy Carnet isn't among them."

Wyeth threw the shell Phillip had given him, and this time, his went farthest. "You want me to take a risk and give her a chance?"

"We both might end up like crybabies out here on the beach soon. I read somewhere that fools try to explain love, but wise men never do. I only know what I've seen since the day you met her, and I'd rather you reached out for this than to live with regret. Like I told you, I'm here to stay at Painter Place, so take that off your list of problems. Go all in."

Chapter Thirteen

Chrissy perched on the twisting red leather and stainless-steel stool at the counter at the soda shop. It was difficult to appear poised on something that moved like a nervous cat. A frosty glass of Southern sweet tea sat on the black marble countertop, intimidating her. What if she overturned her introduction to Southern culinary culture while trying to capture the straw between her lips?

It would be a shame to spoil her fitted white capris, or the nautical blouse. The navy bodice and red trim was smart against the generous white collar, and the stylized anchors on the big buttons made her smile. She inspected the carefully chosen outfit in hopes the long drive hadn't made it look like something she'd pulled from the laundry basket.

Other than the squirrely stool, the picturesque Coastal Corner Drug Store and Soda Shop was wholesome and charming, like a Norman Rockwell painting. There was a jukebox with glowing candy-colored neon tube lights along the machine's outline, luring music lovers to come feed it their spare change.

Another young lady in the soda shop pushed a button to hear a song about how only the lonely could understand how the singer felt. Chrissy didn't like the song because of what it did to the wound it was stabbing in her heart right now. She wished the girl's change had paid for a more uplifting selection.

As of today, Chrissy hoped her loneliness would evaporate. And she never planned to sing anything to re-live the feeling.

She had arrived in Whitehaven early, and a drive around town had told her it was a lazy day along Main Street. The African American teenager who'd pushed the button for the sad song went to the counter to join a friend, about four squirmy stools away from Chrissy. They ordered soda floats, then the girl lamented to her friend, "I feel so awful bad for Maggie Jane, ya know? She's so lonely now without her man Roy."

"Yeah, and my blood boils at that dog callin' her those filthy names in here Friday night! She ain't goin' off to cuddle in the dark with Wyeth Painter."

Chrissy's reflexes were quick. She got her lips off her straw when her stool jerked to the side. Her mother's ring on her right hand clicked against the edge of the counter as she brought her seat back to face the glass of tea. She found a mirrored sign behind the counter that reflected the image of one girl, who waved a hand through the air. "And anyways, Wyeth, he's like a preacher man, or a Sunday School teacher, or the deacon. You don't—"

She broke off, shrugging. "I can't explain it, but there's just somethin' weird about havin' sexy thoughts about a preacher."

The other girl nodded and shuddered. "I wasn't out on Friday night. I had to roll my hair and do my nails for a date on Saturday."

"I was in the Five and Dime, buyin' Mamma a scarf for her birthday. Through the window, I saw folks runnin' up the street. When I looked out the door, there was a crowd." She pointed to the street. "Wyeth, he came stormin' out with his brother and three girls from outta town, from off, ya know. I heard later his brother and the store manager stopped him from forgettin' who he is and just beatin' the daylights outta mean ole Ralph. That skinny troublemaker drinks too much and forgets how civilized folks act, and he keeps bad company. What they said is nigh to unforgivable if ya askin' me my opinion. Can't blame Wyeth none for blastin' off."

The girl sniffed, leaning into the counter to sip her soda float and keeping her stool expertly reigned in. Her friend nodded. After a minute, she observed, "Still, Painters gotta be careful. I know, the Bible's packed with heroes and battles for the Lord, but the Painters, they'd get sued. People always lookin' for a buck from 'em."

"Guess so, but it's heroic to see a man defend a woman, anyways. And those folks on that island don't sin like most people. My mama says it's the White Spirits in that Native American legend, the one with the Wind Songs. If they sing all over your home, you live in a higher place, that's all. Keeps the old Tempter away."

Both teenagers slurped up the bubbles on the bottom of their glasses. Chrissy realized she'd drifted in their direction. She braced her palms on the edge of the counter to adjust the stool with her knees forward again, and she noticed her clenched teeth marks had ruined her straw.

A glance down at her watch told her she'd have to get in her car soon if she wanted to make a good impression by arriving on time at Painter Place. A gawking gas station attendant in town told her earlier that she'd be on the island after crossing the only large bridge in town.

The teen girls at the counter thanked the waitress and paid her. "Anybody know those girls the Painter brothers were with Friday night? I heard there were three, and they're from off."

"No, but a dark-haired girl was cruisin' in Andy's new Corvette the week before, when Justin Gregory was in town. She's cute, that one. Someone joked he showed Whitehaven to that actress, Audrey Hepburn, so she could be in a movie here. But someone else's mama said she's the only child of that big shot surgeon from Charleston in the scandal papers. Don't know if Andy knows who she is yet, but it's a sure thing his daddy don't. She ain't likely to have a family with Painter blood in their veins."

"They inspire me, you know what I mean? The Good Book says to be careful about who ya mix yer blood with, and I plan to. When the boys at school nag me about not kissin' like the other girls, I remind 'em of the Painter and Gregory boys."

Chrissy carefully dismounted the unruly stool. The dainty heels of her open toe sandals clicked over the black-and-white tiles as she made her way to a sign for the Ladies Room where she brushed her teeth and refreshed her lipstick. As she twisted the tube and put it back into a stylish wicker purse, she whispered a prayer thanking the Lord for arranging such an enlightening detour in her afternoon.

She walked out into the bright sunshine and placed her hand on her purse while she scanned her surroundings. There were no suspicious situations and no lurking bodyguards. She was on her own.

Butterflies of hope fluttered their wings against Chrissy's ribcage. The slow drive across the waterway to get to the island was breathtaking, and she suddenly felt small in the scheme of God's creation. The ultramarine blue horizon extended to the world's end in both east and west—or, as the twitching compass she'd set on her console told her, to the north and south from her car.

There was a guardhouse at the end of the bridge that reminded her of an enclosed bus shelter, with a window air conditioner. No one was there, so she crept by in the Thunderbird, hoping she wouldn't be shot.

She shook her head with a resigned sigh. It was difficult to stop thinking that way.

A French Colonial style mansion loomed ahead on her left, and she turned into the parking area behind it. There was another structure shaped like a capital letter L, and it retained the character of stables or carriage houses in an earlier era on the island.

As she turned off the ignition, Wyeth came out of one of those doors. Her heart lurched toward him, but years of discipline over her reactions served her well. He stood rooted in place, staring as if she were rain in a desert. She smiled through the tears that stung her eyes.

He took a few steps toward the car. Then, he started jogging, and before she knew it, he wrapped her in a warm hug. It was a moment she'd never forget.

An older gentleman had come out of the same door Wyeth had, and she knew it must be his father. His build was so much like his son's. They had the same squared hands, the same long artistic fingers, and the same mannerisms. She hadn't expected the magnificent blue eyes, however, eyes that seemed to take you to a faraway place—maybe even infinity—and she became lost there, searching, making connections.

Then his broad, contagious grin forced weathered crinkles around those eyes. He reached for her hand, and his cultured, drawling accent was like listening to Wyeth.

"Well, now, Miss Carnet, as beautiful as your portrait is, it couldn't have prepared me for seein' you in person. I'm Noble Painter, Wyeth's father, and it's a joy to meet you. Welcome to Painter Place."

"The pleasure is all mine, Mr. Painter. Please, call me Chrissy."

"And you must call me Noble," he said, bowing slightly over her hand. "At your service."

"You boys bring Miss Chrissy in, right this minute, before she faints from heat stroke!"

Chrissy instantly loved the voice that chided the men. She turned to the raised garage under the house to see a handsome woman with strong features and graying hair. The woman wore a spotless apron and stood with her hands on her hips.

Noble chuckled. "Chrissy, this is Ida Mae, and she's in charge around these parts. Ida Mae, why don't you take Chrissy inside to meet Savanna?"

Chrissy glanced over to meet Wyeth's eyes, and he smiled and nodded. She handed him her car keys to get her luggage and then walked toward Ida Mae.

The older woman hugged her, then held her out for inspection. "It's like seein' an angel, lookin' at you, Miss Chrissy. A very tall angel though scripture don't mention female angels at all."

Chrissy was delighted at the welcome. "Yes, I'm 5'10", which was embarrassing in high school but comes in handy in my profession. And I can't recall ever being welcomed so warmly as I have today! Your voice is like being wrapped in a blanket of love."

Ida Mae's eyes grew misty as she scrutinized Chrissy there under the shade of the house. "We got a lotta that to go around here, and you have a good heart, I can tell. Somebody would make a mistake to think you're just a pretty face."

She transformed back into her no-nonsense role and gestured for Chrissy to follow up a flight of stairs. "Height is a great thing for a woman. It helps weed out the men in your life. Ya cut out more than half right away and then see what God's doin' in the tall ones, like our Wyeth. He's 6'2", and I ain't shy about takin' a lot of credit for him and his brother shootin' up to the sky. Wyeth's the tallest, though, cause he's the compliant child. Maybe Andy would've grown more if he'd eaten his vegetables every meal, but that boy must learn a few things the hard way."

She opened the door at the top of the stairs and ushered Chrissy into delicious aromas that wrapped around her. She had come into the kitchen area by a back entrance, and despite the sheer scale of the open space, she felt drawn into the intimacy of a place where magic happened.

"Maggie Jane, come on over and meet Chrissy."

Chrissy caught her breath at the name, thinking of the teens in the soda shop who adored her—and of the insinuations in town about her and Wyeth. A young woman put down a spoon and wiped her hands on her apron, then walked over to shake Chrissy's hand.

"A pleasure to meet you, I'm sure," Maggie Jane said. Her voice was earthy, rich, and soft, like the voluptuous curves of her figure. Her dark eyes were clear and alert under thick curling lashes.

"Oh, the pleasure is all mine, Maggie Jane. And forgive me if I'm acting ill-bred within the borders of Southern manners, but I must ask what facial moisturizer you use. You have the most luminous glow I can remember seeing."

Maggie Jane looked surprised, then pleased. She glanced over at an enormous marble-topped table island that ran at least ten feet through the heart of the kitchen. "On the kitchen island, over there, I'm mixin' some of my recipe right now. Come on over. Savanna, Lucinda, and I use it."

"You make your own?"

Maggie Jane pointed to ingredients she'd set out. "That's sweet almond oil. I press it myself, but sometimes I mix in some jojoba. There, that's frankincense, myrrh, sandalwood, rosemary, and ylang-ylang."

"Frankincense and myrrh, like the gifts the Wise Men brought to Jesus? May I?" Chrissy pointed to a decorative glass bottle with a ribbon-bedecked cork stopper.

Maggie Jane opened it and extended it to her. "Yes, they are precious oils since Bible days. I call it Life is Beautiful Facial Serum. Sometimes, I switch to another recipe with rose, frankincense, and sandalwood. Lucinda, she loves it, but Savanna isn't crazy about the rose scent. She uses it in winter when her skin can get cracked in dry heat from fireplaces. Rose oil calms irritation."

Chrissy inhaled the scent from the bottle. "This is heavenly. You are amazing, Maggie Jane. Can I purchase some of this from you?"

Maggie Jane looked back down at the ingredients. "No, but I'll mix up a batch now while everything's out. You try it while you're here."

Wyeth and Noble came through the back door with her luggage, and Wyeth looked surprised to see her in the kitchen with Maggie Jane. "I'm afraid to ask," he drawled. "What are you two cookin' up?"

"A love potion, you goose! Run on, now, get those bags in the Sunflower Room this minute." Maggie Jane pointed him out of the kitchen.

"You could retire on what Phillip would give you for a love potion."

Maggie Jane pretended to throw a dish towel at him, and he ducked away. "That clown," she said indulgently. Then she searched Chrissy's eyes. "You plannin' to call this place home?"

Undaunted, Chrissy held her gaze with the answer. Maggie Jane nodded with satisfaction and fished a small bottle from her apron pocket, which she then pressed into Chrissy's palm. She sandwiched them both between her hands and held them.

"He thinks I'm jokin' around, but I did make a love potion. Wear a drop of this on pulse points when you're with Wyeth, like on your wrists. Throw out any store-bought perfume you brought. He likes this. Be natural. Be his island."

"I wondered what he'd like, and I brought a sample bottle of something light and citrusy. What is this?"

"I'll say later, if it works with your body chemistry. But it has a touch of sandalwood, that draws him like a magnet. I also put in somethin' that made Coco Chanel famous."

She released Chrissy's hand and gestured to put the bottle in her pocket. "It's all natural, good for you. Do what I say, and he'll follow you around like a puppy. But it won't be puppy love, no ma'am, it'll be forever. It's good you're finally here, Chrissy Carnet."

Savanna Painter didn't need to speak to be the attraction in a room. She carried herself like royalty, yet her kindly expression held only grace for anyone fortunate enough to be near her. Wyeth had her soft brown eyes, hair, and coloring, and seeing them stand together warmed Chrissy's heart, though she couldn't have explained why.

Wyeth and his parents gave her a tour of the mansion, and the exterior didn't prepare Chrissy for what was inside. The graceful yet practical architecture outside withstood challenging weather elements, with spacious porches for the ocean views and breezes. But inside, the mansion had the Southern elegance, opulence, and charm she'd only seen in magazines.

She learned how the house design functioned for a large family and guests. The time in which someone built it was when travel was a feat of endurance, and a host could expect extended stays. Special guests visited in the spring, summer, and autumn months. There were cottages built on the island for other guests, usually creative people like artists, writers, and musicians. They came to seclude themselves in their work, or to paint, or to attempt a creative breakthrough.

She learned that Wyeth's favorite room was the library. While his mother and father mentioned some of the books, sculpture, and art in the decor, she strolled the built-in bookcases, many with glass doors to protect against humidity, insects, and dust. The glass inserts were watery with age. Most items were one-of-a-kind or rare. Every piece had a story, which they said they'd share another day.

Fortunately, the room was large and the ceilings high for all the bookcases, because a wall of cozy window seats and sets of French glass doors opened to the front veranda of the house. If the collections in the library didn't offer enough inspiration, there was always the sea.

She admired the ballroom, with its stunning chandeliers and twin French door sets that opened to the veranda on the other side of the house. A graceful pattern inlaid into the flooring brought musical notes to her mind, and Chrissy could imagine this room decorated for a ball over the winter holidays.

Savanna and Noble's suite was on the first floor, among other rooms. After showing her where the service elevator was, they led her to the heart of the house. Instantly, Chrissy knew this was her favorite spot.

Sculptures of graceful herons stood poised amid living palms in huge container gardens, which flanked the wide marble stairs. But it was the sight of the stained-glass dome three stories overhead that stopped her in her tracks. "Oh," she breathed.

Perhaps the Painters were used to this reaction, because they waited. "It's the Creation Account in Genesis," Savanna said. "I remember the first time I saw it. At certain hours of the day, the colors splash down all over the stairs. I love to take off my shoes and follow them, as if I'm stepping barefoot into pools of enchanted paint."

Chrissy gasped. "That's one of the most beautiful things I've ever heard anyone say."

"She's an author," Wyeth piped in, taking Chrissy's hand. "She casts spells over us with descriptions and leaves us speechless. Come on, it will be time for dinner soon, and we haven't shown you how to get to your room."

Grasping the elegant curves of the handrails that led to the second floor, she rose to find the same tile pattern of the ballroom in a hallway and landing. She looked over the railing where the landing opened to the first-floor ballroom below.

A wave of Noble's arm showed her where the bedrooms were. Wyeth had a suite at the back corner of the house, and it had a sitting room that overlooked the marsh. A door in the main room opened to the back veranda, overlooking the converted stables Chrissy had noticed when she arrived. They explained that the building was studio space and a gallery. Wyeth's younger brother, Andy, had a room next to his, opening to the same veranda.

They led her past other guest rooms, all with nine-foot ceilings and seven-foot tall doors, explaining that many buildings in the South had high ceilings so the summer heat would rise. Architecture compensated with proportions for doors and windows in the rooms.

Wyeth opened a door and invited her to come inside. She couldn't help it when her hand went to her heart and her mouth dropped open. She'd entered an intimate paradise.

"Hope you'll like it," Noble said, looking around. "When we remodeled, we opted to use the large closet for a private bathroom. We added more space for the bath by moving a wall that made the sitting area smaller, too, but most guests don't use it much anyway."

Savanna went to a massive whitewashed antique armoire and pulled one of the ornate handles to display the empty interior. "This serves as a closet, but if it isn't large enough, please use the dresser and under the bed. There's also a stool under the bed if you need to place things on top of this. Or, you could ask Wyeth to reach up there for you."

Chrissy gazed around, enthralled. The headboard of a generous sized bed was a reclaimed picture window attached to the wall. Painted over the watery glass inserts was a free-flowing field of sunflowers, separated by the panes, but all coming together to make a single view. Standing as sentinels on either side were tall storm shutters, attached to the wall, weathered and whitewashed like the window frame and other furnishings. Small lamps were mounted through them. The lampshades had tiny sunflowers across them and cheerful yellow fringe trim.

Realizing they were waiting on her reaction, Chrissy gushed, "It's lovely. I've never felt so welcome, anywhere."

She turned to an oversized antique French dresser, where a blue vase of real sunflowers brought tears to her eyes. Beside it was a well-worn red leather Bible, and Chrissy immediately wondered if Wyeth himself had arranged it. She once learned in art classes at school that the red, blue, and yellow triangle formed the basic colors an artist would use.

She sniffed and brushed her cheek with the back of her hand, then traced the sunflower pattern on a cotton quilted bedspread. Noble cleared his throat, and when he spoke, his voice was hoarse. "Well, we'll leave you to settle in. Dinner is at six, downstairs in the dining room, unless you're tired and would like a tray. We eat early so we can all enjoy long evenings."

"Chrissy, dinner is casual here," Savanna said. "What you have on is perfect if you think you'd like to go down to walk on the beach afterwards. Let us know if you need anything at all."

"Oh, thank you so much, I will. I'm looking forward to dinner, and a long evening by the ocean. I'm so—it's all so wonderful that I'm overwhelmed."

Wyeth waited until his parents left before he asked, "Can I help with your suitcases?"

She sniffed again and brightened. "Where are they?"

He turned, and she followed him into the sitting room, where a small upholstered loveseat looking out to the beach was adorned with twin sunflower throw pillows. On an adjoining wall, a slender secretary style desk with a curved feminine chair waited for her to send correspondence or spill out her heart in her journal. Yards of light-filtering gauzy white fabric bunched up on either side of the windows, just as they did in the bedroom.

Wyeth picked up the handles of her oversized suitcases, one in each hand, and plopped them on the bed, where it seemed they'd crush the sunflowers. "Let me know when you've unpacked, and I'll come store these away for you."

As she followed him toward the door, he turned to look over the room once more. "We don't have many resources on the island, which is why my ancestor chose it. The king would consider it worthless and leave him alone. We found other ways to flourish, such as the limited sunflower crop. It's so popular that there's always a waiting list with florists from Charleston to Myrtle Beach when they bloom. The heads that don't become as pretty are used by Ida Mae for oil and seeds."

He glanced at the furnishings and added, "There was once a small cottage on the island where the sunflower fields are now. Some notable people stayed in it over the years, but time and a storm damaged it. We took it apart and preserved what we could for repairs on other cottages, then we dug up the foundation and expanded the sunflower fields. Some of the best parts of the salvaged cottage are in this room."

"Did you paint the sunflower field over the glass panes of the headboard?"

"Yeah. Other windows were smashed in the brunt of the storm, but this one faced the sunflower fields. It haunted me that guests in the cottage had enjoyed that view for decades, so I asked to keep it in the studio until we remodeled this room. One day, I had a vision for what it could be. I couldn't stop painting."

He hesitated with his hand on the doorknob. "The flowers are profitable, but the real reason we grow them is because they make us smile. They remind us that the sun always comes up on a new day, and yellow is the color of hope."

She met his eyes and took an impulsive step toward him. "I've never been so full of hope, Wyeth, and it feels amazing."

"Will you walk with me on the beach later? When we were together in London, you wore a dress the color of last light over the Atlantic. I'd like to show you why I can't get it out of my mind."

"And I want to see all that with you for the first time."

With a small smile, he turned and closed the door gently. She sighed and stood looking after him, wishing he could stay longer.

Remembering Maggie Jane's assurances about the scent in her pocket, Chrissy fished for the tiny bottle. She walked over to stand in front of a rustic, whitewashed old door from the sunflower field cottage, propped against the wall. A full-length mirror replaced the former glass insert.

Then she whispered, "So, this is love."

Chrissy spread her arms wide and twirled barefoot in the surf. "Oh, Wyeth, it's a cotton-candy sky!"

Wyeth couldn't remember the last time he'd laughed from somewhere so deep inside, and it felt as if every tense moment he'd ever stored up evaporated with it. He thought he should join her, but he couldn't resist watching instead. Not that he had never seen a similar reaction from guests who visited for the first time, but it had never been important to him before. Chrissy's face was a study in pure joy, and it was all because of his island.

Well, maybe it's not all for the island, he thought. If he could believe in the way she looked at him, touched him, and the things she said to him, some of her pleasure was because he was here.

He almost doubled over laughing as she ran out of the water from a tiny fish. But he couldn't double over because she ran straight into his arms, laughing along with him. Then she looked up into his face, eyes shining, and he couldn't think of anything else.

"After the cotton candy fades, will the color of my dress happen in the sky?"

"In the sky, in the water, in the shadows, and everywhere," he answered. "It's sneaky, so if you aren't watching, you can miss it. But we'll be ready."

Unbidden, an image of the man watching them on the yacht in London flashed through his mind. He blinked but mastered the instinct to pull away from her.

With a seductive smile, she said, "We'll see it together, Wyeth. And I won't wonder anymore about why you loved the dress so much that night. Shall I wear it again for you? Are there any formal events around here?"

He reached up to tuck a free-spirited lock of hair behind her ear. His fingers lingered on her pearl teardrop earring. "I'd love that. We can look for something formal in the meantime, like in Charleston, but here at Painter Place, we host a formal New Year's Eve Ball every year. Consider yourself invited if you don't mind an alcohol-free celebration."

Her smile enchanted him. "We have a date, and a million dates until then! And for the record, I've never touched a drink."

He wasn't sure how long they stood together like that. Gulls called, sandpipers trotted in a blur to find dinner, and the foamy surf massaged the shore. But all at once, Wyeth knew twilight was pulling misty curtains around them.

"It's happening," he whispered, turning her around to see the horizon. With his arms around her waist, he pulled her back to lean against his heart. She rested her head near his throat.

The fleeting lavender hues became dusky purple, and he heard Chrissy's soft moan of delight. Wyeth drew a deep breath of the sea air. It was the most indescribable twilight he'd ever experienced.

Chapter Fourteen

On Monday afternoon, Andy Painter drummed the beat of a silly rock-and-roll song on the dock railing of the marina in Georgetown, staring at the pay phone. A maintenance crewman passed him with a grin and a salute, heading down the pier.

"Ya waitin' on somebody?"

"No, just gettin' up the courage to make a call," Andy drawled.

The man belted out a rusty laugh. "Gotta be a woman, then, or yer daddy." Then he disappeared, ducking into the cabin of the nearby yacht.

Andy had already handled his daddy. He had a reluctant green light, or maybe it was really a caution light, to follow up on his impulsive invitation to the Island Summer Dance with Valerie.

A serious relationship with her was probably out of the realm of possibility now, but he wasn't ready to let go, either. She hadn't answered his calls, so she still didn't know that he'd found out about her father. But he could hardly wait to hear her perspective on who Andy really was.

He stuffed his hand into a pocket for a tattered piece of paper he carried around. It was her first name, her phone number—and her handwriting. His heart always jumped unreasonably when he saw the beautifully formed cursive letters and clear, careful numbers.

He rubbed his thumb lightly over the ink. Then he looked up again at the grubby pay phone and walked over to pick it up. "I'm givin' you one more chance, girl," he muttered under his breath as his finger turned the dial of numbers.

He was almost startled when she answered. "Hi, Valerie, this is Andy. Hope you're having a great day!"

He bit his lip, waiting on her response. Slowly, she said, "Hi, Andy. It's been an interesting kind of day. I fired some new pottery pieces in the kiln, but a friend made one that had an air bubble. It blew up and damaged another. I hope your day is goin' better than that."

Laughing outright, he replied, "Sounds like most of my days. It's usually not my fault when things blow up."

He imagined the smile on her face, but she didn't say anything, so he jumped in before the conversation lagged. "Listen, I'm down at the harbor. Are you busy? I wondered if you could come and talk face to face."

"Oh. Well, I guess I can, since you're here. I'm in work clothes, though, from the pottery studio."

"No problem. I'm in work clothes, too, with a layover of a couple of hours. A maintenance crew is spiffing up the charter boat."

"Have you eaten?"

"Not since lunch. Is there somewhere you'd recommend? We could talk over dinner."

"Well—" Valerie hesitated. "Why not here?"

Andy almost dropped the receiver. He managed to recover it, and he switched ears. He hoped he sounded suave when he replied, "Sure, why not? How do I get there?"

"I'll come down and walk you back up. Let me tell my mama we're havin' a guest."

"Sure, I'll hold on," he said. With a muffled sound, she covered the mouthpiece of her phone. He pumped a fist into the air and squeezed his eyes shut. *Please, please, Lord, let this happen.*

"Okay," she announced. "I'll be there in five minutes. Where are you?"

Elated, he glanced around. "At a pay phone, near—"

"There's only one. Be watchin' for me."

"I can't think of anything I'd rather do."

Andy struggled to rein in his impulse to eat hardy. It had been hours since an early lunch, and the food in front of him was delicious. But the years his parents had relentlessly spent training him in table manners was paying off in a big way with Valerie's mother, Audrey.

"Please, don't be shy, have more of this," Audrey said, pressing a serving dish with tender cubed steak and gravy in it into his hands. "There's only one left, and we'd rather not put it away."

He accepted the dish and thanked her with the expected courtesies, while she pushed the mashed potatoes closer to his plate. "These will just become potato cakes if you don't eat more with the gravy," she said.

Valerie favored her mother much more than her father, he realized with relief. And he found it charming that though she'd changed into a clean blouse for dinner, there were flicks of clay in her ponytail.

Her mother was a gracious Southern hostess through and through. He recognized the rambling, graceful house he was being entertained in as a home built for the months when plantation owners used to spend time in town. Since Valerie had told him her mother inherited it, it added up to her being from a respectable South Carolina family, despite the unfortunate association with Tony Rush.

While his mouth was full, Audrey kept the conversation going. Valerie related her day in the pottery studio in a small building in the back yard. This summer, she was teaching classes there and creating inventory for the autumn arts fairs.

Andy swallowed and wiped his mouth with an embroidered cloth napkin. "Valerie, I'd love to see your work. How did you become interested in pottery?"

"Oh, I learned it during summer classes with a local artist. After high school, I took business courses, and I have a part time job as an office assistant at my church. But I do well with my pottery at craft fairs. It's a challenging path for a woman, though. There's a lot of work involved in packing up the inventory, lifting the crates, and setting up temporary display shelves."

"Have you approached any local gift shops and galleries? It's a steady market and would cut down on the need for art fairs."

Valerie seemed flustered and a look passed between her and her mother. She replied, "Maybe I will when I build my reputation a while longer."

Instantly, he realized that it might be her father's reputation, not her own, that was robbing her of the confidence to approach pottery venues. He changed the subject, and since her mother had introduced herself to him by her first name, he avoided using her last when he said, "Audrey, tell us about your day."

"How kind of you to ask," she replied, genuinely pleased. She sat back and relaxed. This was a big mark on his scoreboard that would pay off.

"Let's see. I'm sure my day wasn't close to the excitement of bein' out on big water in your sport fishing charter, but I think it counted for something. My dear friend at church looks after her grandchild, but she strained her back yesterday. I went to watch the little one, so her daughter could work. You see, it's a true financial hardship for the mother to lose even a day's income right now. I am blessed for the chance to enjoy that little sprite!"

Andy cleared his throat and took a sip of water. "So, you love children?"

Audrey beamed. "Oh, yes! Do you?"

He saw Valerie scowl a warning at her mother. "Yes, ma'am, I do. I'm on the rotation schedule at my church to help in the children's classes once every seven weeks, and it's fun because I can act silly and get by with it. I want three or four children of my own someday, and when they're grown up, maybe I'll have a bunch of grandkids to start the fun all over again."

Valerie put her napkin on the table and started to rise from her chair, but Andy jumped up to pull it out for her. Audrey said brightly, "Valerie, why don't you show Andy the pottery you finished today? He will return to the harbor soon. I'm goin' to help Lulu clear the table and tidy up."

Andy reached for Valerie's hand. "Audrey, may I ask you for a favor first? There's a dance on Saturday, and I'd like your permission to have Valerie as my date. But I won't be able to pick her up here in Georgetown, because I'm committed to help there. If you approve of letting her attend with me, maybe we can work out a way for her to be in Whitehaven again with her friends."

Audrey opened her mouth to answer, but Valerie rushed in. "Mama, I already checked, and no one can go up with me." She turned to Andy. "I'm sorry, I was goin' to tell you when I walked you back down to the boat. I can't come up this weekend."

Unfazed, Andy looked at Audrey again to make his plea. "I have an alternative plan. I'm workin' a sport fishin' yacht on Wednesday. We'll pick up a tour group here and head out to deep water. After we drop them off, we'll be takin' the boat up to a marina near Whitehaven, where a potential buyer wants to have a friend look it over. If you'll allow Valerie to come with me, she can stay with my family until Sunday, then I'll drive her home."

"I assume your parents will chaperone her?"

"Yes, but if it would put you more at ease, you're welcome to attend with her. I'll arrange for you to stay overnight."

Valerie pulled her hand from his to grip the back of her chair. She blurted, "Mama, he's Andy Painter! He lives at Painter Place, the landmark. That's where the dance is."

He pulled her arm to get her to turn to him. "Why are you holdin' my last name against me? I don't hold yours against you!"

She paled and gasped, staring wide-eyed at him. He tore his eyes from hers to look at her mother. "Yes, my parents know my plans, and they approve. Since you know who I am, you know I'm a man of my word. Valerie won't be in any compromising situations."

Slowly, her mother rose from her seat. She said solemnly, "Andy, I will be thrilled if you can convince my daughter to come with you to Painter Place and be your date for the dance. But the decision is hers."

Wyeth grinned as the road jarred Chrissy in the creaking seat of his dad's rattling truck. But she didn't seem to notice. She looked out the windows like a child viewing Christmas lights. Apparently, she saw something he didn't, and not much would happen in town on a sleepy Tuesday afternoon.

No doubt, she thought she was casually dressed, and maybe that was true where she came from. But in Whitehaven, she still looked like the star of a commercial who brainwashed viewers into thinking she could scrub the toilets and look perfect when her adoring husband came home to a spotless house and flavorful dinner.

Breathless, she turned from the window. "Wyeth, can we go into that antique store sometime? Something about it begs me to explore."

His quick reflexes fired to jerk the wheel and pull the truck into a parking space near the sign for *Antiques on Main*. "Your wish is my command. Let's go on a treasure hunt."

A patron to the store walked out the front door before they could get to it, holding it open with one hand and gripping a box against his side with the other. "Howdy, Wyeth. Good day, ma'am."

"Hi, hope you and your family are well, Tom." Wyeth leaned on the door, which jiggled the little bell and set it to ring again. He reached to shake Tom's hand.

"Oh, yeah, sure 'nuff. The Lord's good." Tom said.

They both waved, and Wyeth followed Chrissy inside to a treasure trove of things people had parted with. It was a well-known store along the coast, and it drew an eclectic array of tourists into town. There was always an enormous glass jar of peppermint sticks on the front counter, and Wyeth loved the refreshing aroma when the owner opened it.

"Are you a collector?" he asked Chrissy.

"Oh, no, not at all. This is the first antique store I've ever been in. But the Big House has captured my imagination, making me wonder about the people and stories behind things. Like what you told me about the Sunflower Room. I keep imagining the guests who looked out over the sunflower fields through that window, and whether a billion joyful yellow sunbursts soothed their hearts from the wounds of life. This place just seemed like it might be full of similar mysteries."

"That's a very insightful thing to say, Chrissy Carnet. You like mysteries?"

She turned a coy smile up at him. "Yes, sometimes. I like you, Wyeth Painter, and you're mysterious."

She directed her attention back to a table laden with decorative things, leaving him to consider what that meant. He hesitated. "I—okay, you got me. I have no appropriate response in my thick head."

Scrutinizing a small, ornate bottle she'd picked up from among the other intriguing things on the table, she replied, "It means I like you much more than a friend, and that you'll always fascinate me."

Behind them, a bright melody skipped out from a music box like a child frolicking on a playground. Chrissy's head jerked up to see where it came from.

At that moment, Wyeth knew it was his mission in life to have that music box. He leaned near her ear. "It must be ugly. The lady who looked at it put it back down and moved on."

She gasped and punched him with her elbow. "Maybe it is, but I don't care. The music—it's lovely, and I can't recall ever hearing that melody. Aren't music box songs always something everyone knows?"

"All I know about music boxes is how to wind them," Wyeth replied as he followed her to the shelf where a customer had set the porcelain box down and left it open. They saw it at the same moment and turned to look at one another in shock.

Chrissy recovered first and took a step closer to the shelf. She leaned over to touch a tiny sculpture of two kissing doves inside. Then she picked up the piece with both hands, as if it was a magician's illusion that would disappear. Another bright note escaped the music mechanism.

Intrigued, Wyeth came close and wasn't sure why he almost whispered for her to close the lid. When she did, they stood spellbound, staring at the tiny painted sunflowers that joyfully spilled across the porcelain top.

Chrissy traced her fingertips over the flowers as if to be sure they existed, then ever so gently, she turned the music box over to see the markings on the bottom. Disappointed, she said, "The name of the song isn't here."

"Then let's call it 'Our Song.'"

She beamed. "That's a wonderful idea! It's our song."

The owner of the store peeked around the aisle. "Can I help you find anything special today?"

Chrissy and Wyeth laughed, and Wyeth replied, "No, sir, something special found us."

"Ah, I see you've discovered the music box. I got it at an estate sale here in the Lowcountry. Tried to find out more about it, and the auctioneer told me everyone who could help had passed on. The only info he had about the box was that it was custom made, and the tune was an original composition by the person who commissioned the work. It's an antique, and the artisan's stamp places it at about the turn of the century. I can't guarantee it isn't on this side of the century, though."

"We don't care. I'll take it. Can we have it engraved?"

"Great thinking, Wyeth," the store owner exclaimed. "Leave a trail for future owners."

At Wyeth's blank expression, he rushed to say, "I mean, well, I was assuming it was stayin' with you at Painter Place. Sorry to overstep. Maybe this is a gift for the young lady?"

"Oh, yes, this is for the young lady. Chrissy, what would you like to have engraved on the box?"

The owner wrote down what Chrissy told him and asked her to check it for accuracy:

Painter Place, 1960

Our Song

CC & WP

Sunflower Detail from *Tall Ships and Sunflowers*
by Pamela Poole

Back in the truck, Chrissy clutched the small, stuffed wooden crate which held the music box. Neither one of them said much on the way to the hardware store, but it was a companionable silence.

Just as he had in London, Wyeth questioned the way he was running open throttled in this relationship. He'd been around Chrissy only five days. Five days! That was not enough to be thinking about forever. In fact, with the music box purchase, he'd just placed them both in the position of being seriously hurt.

But she had professed something in the antique store that kept echoing through his heart and mind. She had much more than a passing interest in him. For her, the waters of time in their relationship were flowing into the future.

When Wyeth took Chrissy's hand and went inside the warehouse of the hardware store, he had to speak over the whoosh of enormous fans to let the clerk know he wanted to pick up his dad's order. The clerk waved and nodded before disappearing into a back door.

While they waited, they moved out of the worst of the gale from the fans. The scents from some potted herbs helped them escape the smell of oiled machines, and Wyeth pointed out examples of some of Maggie Jane's stand-by plants from the kitchen garden at Painter Place.

"There was a time in history when people might have been suspicious of Ida Mae and Maggie Jane," he said. "But herbal folk remedies and healing through food is just chemistry. There's nothing evil about it. In fact, they are some of the most Christian people I've ever met. Their family passes down recipes from generation to generation, and they brought them to Painter Place long ago."

"Has anyone ever accused them of something darker?"

"My dad says there was a brief time when Ida Mae had a rival for the affections of Maggie Jane's dad. The rival insinuated things about her. Big Jim, he was a single man who came over to the island to ask about workin' for food. He was a hobo, about age thirty, travelin the rails from the north. He'd been an itinerant preacher who took on the mantle of traveling evangelist while he worked his way down South. There were a lot of new souls bound for heaven all along the way, but he gave all the credit to the Lord."

Wyeth traced over a sprig of thyme with his finger. "My dad, he said Big Jim was done for the moment he rested his eyes on Ida Mae. He was sick from a hard life when he showed up at the door. But he wouldn't take any help without workin' for it, and Ida Mae used her skills to bring his vitality back. He and Dad became fast friends, and he kept Big Jim on as a trusted jack-of-all-trades. Then Ida Mae married him, and they had Maggie Jane."

He suddenly became aware that he was being watched. But Chrissy had assured him she would be coming alone. When he forced himself to look up and around, it was not the mysterious man in London that waited for him. It was Ralph.

Ralph's demeanor was nothing like it had been in the soda shop. He humbly asked if he could speak to Wyeth alone, pointing to a spot near the door. Chrissy nodded to Wyeth and said she would be learning more about the herbs so she could impress Maggie Jane.

As he stopped and stood in front of Ralph, Wyeth crossed his arms. Ralph said, "Wyeth, I need work on the island for the dance. I lost two days' pay here 'cause they told me not to come in. They expected trouble after last Friday night. I gotta—" Ralph looked away. "I'm helpin' Mama."

"Are you fixin' that roof?"

"Yeah. She ain't got no business liftin' that tin tub she uses when it rains, and sometimes it gets fuller than she can manage before I get there. I know what you said, about askin' for work again. But this is for her."

He drew a ragged breath and clenched his jaw before turning to Wyeth. "I am sorry for what I said. That was the beer talkin' about some rumors I heard around town. It won't happen again."

Wyeth wanted to take the easy road. But then, what would Ralph learn? "Ralph, the beer may've loosened your tongue and your judgement, but what you said was from your heart. You don't like me. You use me when you need somethin'."

"It ain't like that, Wyeth, I mean it! I do like you. What I don't like is that you have money, and I can barely make it. I hate to beg you and your dad for extra work when I'm down and out. Only way I can stomach it is 'cause you break your own back out there with the rest of us. It's a hard place, that island."

Then he pointed a finger at Wyeth. "I know you offered to help my Mama. She told me, and don't think for a split second I wasn't tempted to make you do my job!" He waved through the air in resignation. "But she's the one I got my stubborn, proud streak from. I'm gonna pay for fixin' that roof and I'm gonna do the work. I know how, I just gotta get the supplies. We don't take charity and ain't beholdin' to anyone."

"I'm not in charge of how God distributes His blessings, Ralph. I forgive you for what you said about me, but you'll apologize to Maggie Jane before I'll arrange work on the island."

Ralph's eyes popped. "I can't go where she lives, Wyeth! I'll get shot!"

"You don't have to. Come to Painter Place when you get off. You apologize to her there, at the Big House, in front of her mama. From now on, when anybody in town says she's what you called her, you say you know better. Say you got it straight from me, and to leave Maggie Jane alone to grieve Roy in peace. I've already hired the labor for the dance, but if you do all this, Ralph, I'll pay you myself, to work my part. I could use the time, since I have a guest."

Ralph looked miserable. He pulled off his cap and swiped it through the air. Wyeth stood still, arms crossed, waiting. Ralph finally jerked the cap over his head and extended his hand to shake on the deal. "I'll be out there. Thank you," he muttered.

Wyeth was drenched in sweat and grime. After arriving back at Painter Place and helping the grounds supervisor unload the pickup truck around the pavilion and pier, he parked it in the ghostly shade of a twisting old oak behind the Big House.

He reached for a gleaming stainless-steel thermos bottle on the seat and carried it around to the back of the truck, then leaned against the tailgate to cool off. As he twisted the cap from the thermos and gulped water, he wondered what to do next. If he went inside now, Chrissy might see him like this.

Not that he wanted to hide this part of his life from her. If it mattered, she should know about it. But not today. Today, he clutched at a lingering afterglow from their experience at the antique store. Running into her now, the way he looked and smelled, wasn't remotely romantic.

What would his parents think about his purchase in the antique shop, or the engraving that Chrissy had done on her music box? All he knew for sure was that he hadn't asked the store owner to keep the purchase a secret. Word would spread like wildfire after that incident last Friday night when Ralph implied that there was something going on between Wyeth and Maggie Jane.

A swipe of his forearm dried his brow, and he shook strands of clinging dark hair away. There was a clean shirt in his studio, and he could dunk his face, head and hands in the sink. That was at least half better a condition for Chrissy to see him in.

After a lazy pull at the door to the building, Wyeth stopped cold at the sound of his little sister's voice. She was talking about Chrissy's portrait. And it was very much like the version she'd given him and Andy.

He barely had time to catch his breath and wonder who she was talking to before he heard Chrissy's voice. With stealthy steps, he moved toward his studio.

"The blue reflection in my earring, you're sure that's his apron? You're sure he meant to put himself into such an intimate place in the painting?"

"*Everything* my big brother puts into a painting means something, if only people knew to look. He taught me his secrets. See over there, at his stool? His apron is the same denim blue, and it's different from the scarf. Lots of artists wear black aprons and that might be hard to spot in a reflection. Wyeth never does, and he doesn't use that color in his paintings, either."

"He doesn't like black?"

"Oh, he likes it well enough on other people. But he has bad memories of it. My grandma wore black all the time after my grandpa and uncle were lost at sea, and when she died, Wyeth and Andy were little. He had to wear that color to her funeral and realized for the first time what it meant. He loved her so much, and she loved his grandfather and uncle like that. Other people were wearing black around town, because they lost family members in the war, and he started noticing. He wouldn't wear it anymore because he feared someone he loved would die, like Mama or Daddy. Then when he got really, truly sick one time, there was a chance he wouldn't make it, and he didn't want everyone at Painter Place to wear black."

Wyeth squeezed his eyes shut and grimaced against a stab of pain he hadn't felt in years. He leaned back against the wall.

"Juliette, you are a remarkable young lady, and your brother is a remarkable man. I haven't met anyone like either of you. I can tell you are close."

"Yes, as close as anyone gets to Wyeth, except my parents and Phillip. They are blood brothers, you know. Sometimes, not even your own real brother can be as close as blood brothers can be. That's why my other brother, Andy, gets jealous sometimes. He needs Wyeth, and he wants his attention, so he acts up to get it. It's the wrong attention, but he'd rather have that than nothing."

Wyeth drew a sharp breath. Juliette had never told him this. Had she overheard it from his parents? No. No, she knew it from watching them. She was wise beyond her age, and that was her way.

"Would Andy be jealous of a woman, if Wyeth ever got married?"

"No, that's a different thing altogether. Andy will get married someday, too. They will have wives that will be great friends because that's how it is if you marry someone here at Painter Place. Andy wants Wyeth to need him and respect him, to spend time with him. He wants deep conversations with Wyeth. You know, brother stuff. Wyeth, he's so—" Juliette sighed.

Wyeth hung on the edge of her sentence. With a rueful smile, he figured she was trying to think of grown up words. But he wasn't ready for the description she chose.

"He's high up, above things most of us concern ourselves with. He's always creatin' imaginary scenes in his mind to see if they work out as a painting, so sometimes, he doesn't notice everyday things. And he's super smart, like my mother. That's how he got into a top university."

"Yes, I've noticed. You said you were bringing me here to explain why he won't sell the painting. Do you think I'm ready to hear the reason yet?"

"Wyeth doesn't know how to explain it to you himself. See, it's not just a portrait of you, like everyone thinks. My dad and I talked about it and we know it's a dream. A daydream about you, him, and

Painter Place. He can't sell it to you, even if you go away, because you'd be takin' his dream with you."

Chrissy's tone was quiet when she said, "Oh, Juliette. Thank you for your help in understanding why I should stop asking him for the painting. I love being here in his studio, and I don't want to leave it yet, but do you think we should go get cleaned up for dinner?"

"Sure! Can I help you pick out what to wear?"

"I wish you would! I plan to ask Wyeth to help me brush up on my dancing in the ballroom tonight. Would you like to join us? When I was little, I took ballet and jazz, and I still do ballet workouts to stay fit. But I heard there's a popular dance around here called the Carolina Shag. I don't know what that is, and I don't want to embarrass your brother on Saturday night."

"Oh," Juliette gushed. "That's a lovely idea! You can practice in any outfit, but when you go to a dance, always wear something that sways with your movements."

Wyeth was trapped in the hall and he heard them getting closer. He backed up and slid in the doorway of his dad's studio, then closed the door soundlessly. Rushing to the sink, he stuck his head in to wash his hair, face, and neck, then pulled off his shirt and scrubbed with a bar of soap.

When he'd toweled off, he opened the door and stood in the hallway again, listening to be sure his studio was empty. All was quiet, so he went to grab his clean shirt. He managed the buttons while he went to admire the portrait of Chrissy. It was always fresh, that overwhelming desire for her to be part of Painter Place, as his wife.

Juliette was right about how he'd painted his dream. But the day he had painted it, he knew the same truth he admitted now. Not all dreams come true.

Chapter Fifteen

Valerie Rush cast covert glances at Andy Painter, watching how he worked as part of the crew on a fishing charter boat. When he'd picked her up at the marina as they'd planned, she'd known he'd be busy.

It was only Wednesday. There was something she needed to tell him, but five dreamy days stretched ahead, and that was as far into the future as she wanted to see.

An open volume by Jane Austen lay in her lap as she relaxed inside a spacious, comfortable cabin. It had been unsettling, at first, when she saw how the windows wrapped around and made her feel like she was part of the Atlantic. Once she grew accustomed to the reality of the invisible barrier, she found it exciting.

Andy stuck his head in to check on her again, sporting the charter crew logo on a long-sleeved cotton shirt and a hat over his sun-bleached blonde hair. His perpetual grin was infectious, so she returned it to him. "I'm doing fine, really I am. It's relaxing to be on the water like this. I might even have a catnap."

"But when you came aboard you were a little apprehensive." He leaned in, strong hands gripping a rail overhead.

"Well, it would be scary out at sea if bad weather came in. I've heard stories."

He looked serious now, searching her eyes for fear, and her pulse leaped. She knew a girl could get lost in those blue eyes and forget everything, because she'd already done that.

"Well, it's supposed to be clear today, but I understand your reaction to the stories. Weather is weather. A lot of factors have gone into our readiness on board, so we've got that going for us. We know all we can about the boat itself, because if we get surprised, we focus our energy on dealing with the wind and water."

He paused, studying the cabin and looking out the windows. "Besides, she's named *Fair Weather*. When you first saw her, did you notice the proud Carolina-style bow she boasts? They built her in Florida, but her owner asked for a few Carolina hallmarks of style for her design. She's huge but sleek, and she's made to handle surly conditions that might keep other charters from going out to fish. I like this crew, too. They're in shape to handle a storm, mentally and physically."

Since she couldn't take her eyes off his, she stared back and nodded. She knew the bow was the front of the boat, cutting into the water, but she wasn't sure what Carolina-style meant. When she realized the silence had stretched into awkwardness, she smiled weakly and told him that in that case, she trusted them.

"Okay, but don't put all your trust in us. Pray."

Someone shouted his name, and he twisted to look over his shoulder. When he turned back to her, he winked. "You pray. I'll go to work."

She stared out the tinted window into the horizon and the cresting caps along the sea. She prayed, but not only for protection on the *Fair Weather*. She poured out thanksgiving for the way Christ was healing her broken heart. And she asked Him to help her know for sure if Andy Painter was what she and her mother had asked Him for.

Valerie awakened with a start. She'd been dreaming about her novel, *Pride and Prejudice*, which slid against the back of the seat, abandoned when the boat lazily rocked her to sleep. In the real world she found herself in, the captain of the *Fair Weather* was shouting orders to the crew.

She went to the restroom in the cabin, and when she came out, she heard the captain shouting to the crew again, ordering them to keep an eye on a distant bank of clouds. Curiosity led her to go out on the deck, holding on to the rails. In the cockpit over the cabin, she heard the captain and Andy discussing sea state conditions, which the captain was reporting over a radio. Andy checked a chart, and the tension in his movements sent a sudden spike of dread through her heart.

He turned to answer another crew member's question and caught a glance of her. He looked back to finish his brief conversation and then said something to the captain who nodded and replied, "Get her into a life jacket and secure her in the cabin."

Andy nimbly climbed down the ladder. His expression frightened her as he opened a hatch to get a life jacket. But he teased, "All right, that's it. Next time, I'm assigning prayer duty to someone else."

She attempted to smile. "I prayed, but I fell asleep. I don't think Jesus holds that against me. It means I trust Him to surround me with His protection."

Andy chuckled as he handed her a life jacket and pointed her to the cabin. She fumbled with the clasps, and he adjusted the straps to fit her. There was tension in his voice, but he seemed to think he was calming her as he said, "We'll be fine. But you know if you ever find yourself in the water in an emergency, you grab whatever floats, right?"

She nodded, wide-eyed. He pointed to the life rings she'd seen on the deck. "Those will float."

"Yeah, so I've heard. Will you have one?"

He slipped his hand from the life jacket strap down to catch hers and he squeezed it. "I'll wear safety gear and a tether. I have to get out there now. I don't like it, knowin' you're scared, but the best way for me to keep you safe is to go do my job. Pray, and maybe it will stay calm enough for you to take another nap. Then you won't be sleepy if we stay up talkin' in the moonlight on the veranda at Painter Place."

In the awkward bulk of her life jacket, Valerie leaned over to hug him. "I'll pray, Andy. I'm holdin' you to that moonlight rendezvous. Don't stand me up."

As the wind gusts grew unruly and powerful, Valerie watched an ominous cloud bank. She wasn't sure why, but the sight of it struck the deepest terror she'd ever known. It was chasing them down. Or were they charging into it head on? It was impossible to tell.

She didn't understand nautical terms, but she knew weather descriptions. The captain had shouted into the radio that the *Fair Weather* out of Georgetown was facing a squall. She'd only heard stories about seamen caught in squalls, but they created violent wind gusts that lasted at least a minute, often longer. The storms were thankfully brief, but they spawned tornados, thunder and lightning, and hail.

Unless it was a white squall. Those were deadly, the stuff of legends. And her mind wouldn't take her there.

A deafening roar came from everywhere at once, and a ferocious gust of wind blasted against the yacht. Then came a wave so high that Valerie cried out and cowered down to the floor as it slammed into the side. She felt the concussion and squeezed her eyes shut, unwilling to watch the horrifying sight of the powerful ocean that might break the window and drown her.

But when the crash subsided and her lungs didn't fill with water, she peeked out to find that the window was a resolute shield. Torrential rain now pummeled the *Fair Weather.*

Panting, she scrambled to her hands and knees to press her back against a cabinet. Her shaking arms could barely obey her will as she searched frantically for something to hold on to, and she stifled a sob.

"What's that verse?" she asked herself between her chattering teeth. Since meeting Andy, she'd been memorizing Bible passages about water and the sea. If he loved it so much, she wanted to love it, too.

Then the words from Psalm 89:8-9 tumbled into her mind, and she anxiously sorted them to pray out loud. "O Lord God Almighty, who is like You? You are mighty, O Lord, and Your faithfulness surrounds You."

She gulped back her fear as the roar increased outside the yacht cabin. "You rule!" she gasped. She held on and struggled to recall how the verse went. "You rule over the surging sea; when the waves mount up, You still them. When the waves mount up!" she repeated as the boat tilted.

With a pitiful groan, she watched in terrifying slow motion while the *Fair Weather* rose on the dragon-back of untamable water. Only her firm grip kept her from tumbling backwards and being hurt.

"You still them!" she called out, praying the Bible verse. "You rule over the surging sea!"

A sharp maneuver of the vessel jerked her arm taunt as the crew battled the squall. Andy had assured her that the vessel and crew were ready for any rough conditions, and she remembered how he'd searched her eyes earlier that day to determine if she was nervous.

His eyes were the color of the ocean on a clear day. He seemed to spring from it, to be part of it. And he'd told her not to be afraid.

"Protect him, please, shield him, in Your own hands!" she prayed.

But then came the next vicious gust, and this time, she expected the yacht to capsize. Her eyes darted around the cabin for a way to escape if she became disoriented. Outside the window, one of the crew members was being hauled back up to safety. With her heart in her mouth, she frantically got to her knees and braced herself to stand.

Then, she screamed and planted both palms on the window. Andy wasn't even on the *Fair Weather*. He was fighting the wild sea. And over his head poised a wall of water so monstrous that she couldn't even see its crest.

That's why my other brother, Andy, gets jealous sometimes. He needs Wyeth, and he wants his attention, so he acts up to get it. It's the wrong attention, but he'd rather have that than nothing.

Wyeth stood on the dock at a marina near Whitehaven and rubbed his face with his hands, haunted by what he'd heard his sister Juliette tell Chrissy yesterday. He wrestled with the wringing sensation in his stomach. *Andy wants Wyeth to need him and respect him, to spend time with him. He wants deep conversations with Wyeth. You know, brother stuff.*

Juliette was at a friend's house for the day. She didn't know about the distress call from the fishing charter her brother was working on. And she hadn't met Valerie yet.

But he had. Looking back, Wyeth was grateful for the evening he'd spent going out cruising with Andy. At first, he'd thought it was a move of desperation on Andy's part for some entertainment in town, veiled as a request for Wyeth to meet a young lady from off. Wyeth's own heart was aching from what he thought was the end of a lightning strike relationship with Chrissy, so he only went to keep Andy from getting involved in a dead-end relationship.

He hadn't valued it as quality time with his little brother. He'd been away from the island for long stretches of time the last four years while he finished college. Wyeth had grown accustomed to distance from everyone but Phillip, but Andy was fighting for his rightful place now that he'd come home. It made sense when he remembered how Andy had asked him to come to town without Phillip.

You're perfect. I'm the Painter family's risky business. But who had his dad praised for getting Wyeth out of trouble that Friday night? Andy had stepped up. He was a lot more capable than he let everyone think he was.

Wyeth needed to stop acting as if he was going back to another semester of school. He was home to stay, and his relationships needed freshening up. There was no option for being sidetracked anymore. It was time to step into his role as the heir to Painter Place, and he needed his brother.

Beside him, Chrissy took his hand and knit their fingers together. She had made no empty promises about how everything would be okay, and she didn't soothe him by telling him not to worry. She simply stayed by him, and he craved the comfort of her presence.

But what if the worst happened? She'd see him at his weakest. He glanced at his father, who remained outwardly calm and positive. But Wyeth caught the tremble in his voice and other telltale signs of distress. When his father was younger than Wyeth, he lost his own father and older brother in these same seas. How it happened was a mystery, but other boats in the area that day reported a sudden storm they barely escaped.

An engine growled in the parking lot, and Wyeth turned to see Phil Gregory's Mercedes pull into a space near the dock. Phillip burst out of it and jogged toward him with his face full of apprehension.

"Where is he? Have they heard anything yet?"

"No, not since the Coast Guard sent out warnings about the weather. The captain's last radio contact claimed something like a white squall."

"What? Are you sure?" Phillip didn't hide how anxious he was, and Wyeth's anxiety rose. If anyone knew how important Andy's safety was to the future of Painter Place, it was Phillip.

Phil and Lucinda rushed up to Wyeth's mom and dad, and a sports car squealed into the parking lot. Behind it, a gleaming Chrysler Imperial drove in and slid into a space beside the Mercedes. The driver of the sports car stood quickly to his full height and trotted over to open the door on the Chrysler.

Wyeth gaped, and Phillip jerked his head around to see. They recognized Dr. Anthony Rush from his photos in the society pages, and the woman he was arguing with must be Valerie's mother.

Phillip and Wyeth exchanged looks. "I thought the papers just picked the best shots," growled Phillip.

The woman coolly ignored Dr. Rush as she headed toward the dock with a purposeful stride. Wyeth's parents solemnly stepped forward to greet them. Dr. Rush was terse through the introductions, then he asked for the man in charge of any rescue efforts to find his daughter.

Phil Gregory pointed to a small office and explained that they were waiting for an update. Dr. Rush turned on his heel and marched that direction, but Valerie's mother stayed with the Painters. Once her estranged husband jerked the door of the building open, Audrey allowed herself to wilt.

Wyeth watched as she took his mother's hand. "The prayer chain at my church is waiting for news." He saw fear in his mother's eyes as she hugged Audrey, and it sent another strike of unthinkable dread to his heart. He silently prayed for the hundredth time that his family would be spared another tragedy at sea.

Dr. Rush stormed out of the office without the information he went in for and marched back their way. That's when he noticed Chrissy. He hesitated, calmed, and slowed his pace. By the time he'd reached his estranged wife's side, he had taken a full assessment of the young lady beside Wyeth.

Chrissy pressed against Wyeth's arm. She knew what was on Dr. Rush's mind. He felt a surge of possessiveness but didn't mean to make a fist. The instant he realized what he'd done, he opened his hand.

But Dr. Rush had already noticed. "The older brother, I suppose."

"Not old enough to be her father, though," Wyeth coldly responded.

Phillip's sharp breath was audible. Dr. Rush fixed a narrow look on Wyeth, but it was full of wary respect. He ignored the comment.

"White squall is a myth," he announced to them all, turning to Wyeth's father. "Mr. Painter, how long has Andy been workin' on boats?"

"Ever since he was old enough to wear a toddler-sized life jacket and captain's cap."

"He's a pup! He had no business takin' my daughter out to deep water, riskin' her life!"

"Beggin' your pardon, Dr. Rush, but Andy's not in charge of that yacht. He's only a part of the crew. There was no storm on the radar when the captain left port. Andy's highly trained in gales and heavy weather in all kinds of sea state, but no two storms are the same. Take your problem up with the captain. He's seen years of bad weather."

Dr. Rush stabbed a finger at him. "When—if—my daughter gets back, he is never to contact her again, you understand me? My daughter is from the best bloodlines in South Carolina. She's been raised better than to end up with a deckhand!"

Wyeth trembled in fury and he saw Phillip's jaw clench. They watched Noble, who pursed his lips and slowly raised a tanned, work-roughened hand. He ran it through his sun-bleached blonde hair and drawled, "Well, Andy has higher aspirations, you know. He only asked for a date, not her hand in marriage. He went through the proper channels, askin' me first, then askin' permission from the spiritual head of Valerie's household. Christ's bloodline is the only one that matters."

A calm look at Audrey's nod confirmed his claim, so he added, "Since that isn't you, Dr. Rush, and since in fact you haven't lived with them since Valerie was a little girl, you don't have the authority to approve or disapprove of what your twenty-year-old daughter does. That's a matter between the believers in the house."

Dr. Rush's face flushed. He sputtered, "That's the perspective that gives you a bad reputation among normal people, Mr. Painter! You're a zealot livin' in a fantasy world. Here's somethin' real you can believe in! When I get back to Charleston, I'm seein' my lawyer."

"Give me his number, and I'll have mine call him," Phil interrupted, handing Dr. Rush his Gregory Global business card. "The *Fair Weather* is fully insured against all claims. Andy is on that boat today as a favor for a friend of mine, who may invest in it—and in Andy—as a charter business."

Wyeth and Phillip had watched this teamwork all their lives. If anyone could diffuse a burning fuse on dynamite, it was Noble Painter, but if he failed, there was always Phil Gregory. No one got past them if they teamed up. Someday, Wyeth knew, he and Phillip could learn to rein in their tempers and be the two men no one could get past.

Audrey's tone was venomous as she turned on Dr. Rush. "While you're at the lawyer's office, get the divorce papers completed. I should have done it myself, years ago. Your behavior is despicable and you're a disgrace to your father's bloodline. You're not fit for polite society!"

He glowered at her and said their issues would be a private discussion for later. She ignored him and grasped Wyeth's mother's hand again, apologizing for the rude domestic quarrel when the important topic was the safety of their children. She stood with the Painters and Gregorys, lined up in a stand-off with Dr. Rush. Then the door burst open from the yacht club office, and a uniformed manager walked out.

"I have news!" he shouted.

A Coast Guard escort waited in the distance as the captain of the *Fair Weather* brought the charter fishing vessel into the marina. She had been doused by heavy seas, but she floated in with dignity.

Phillip whistled softly and commented to Wyeth about his admiration of her size and the proud Carolina bow. Wyeth nodded, but his eyes scanned the vessel for his brother. He jogged on the plank dock toward where the Fair Weather would be secured.

Then he saw Andy climbing and hustling with the crew in methodical tasks to secure the boat. Wyeth swiped away tears of relief with the back of his hand. *Of course. That's what he'd be doing. This is who he is!* And at that moment, he knew he'd help Andy have his dream of owning a marina someday. He might even buy a boat they could work on together and take out on weekends.

As he stood waiting on Andy to step off the decks of the *Fair Weather*, his heart gushed with thankful prayers. Chrissy, Phillip, and the others had caught up with him by the time Valerie disembarked. Andy followed, and when his feet landed on the dock, he set down his duffle bag and Valerie's suitcase. Then he staggered back when she flung her arms around him. She sobbed wildly, then grabbed his shoulders and cried, "Never, ever scare me like that again!"

He steadied them both with hands on her waist and flashed his characteristic white grin. "I told you we'd be fine if you'd pray!"

Indignant, she gasped. "I was prayin' as hard as I could! And you—"

Valerie pointed emphatically out to the water, and cried out, "You were overboard, in a *squall*! The waves were like mountains! I thought I'd lost you."

Wyeth waited, unsure if Valerie would slap Andy or hug him again. But all she did was stand there, weeping. With a helpless gesture, Andy softened his tone, "I told you I'd be tethered to the boat, in a life jacket. I couldn't let Jack drown out there! He banged his shoulder goin' overboard."

"I know that!" she exclaimed. "His arm was dangling when they brought him up. He's safe, and you're courageous. But you could've drowned before my eyes, Andy! Give me some credit for knowin' how dangerous that storm was. Don't pretend it was nothing!"

Andy sighed and pulled her closer, patting her on the back as if she were a child, and Wyeth knew his brother did not understand how to make her feel better. "I'm okay now, Valerie. Please don't cry. I didn't know it mattered so much, or I wouldn't have been so flippant."

"It doesn't matter, not for her," Dr. Rush boomed, and Valerie's head jerked around to look for him. Andy stiffened and dropped his arms, but he didn't step away. Valerie's father ordered, "Come on, Valerie, let's get you home before the reporters arrive. I don't want you photographed here, with—them."

Valerie sniffed and swiped tears away. Her eyes flashed in defiance. "No. You're the one who needs to leave. I didn't endure all this today just to turn around and go home. I've been plannin' a visit to the island for a long time, and I'm old enough to decide for myself. If reporters come, fine! Maybe we'll both make the papers this week, only I'll be praising a guy with virtue, and readers can see your lack of any."

Dr. Rush opened his mouth for a scathing retort, but Audrey rushed to Valerie's side and hugged her. "I know you're upset, but disrespect won't help. Everyone's been prayin' for you and the crew, so let's go make a few phone calls to let them know you're okay. I packed to stay a few days, and it's a good thing, too. The Painters invited me to visit while you're there."

She turned to Andy and hugged him as she poured out thanks for taking care of Valerie. "Why don't you both ride with me to Painter Place? You can show me the way."

Abandoned by everyone, Dr. Rush turned on his heel and left the docks without a word. The captain and other crew members disembarked, one wearing a makeshift sling on his left arm. They all shook Andy's hand and tipped their caps to Valerie. The man in the office came up to the captain with a clipboard to take a report, and a maintenance crew arrived.

"Go on, Andy, before the press gets here and makes a big deal outta this," the captain said gruffly. "Hope we can work together again real soon."

Then he turned to shake hands with Noble and Phil. "Get 'im and his girl outta here so he won't have to start makin' statements to reporters. He did his job well and everything's tidy with our records. Mr. Gregory, you'll have an official maintenance report on the *Fair Weather* by tomorrow for your potential buyer."

As the group going to Painter Place piled into their cars and turned onto the main road, the first news station van was pulling into the marina parking lot.

"It's magical, Andy," Valerie said, keeping her voice low as they stood watching the moonlit sparkle that stretched over an inky Atlantic Ocean. "You have a wonderful home and family. I don't know how you can bear leaving the island every day to go to work on the charter boats."

Andy shrugged. "We all have to earn an income somehow instead of living on Painter Place money. Wyeth and Dad handle business for the island and try to paint for the gallery, commissions, and shows, Mama helps represent Painter Place as an ambassador, writes novels, and speaks at conferences. I work for charter fishing captains in marinas. We all pitch in around here with odds and ends, and I'm good with outdoor work. After so many years, it's likely that I know every demolition and construction trick there is. But my dream is to live on the island and have a marina in Whitehaven, not go out on the water all the time like today."

"Why is it the artist in each generation who inherits the island?"

"It's not that other children inherit nothing, they get a portion, like land and a house. I get to build a pier and a big house of my own when I marry. There's more money set aside for me and Juliette, and she will get land if she remains here. But she isn't likely to. She says she'll be an actress someday. The Gregory family only gets land if they buy more from the Painters. Anyone who commits to living here must pitch in to help with maintenance."

Andy leaned one arm against a column, looking out over the dunes and the pavilion. "The artist in each generation gets the biggest portion because managing Painter Place is a daunting task. I sure don't want it! Wyeth's part is no picnic, but he's a genius. Since he came home from college, he's already influenced Dad to make changes that will cut costs and streamline operations. Besides, an artist's income is uncertain. It often takes years for the right collector to come along to purchase a painting. Painter family artists get the financial shelter of the island, assuming they remain here and run it according to the requirements from my ancestors."

"People who don't live here don't realize all this, do they?"

"Some who come work for us do. Others think we're snobs who live on a playground."

Valerie sighed, staring out at the water, and leaned forward with her hands on the veranda railing. Instantly, she winced and pulled back, shaking her wrists.

Andy scowled and reached for one of her hands. "Are you hurt?"

"It's nothing. My wrists, hands, and arms are sore from holding on during the storm today. It will go away. It would be worse if I wasn't a potter. Handling heavy clay gives me more strength that most women."

He massaged her hand and wrist, saying, "When we go inside, I'll get you some of Ida Mae's balm and pain reliever. I don't want to be redundant, but I wish I had known we'd run into that storm. I could have worked out another way to pick you up for the dance."

"If I hadn't been on the *Fair Weather* today, I wouldn't have known about what happened, would I? You'd have just said you were in a storm."

Andy shrugged again and turned to look out at the beach. Valerie said, "That's fine for most people, but it's something I need to know about who you are. The first night we met and went cruisin' in the Corvette, you said I'd get to know you better on a boat. As scared as I was, I'm glad I was there."

She put her other hand on his cheek. "This afternoon, Mama told me life is like this. We're not in control of the storms, but we should surround ourselves with people who handle them well. You handle storms well, and you're alive, that's what matters."

As they stood looking at one another in the shadows of midnight, he lightened the mood with a lopsided smile. "You told me not to stand you up for a rendezvous on the veranda at Painter Place. I'm just gettin' used to followin' your orders."

Chapter Sixteen

The sea was bountiful on Thursday evening as the island families gathered with their guests to surf fish on the beach. A blinding array of sunset colors sprinkled over the water and streaked the horizon in layers while Noble explained to Montgomery Heyward the importance of having a sand spike for the fishing rods.

Andy taught Valerie, her mother Audrey, and some other guests to cast in close to the breakers, where the smaller fish were. Wyeth helped Chrissy manage her rod to bring a wildly flapping catch in while Juliette laughed at her efforts, and especially at her squeal when the dangling fish banged against her bare leg.

Nearby, Phillip helped his dad and a few other guests build a bonfire site. Camellia didn't want to fish, so she helped Savanna organize the refreshments. A trio of artists who'd been painting on the beach wearily lay down their load of supplies and easels to watch the fun.

When the sun went down, the bonfire became a beacon on the beach. The surf fishers put away their rods and cleaned up their hands, and everyone grabbed something to drink from coolers. Someone handed small paper bags of fresh popcorn to guests as they plopped down on beach blankets. Soon, they were telling fish stories and listening to guitars, bongo drums, a saxophone, and some samples of songs by four musicians who had spent the week finishing an album.

Juliette popped marshmallows into her mouth and huddled next to her dad's side. Though Noble was talking with one musician, he raised his arm to gather her closer. After a light kiss on the top of her head, he went back to his conversation.

Wyeth caught the faraway expression on Chrissy's face as she watched them. He reached over to put his arm around her. "Chilly? I can get you a beach towel or blanket."

When she bit her lip, he blinked at the mischief in her expression. Then she tickled his ear with a smoky whisper. "I like your arm around me better than a beach towel."

He grinned and checked to see if anyone was watching. Then he whispered, "How am I supposed to respond to that? Remember to take it easy on me. I was raised to restrain myself from public displays of affection with gorgeous single young ladies."

"Oh, yeah? Well, try living under the watchful eyes of guards, and attending private schools in uniform under the scrutiny of security cameras. See what that does to discourage any display of affection, public or private!"

Then she leaned into his shoulder. "However, at sleepovers with my friends, someone inevitably sneaked in a kisses-only romance novel borrowed from an older friend. We looked for the romantic parts and took turns reading them to everyone."

Wyeth chuckled. He glanced around again, but the only one that seemed to have noticed them was his brother. All he did was grin and wink, then he looked away.

"Okay, so, I have a story about books," he whispered. "In college, an art professor of mine was determined to give me a failing grade for figure painting if I didn't come to class and paint a nude. He made it his mission to free me from my oppressive religious upbringing. So, I asked if I could get credit if I proved I understood the human frame by hiring and painting a dancer to model for me, wearing a leotard and a clinging skirt. Phillip went with me to the library to study up on the female muscular system beforehand, which was difficult to do without running across much more information than we'd seen in Biology class. Then he and a female art student friend of ours sat with me to sketch the model while I painted. My professor relented and gave me credit for 'an outstanding depiction of athletic grace.'"

Chrissy's eyes danced. "I suppose you could say we both learned a life skill, but yours was an honorable quest for a grade while mine was for a girls' night out."

He had to look away and covered his laugh with a cough. When he saw no one was watching, he came closer with a husky whisper. "Why didn't you rely on movies or television, instead of takin' the chance of gettin' caught with the contraband novels?"

"We didn't see many movies, and as I became a teen, my mom kept me too busy with dance, modeling lessons, and pageants to watch much television. Besides, reading those descriptions in words made it easier for me to understand the motions, and to know what motivated the characters."

Wyeth allowed himself to groan under his breath. "I'm sure you know by now I can't measure up to the suave swashbucklers in novels. But tonight, there's nothing I'd rather do than put my arm around you to keep you warm."

When he met her eyes, she wasn't smiling anymore. "You and I, Wyeth, we are real. When we can show our love for one another, the way we touch and interact will become more natural each time. We won't be thinking about movies or books."

Phillip desperately wanted Camellia to love Painter Place. She had enjoyed the island since arriving that afternoon, but she also seemed aloof, like an observer rather than a participant. It was a relief when she was delighted with the Gregory estate where her family would be guests until Sunday.

He drew a deep breath to tame the anxious feeling that shadowed him lately. None of the scenarios that came to mind for having a second home in Charleston with her would be a happy outcome. His father and Wyeth were right—if she didn't come around to see herself spending her life here, they should end their relationship.

Though he sat close by her side on a beach blanket in the sand, she was looking the other way. Her attention was on the conversation between a musician and Noble Painter, about how the family had held on to the island for hundreds of years.

Noble told the Bible's account of how Joshua led the Israelites to set up twelve stones as a memorial to what God had done by bringing them across the Jordan River into the Promised Land, so they could tell the next generation what the stones meant. He added the story of the time the prophet Samuel raised a large stone as a memorial when God gave Israel a great victory. Noble said his father's name was Samuel, to honor the Bible hero who set up the stone and called it Ebenezer, which meant "stone of help." Samuel charged the Israelites to look at the stone as years passed and remember how God had helped them.

"You see, people forget what things mean," Noble said in his languid Southern drawl. "My ancestor settled this island as a refuge from religious persecution and declared it to be a landmark, an Ebenezer, a memorial—proof for future generations of what God did in delivering him, his mother, and his grandmother. Every generation of Painters teaches the next about how God provided it for us. As Psalm 90:1-2 says, from generation to generation, the Lord is our dwelling place."

"It feels so peaceful, like what you called it—a refuge," agreed one of the band members. "When I drove across the bridge to the island, there was a difference I could feel. We even commented on it, didn't we, guys?"

He turned to his band, and they nodded. One said, "Things out there in the rest of the world, they are scary, unstable. In our business, the last decade was the first one for rock-n-roll, and we feel like we're riding on a powder keg with an invisible fuse. Much of the new trend is exciting, and it's not really the sound, or the beat, that's a problem. Those are just expressions of creativity. It's the things people get away with singing about!"

He lightly slapped his own face, and everyone chuckled. "My mama would've washed out my mouth with soap!" the band leader declared. "At the least, I'd have had a lecture on Philippians 4:8, and she might have made me copy it twenty times to be sure I didn't forget it again."

Noble's nod was sympathetic. "Well, the evil one, he cloaks his endeavors in a guise of progress. Otherwise, no one would fall for them. Music evokes feelings, stirring us, and we get carried away with it."

Someone asked what rules applied to the music that would be allowed this weekend at the upcoming Island Summer Dance, or at any other time on the island. Noble explained that it didn't matter if the sound was classical or new. Everyone had different tastes. The songs for the dance would be selected based on the lack of coarse words to express a reasonably wholesome message for both single and married couples since they'd be the audience that occupied the pavilion dance floor.

Phil said, "I've heard claims that if someone can control the words of the music in a society, they can control that population. People memorize and internalize the words. I believe that, and I try to keep my head and heart tuned to messages that bring glory to Christ, not excuses for my darker human passions. Here at Painter Place, the influences of music can contribute to a wayward child. Once grown, that offspring can ruin what it took generations to build. Still, as Noble explained, it would only be an earthly place, given to us for an allotted time. The faithful are bound for glory."

The musician across from him grinned and quickly picked a few chords on his guitar. His band members took his cue and soon the crowd clapped to the beat as they belted out a popular gospel song about a train bound for glory.

Phillip leaned closer to Camellia to enjoy her voice, and she turned with a smile in her eyes. Encouraged, he touched his shoulder to her sweater, forcing himself into one of her best memories. She reached up to tidy a blonde strand of hair tickling her pretty ear, and a dangling diamond earring flashed tiny prism stars from the bonfire.

The band members kept the songs coming and asked for requests. Other guests in the cottages on the island came out to plop down in the sand with them.

A shy light winked in the darkness and caught Phillip's attention. There was nothing unusual about a small vessel near the shore. Nevertheless, Phillip sensed this one was lurking.

Maybe jilted reporters were trying to get zoomed photos of Andy and Valerie. They could use them as emotional bait in a piece about yesterday's near-tragic storm at sea aboard the *Fair Weather*. His dad shared the official ship's log with him and Noble, and it was sobering, though the boat's performance in bad weather conditions was excellent. Reporters might play up the angle of whether the captain had encountered the myth of a white squall and dramatize Andy's heroic rescue of a crew member at sea.

Or would Valerie's father, Dr. Rush, hire a private detective to keep tabs on her and her mother? Phillip's gut told him that Valerie's father didn't want her mother to divorce him. In fact, despite the man's behavior, he thought Dr. Rush still had feelings for his wife, and he thought she knew it.

The idea of surveillance almost jolted him. He blinked and sat upright, then looked over at Wyeth. His friend was staring out to sea, absorbed in the view of the same light, and Phillip saw him shiver.

Chrissy smiled, assuming Wyeth had a chill. She reached behind them for a giant beach towel. Wyeth tore his eyes away from the light to help settle the wrap around both their shoulders. As she moved closer beside him, a lingering look passed between them.

If Wyeth asked, Phillip felt sure Chrissy would rush at the chance to marry him. She turned her attention back to the bonfire group, singing along, and Wyeth sang the long-memorized lyrics of a folk song without thinking. His eyes became thoughtful again as he peered out at the tiny light, and he scowled.

Then Phillip realized Wyeth wasn't ready to allow Chrissy to be a permanent part of his life, no matter how much they both may want that. His friend hadn't accepted who she was, or what that meant for Painter Place.

"I'm not sure I'm with you on this, Wyeth," Phillip said. They stood together at the end of the pier on Friday morning where they'd taken a walk out to oversee the men securing the lights for the dance the next night. "It's not a bad thing to have someone guarding the island, someone who can help if the worst happens. You and I, we'd be on a short list, just like Adolf Coors."

The unsolved disappearance of the Coors heir had bothered Phillip since the day it happened, and Wyeth wondered if he'd been in contact with him before the apparent kidnapping. But unless Phillip offered to mention his connection, Wyeth knew better than to fish for clues. The Gregory men were stalwart about handling confidential information.

Still, some interaction with the missing heir would explain how hard Phillip had taken the news when Coors' still-running car was discovered on a bridge near his home in Colorado. At first, it confused Wyeth that Phillip took the kidnapping to heart, since he had less than zero tolerance for alcohol consumption. Then, Phillip told him Ad Coors didn't drink and was in fact allergic to beer, and he didn't want to work at the brewery. How had Phillip known this?

Wyeth had been praying that Ad Coors would be found in good health and his abductor brought to justice, but every passing day stacked the odds against the best outcome. He knew Phillip saw himself in Ad's shoes, perhaps a victim someday because of family business. Worse, he must wonder about his future sons.

"I wish I knew how to contact Chrissy's dad," Phillip mused. "If he's all you said he is, I wish they'd put him on the Coors case."

Wyeth swallowed and stroked the nape of his neck. Sometimes, he dared to hope that his encounter with the ghost-man in London was a dream. Other times, he couldn't get the guy's face out of his mind. But he was certain that if the man he saw existed, he never failed a mission. He was the one Wyeth would want to handle any kidnapping situation that might arise at Painter Place.

"Okay, Phillip, maybe someday we'll be forced to have more security on the island. I trust your foresight and I know you have the best interests of our families in your mind. And maybe you're right, I could be miserable about it when the real problem is that I'm—I'm—"

He waved a helpless hand over the weathered railing. What were the right words?

Phillip smirked. "You want a reason to put the brakes on this relationship. It's too easy, right? To make things worse, soon she'll have nowhere to go. You feel responsible for takin' care of her. It's hard to remember that she's only eighteen."

"It's reckless of people to lose their hearts right from the get-go, not takin' time to get to know one another."

Phillip stared out over the waves and kept his tone even. "You've lost your heart, Wyeth?"

Wyeth snorted. "Didn't you lose yours that night in Charleston?"

His friend shrugged, but he stared ahead as if at an absorbing view. His deep voice took on a matter-of-fact tone. "I thought I had.

I was so sure about her, but now—well, now I wonder if my first love will be my first break-up. Like you said, it's reckless to rush things. Some differences can't be overcome. Your mama warned us, it's a silly romantic notion that love conquers all. That's not what life is like."

Wyeth tugged his hair back over his ear. "Yeah, my parents get smarter every day. Remember when my dad said we should treat anyone we think we're in love with as if she's our sister in Christ, until we put a ring on her finger at the altar? No matter how certain we may feel, until that moment, anything could go wrong—like with Maggie Jane and Roy. Her heart may be the worse for losin' him, but he respected the next guy who might come along. Dad insisted we should treat a girlfriend as if she may be someone else's wife someday, not ours. He told us to think about the purity we hope for in a woman, and we should leave that for the next guy."

Agitated, he tapped his palms on the railing. "Now, Chrissy has come along, and half the time, my emotions are wanderin' like homeless balloons. I want all my firsts to be all her firsts and don't care about the possible next guy."

Phillip glanced sidelong at him. "Yeah, I saw that last night. Chrissy knows her mind, and she's headin' straight for what she wants—you. I predict a short engagement."

Wyeth grinned sheepishly, and they stood in companionable silence. Phillip looked thoughtful and said, "Once, I overheard Noble become exasperated when Andy challenged his 'old fashioned' ideas about relationship parameters. Your dad, he pointed at him and said something like, okay, if it's no big deal, try it. He told him to come back and let him know if his mind hadn't gone further than her lips, and to tell him if he still didn't believe the kiss he wanted in privacy was dangerous. And then, he told Andy to burn that experience in his mind and think of it when he met the woman he hoped to marry. Your dad asked him if he wanted her to be out enjoying harmless kisses with all her dates until Andy came into her life."

Wyeth groaned and tapped the pier railing with his palm again. "What did Andy say?"

"He turned and stormed away. That's the last I heard of it."

A warm breeze stirred Wyeth's hair while they stood in companionable silence. "Phillip, what if Valerie thinks kissing a date is harmless? Word will get out, and unless Andy has done the same, he will face the ridicule of savin' his first kiss for a wife who didn't do the same."

Now, it was Phillip who tapped his palms distractedly on the weathered railing. "I really don't know. But we'd hear about it around town if Andy did. Justin says Andy doesn't date; he just throws his adoring entourage clever, evasive bait."

Wyeth recalled the girls engulfing his brother's Corvette in town. "But I was with him the second time he met Valerie, and she wasn't chasin' him. Maybe that's part of her appeal. She's really cute and oozes personality."

"I agree. Valerie would turn my head, too. But she's also sentimental, Wyeth, and at least a little insecure. She was rejected by the man in her life who should have valued her the most. To marry Valerie, Andy will have to reassure her often that he's faithful. She will have to adjust to having the leadership of a man around the house. He will take on her family issues and try to explain them to his children. Would you want your kids to grow up seein' their grandfather in the papers with a different woman now and then? How early in their lives would you explain it before they hear it from the kids at school? If she's the right one for Andy, the island is a terrific place for her, but he'll need a lot of your dad's wisdom."

Chapter Seventeen

Chrissy parallel parked her two-door white Thunderbird convertible in a space on Main Street. It was Friday morning, only a day before the Island Summer Dance. Beside her, Camellia said, "I think you're wise to consider askin' Noble Painter and Phil Gregory to weigh in on whether to accept the contract for your house. Your realtor and financial manager may be right, but you should have advice you trust before signing anything. When you sell it where will you live?"

A jewel studded key chain winked in the sunlight as Chrissy pulled it from the ignition. She squeezed her eyes shut and put her hand over her mouth.

Camellia glanced into the back seat at Valerie, and they waited until Chrissy shrugged and said brightly, "Here! I will live here because I love it. I'll look for a beach cottage. It's time to move on with my life."

"You may like it now, while romance is in the air," Camellia noted. "But what if you hate it a year from now? You grew up in an important city. You're a model who can travel, see places, and mingle with the rich and famous. What if you change your mind about Wyeth?"

Chrissy glanced all around them to survey their surroundings. She checked to be sure the pocketknife housed in the glamourous key chain in her hand still flipped out easily, then she popped it into an outside pocket in her purse.

Camellia raised a delicate brow. "Is this how a lady gets out of a car where you come from?"

"Only if she doesn't want to become a victim. It's called 'staying off the x.' And I won't change my mind about Whitehaven or Wyeth. I've dreamed of a small, quiet coastal town. I want to live in a place where my neighbors know my name, and where they gossip, brainstorming solutions to my problems when they're concerned about me. I want to marry someone who has an amazing family, and those men are hard to find."

"Marry?" Valerie exclaimed. "Chrissy, are you and Wyeth secretly engaged?"

"Not yet," Chrissy grasped her door handle and checked for traffic in her lane. "But if he doesn't ask, I will."

Camellia opened the passenger door and gracefully arranged her legs with her skirt to get out of the car. When she stood on the sidewalk, she pulled up her seat to give Valerie room to get out of the back. When Chrissy came around to join them, Valerie said, "Chrissy, you're just jokin' with us, right? You wouldn't actually propose to a man!"

"She's dead serious, Valerie. She's not from around here, either, so she's free from the Southern Belle code. Anyway, she's the most mature, straightforward teenager I've ever met. And she's packin' heat in that cute high-dollar handbag."

While Valerie gaped and stepped back from Chrissy's purse, Camellia's eyes scoured Main Street. She scowled, and Chrissy told her to stop because it would make permanent wrinkles. She smoothed her expression so as not to ruin her looks, but she didn't veil the sarcasm in her voice. "What a quaint town! Are there any good restaurants, parks or concerts? What about beauty salons and shopping?"

Chrissy shaded her eyes from the glare on storefront windows. "I've only been in town twice, once when I looked around before crossing the bridge when I arrived, and once with Wyeth." She pointed. "There's a wonderful antique and collectibles store, down that way. That's all the shopping I know about yet. I'm glad you and Valerie needed things, so we can explore."

Turning to the movie theater marquee, she said, "That was on in Washington weeks ago, so I'm guessing Whitehaven doesn't get the first showings of the movies. Fashion trends are behind a couple of years. But the little soda shop on the corner makes me feel like I'm in a wholesome Norman Rockwell illustration. Let's have lunch there."

"The homemade ice cream place is the best," swooned Valerie, pointing at a sign. "I want a sundae before we go back home."

Chrissy laughed. "Back home? When did Painter Place become 'home' to you? Guess I'm not the only one, after all!"

Valerie blinked when she realized what she'd said. With an evasive shrug, she replied, "Oh, I don't know, really. Let's shop there, in the boutique. I love the window display!"

Few other customers browsed the merchandise in the small specialty shop. Chrissy and Valerie couldn't find any casual beach clothing that suited their height, but they discovered sandals that Valerie insisted were the most adorable she'd ever seen.

At first, Camellia was as unenthusiastic about the inventory as she'd been about the town. But as the other two friends sought her opinion of some items they were looking at, she relaxed. She was laughing along with them as they all tried on hats and made movie star faces in a gilded oval mirror.

Then she noticed a wispy shawl. She gasped softly as she pulled it from a hanger. "It would be perfect against the chill of an ocean breeze, on summer evenings."

"Yes, like last night. The palm tree pattern is gorgeous!" Chrissy traced her fingertip over the design on the fine cotton. "It's a lot like your bracelet. They're both perfect for the island."

Valerie came to admire the shawl. Then she took Camellia's arm to study the bracelet. "Oh, Camellia, this is beyond beautiful! Where did you get it?"

"Well—a jewelry store. In Charleston." She hesitated, then blurted, "Phillip bought it for me."

She looked up anxiously. Valerie's jaw dropped, and Chrissy reached out with a reassuring touch on Camellia's arm. "It's a lovely, thoughtful gift. He was decorating you with Painter Place motifs. It can only mean he wants you to be here, with him."

"Camellia, this is—" Valerie waved a hand through the air beside her. "Something so nice is like a ring. Do you love him?"

The jingle of a bell on the door announced a few others coming into the store. They laughed together about trying a new recipe that became a cooking disaster, and the clerk called out a greeting to them.

Chrissy, Camellia, and Valerie huddled closer. "Never mind, Camellia, we'll talk about it over lunch. Let's make our final choices here and go to the soda shop."

"I like this place," Valerie purred as the three friends entered the Coastal Corner Drug Store and Soda Shoppe. "This is where Andy and I had our first dance, the night—"

She glanced furtively at Chrissy, who chose a place for them at a nearby table. A young man with a contagious grin welcomed them from behind the counter where he placed a tempting slice of pie in front of a patron.

"It's all right, Valerie, I know about your friends being with Wyeth and about his aggressive encounter that night." Chrissy reached for the small menu in a metal stand in the center of the shiny laminate tabletop.

Camellia stopped looking around. "What? I don't. What happened?"

Silverware clinked on plates around the soda shop as the counter waiter made his way to their table, dancing to the music on the jukebox. "Mercy, it must be my lucky day!" he teased. "What can I get for three beautiful young ladies?"

Chrissy laughed and looked at his name tag. "I think it's our lucky day, Barney! Your cheerful face and happy dance are an inspiration. We should all remember to enjoy life that much."

Barney's face split into another grin. "Ma'am, the Lord Himself makes every day, and we're supposed to rejoice and be glad in it. That's what the Good Book says!"

His words and attitude charmed Camellia, and they placed their orders while the jukebox throbbed to the next song. Chrissy gestured for the other girls to grasp her hands to say grace.

When the exuberant waiter brought their lunch orders, Valerie had almost finished telling Camellia a hushed overview of the night Wyeth was accused of being intimate with Maggie Jane. With a direct look into Chrissy's eyes, she said, "Andy told me that people think Wyeth is the deep water in a river where you can't be sure what's really under the smooth surface. I think the guy who was tryin' to start a racial incident knew about somethin' people don't see, somethin' that would set Wyeth off. I hope you're not jealous of Maggie Jane, 'cause they're close, like brother and sister."

Chrissy swallowed a mouthful of her sandwich and patted her lips lightly with a napkin, trying not to disturb her lipstick. "I'm not the least bit jealous of her. I suppose Andy has told you that the guy who insulted Wyeth and Maggie Jane told Wyeth he was sorry, then Wyeth made him go out to the Big House and apologize to her in front of her mother. She was so dignified and gracious! The first time she saw me, she made me feel like a trusted friend. She gave me a bottle of what she calls a 'love potion' perfume so I'll smell like Wyeth's island. And then, she did something that still touches me. She asked if I was there to stay and read my eyes to be sure I was honest. Then she told me it was good I was there. I'm glad I'd already heard about what happened here, because I think she was referring to Wyeth having a girlfriend, to deflect suspicion from her."

She stopped to sip pink lemonade from a gaily striped straw in her glass and added, "I'm not jealous of your friends being with him that night, either. He came to town as a favor to Andy, to meet you, so he wasn't here to find a girlfriend. On the day I arrived in Whitehaven and stopped in here for my introduction to Southern sweet tea, I overheard two girls talking. It was as if Jesus gave me a glimpse at what the locals think about the Painter family, especially Wyeth and Andy. The girls discussed the sterling reputation of Wyeth, Maggie Jane, and the Painters. They're inspired by how the Painter and Gregory boys don't date like other people."

Wide-eyed, Valerie reached for her glass. Camellia said, "My parents asked me to consider that, too. They told me that someday I'd understand that a sweet kiss could easily become one that awakens stronger feelings. They also said a guy could misconstrue it as an invitation even if the kiss was innocent enough. Ever heard the term 'kiss and tell'? Guys where I'm from like to kiss and exaggerate. When my parents asked me to do everything possible to keep my reputation from being damaged, I made a personal decision to wait for the man I marry to be my first kiss. Some of my friends think that's extreme, but they're always the ones crying on my shoulder about their latest break-up."

"So, you've never had a real kiss?" asked Valerie.

"Not the kind you want when you're in love. But yes, sometimes on the lips, butterfly kisses as greetings and goodbyes among my friends and relatives. My youth group researched it, and kissing isn't a universal practice. Historically, it was slow to spread, and it wasn't a part of some cultures until Europeans settled there. Here in America, we've let Hollywood dictate what's healthy for our society, and they get most of it wrong."

The theme to a popular film poured from the jukebox. Chrissy sighed. "Speaking of Hollywood, they have some wonderful movie theme songs. This one is so hauntingly beautiful. It makes my heart ache with dreams of romance on the beach, and those dangerous kisses Camellia's talking about."

Camellia swallowed a dainty bite of her sandwich. "You sound melancholy, Chrissy! Did this song inspire your love of an island like Painter Place?"

"Oh, no. I've daydreamed about it for so long I honestly can't recall when the Southern coast sent a siren call for me to come home. It was a puzzle to my mother."

Valerie pushed her empty sandwich wrapper into the small basket the waiter served it in. "You described the music perfectly, Chrissy. I haven't seen this movie yet though. My mom wouldn't have kept me from going, but she'd have wanted me to talk about it afterwards, so she could see if I have the right perspective on things. I only go to movies with friends for entertainment, to escape reality. It wouldn't be entertaining for me to watch all the dysfunctional relationships in that story."

Camellia nodded sadly. "An unplanned pregnancy is a reality to some dear friends of mine, and it's tearin' them apart as a couple. Some people may think it's romantic to just throw caution to the wind and follow your feelings, but it's not. Too many will use it as an excuse to imitate the young couple, like the character played by Sandra Dee."

"Chrissy, you remind me of her. It's your hair, I think. Did you see the movie?"

"No, but my opinion would be the same as yours and Camellia's. I didn't go to any movies last year. My mother died, so I was grieving and trying to hold together during my last year of private school so I could graduate."

Valerie made a small groan of sympathy and reached out to touch Chrissy's hand. "Andy told me you lost your mom, but I forgot that it would have been the same year as the movie. I'm sorry to have been so thoughtless."

Weaving her fingers into Valerie's, Chrissy waved airily with the other hand. "Please, don't be concerned. Our own lives are challenging enough to get through without trying to tip-toe our way through all the landmines of things that might bother someone else. I am doing well now, and my grief counselor thinks the fresh start I'm planning will be a leap forward."

She shifted in the small metal chair and looked directly into Valerie's eyes. "Like you, I didn't grow up with a father, Valerie. We aren't what the Painters would have wished for as wives for their sons. I'm told that marriage is hard enough without partnering with someone who brings baggage into it, and I decided before I met Wyeth that I would never expect a spouse to be all the things I've missed. That was someone else's failure, not a husband's role. I will be realistic about my insecurities as I learn to trust Wyeth on his own merits."

Camellia squeezed her eyes shut and touched her fingertips to her mouth, then shook her head in admiration. When she looked back at them, she sniffed and blinked, then smiled. "Chrissy, I've met no one like you. I get the impression you were never a little girl, and I'd love to get to know you better."

Chrissy laughed brightly and reached for her glass to finish her lemonade. She paused before putting her lips on the straw. "If you'll promise to stick around, I can tell you true stories that are stranger than fiction."

"And speaking of true stories, I want to know what you didn't tell us in the boutique, Camellia!" Valerie leaned forward and glanced around as if someone might overhear.

A song about a love affair breaking up was flowing from the speakers of the juke box. With an evasive look over to the young man who was putting spare change into it, Camellia bit her lip, then said, "I have the right man. But he's in the wrong place."

"You'd better decide if you're hiring a moving company soon," Chrissy warned. "One thing about living at the Big House is that I overhear a lot. My room opens to the ocean from the second-floor veranda. As I stood there yesterday, I heard Phillip telling his dad he wants to see if you'll agree to look to the future with him before Victoria and her father dock at the port in Charleston. He wants no one to think he's trying to decide between you two, and the papers will pick up on the story she's here. Phil doesn't know how much longer he can make excuses. Victoria wants to visit Painter Place and stake a claim, and she's armed with sturdy ingenuity. Only you can stop her."

Camellia jerked her head around to stare wide-eyed at Chrissy, who put both hands up in surrender. But the steely look in her eyes remained. "Sure, I'm gossiping. And it was a private conversation. I'd have kept it to myself if you hadn't confessed where that bracelet came from. But hear this, Camellia," she said, pointing a finger at her friend. "If my dream for a future at Painter Place with Wyeth comes true, I want you there, not someone like Victoria."

"Can I assume that Victoria's not from around here?" Valerie ventured. "Maybe she even lacks the grace and charm of a Southern-bred lady?"

"Victoria is a beautiful, accomplished British socialite whose daddy has a super-yacht named *The Dominator*," Chrissy informed her. "She expects to marry someone who fits that description, and it was Phillip's nickname the night we attended a reception aboard that ship. She's also a well-connected, first-class event hostess that would be an asset to anyone with high-class clientele. If motivated, she'd be a quick student of the graces and charms of a Southern-bred lady. She has her sights locked on Phillip though her daddy wants her to marry a guy in London that escorted Camellia to a reception we attended. But her daddy and Phil Gregory had at least one conversation about the possibility of a high-profile engagement between Victoria and her heart's desire."

"She wants to change him," blurted Camellia, leaning forward and knitting her fingers together. "Before she found out I knew Phillip, she told me Whitehaven was nowhere, that she'd rather die than live here. She said she'd deceive him into thinkin' she'd live here if they married, but after the wedding, she'd either force him to go with her to live somewhere else or they'd have a long-distance marriage. She believes she can make him love her and do anything to make her happy."

Chrissy slowly leaned forward and placed her hand on Camellia's. "Is that so different from what you want him to do?"

Chapter Eighteen

Wyeth saw the sleek Thunderbird pulling slowly onto Pavilion Avenue from the bridge. With the top down, Chrissy, Camellia, and Valerie were hard to miss against the bright turquoise leather. He grinned at the long stretch of sculpted white metal and three beauties dressed for summer. They'd make a great television commercial for the car manufacturer, or a famous brand of sunscreen.

He shouted to Phillip and Andy, then pointed at his chest and the gleaming car. Phillip nodded and turned to hand a box to someone next to him. But Andy shrugged helplessly, his hands full of tools for a group of men repairing a bench near the pavilion.

Chrissy turned off the engine in a parking space under a melancholy old tree, and Wyeth trotted up to grab her door handle. She rewarded him with a beaming smile as she pulled off her sunglasses.

Unable to take his eyes off her, he stood waiting for her to step out. Phillip jogged up and opened Camellia's door, and Andy was breathless when he ran up in time to push the front seat forward and hold Valerie's hand to help her out.

Chrissy kept her eyes locked on Wyeth's as she rose gracefully from the driver's side. "I love driving up to the Big House. There always seems to be a welcoming committee. Is it like this everywhere in the South, or just Painter Place?"

Wyeth reached into the back seat for their shopping bags. "I never really thought about it. I suppose it's a Southern thing, but honestly, I only notice when I'm waiting for you."

The girls were cooing over Wyeth's answer while Andy asked where they'd had lunch. Valerie gave him an animated description of their orders at the Coastal Corner and the ice cream sundaes that followed.

Phillip studied Camellia's face. "Did you find anything you liked in town?"

When she smiled and nodded enthusiastically, he visibly relaxed. Chrissy took a bag out of Wyeth's hands and motioned for Phillip to come closer, then she displayed a peek at the shawl. With wide-eyed innocence, she said, "It reminds me of her gorgeous bracelet. Don't you think so?"

He reached out as if to touch the fine pattern, then realized his hand was dirty from working outside. He impulsively wiped it on his jeans and looked at Camellia. "It's perfect. It's classy, like you."

Ignoring the dirt, she reached out to grasp his hand. With a warm look and a silvery voice, she replied, "The moment I saw it, I knew it was made for Painter Place. I can't wait to wear it!"

Phillip blinked and swallowed. His voice was thick when he replied, "And I can't wait to see it."

"Hey, what about tonight?" Andy piped in. "We haven't taken you to see the Painter family chapel, or Dog's Head, or the old boathouse. You don't know the island until you've heard about them. We have some spooky legends, so stick close to us."

He winked, made a ghoulish sound, and reached for Valerie's hand with his dirty one. She grasped it without hesitation and pretended to shiver as she leaned into his side. "I've heard about the Legend of King's Ransom, and a friend of mine did an essay about the history behind the one with the wind songs. I hear there's one about a mermaid and one about some hidden treasure. Andy, can we take flashlights?"

"Sure, but I always heard girls with green eyes could see in the dark, like cats. Who needs a flashlight when we've got you and Camellia? I could save money on batteries if I'd just marry a girl like that."

Wyeth cupped Chrissy's elbow and led the group toward the house. "When we were boys, we'd brag we knew this island like the back of our hands. But the wind, water, and wildlife change it. Every spring, or after a big storm, we get out and chart any differences. My dad keeps a record in the library. Year to year, we might have more island, or less."

Camellia turned to Phillip and asked if he had a camera. "I forgot to pack mine, and I'd love to take the film back with me to Charleston and get the photos printed, so I can remember this weekend."

Encouraged at Camellia's new excitement for the island, Phillip assured her he did and would put a fresh roll of film in. Chrissy said photography was her hobby and she would also take plenty of photos to share. Then Wyeth piped in, bragging about how great her photos from London were.

"That's because you are such a handsome model," she teased. "You painted my portrait and I created yours with a camera."

A sweaty teenager ran up to them, calling for Wyeth. One of the work crew had a question about a foundation for a torch being used in the Island Summer Dance.

"Tell him I'm on my way. It's easier to show him than to explain." Wyeth handed the bags to Chrissy. "Are you okay carrying these in? We're almost finished, and we'll clean up. Go nowhere without me, promise?"

"Promise! If you're sure there is nothing we can do to help, Camellia will hang out here with me and Valerie. She's a decorator and hasn't seen the Sunflower Room. I want to talk about it to anyone who will listen. Your family should have it featured in a magazine!"

"Is this goin' to be anything like the girls' night out you told me about?"

Airily, she answered, "The only reading material in my room is a Bible and some fashion magazines. But any confidences shared will remain among the sunflowers."

He threw back his head with a hearty laugh. The others smiled and glanced at one another to see if anyone knew what the couple was talking about.

Wyeth said, "Private joke." And with a peck at Chrissy's cheekbone, he jogged off back to work.

After dinner at the Big House, the three young couples at Painter Place put on insect repellant and set off with flashlights and cameras. Wyeth drove Chrissy's Thunderbird up Castaway Drive while Phillip and Camellia followed in the Maserati. Andy acted as a tour guide to Chrissy and Valerie from the back seat of the convertible.

The Atlantic Ocean filled their sight on the passenger side, and Chrissy seemed torn between looking out at it or turning around to ask Andy questions. "How did this road get its name? That sounds like a story."

"It's a story all right, but you'll be disappointed if you're expectin' *Robinson Crusoe*. The first Painter who settled this island referred to himself as a Carolina castaway because he had to live on a deserted island. The nickname stuck. His real name was Patrick, and that's how he signed all his paintings and legal stuff."

"Patrick? Oh, Andy! I really like that. It has a wonderful ring to it—Patrick Painter," Valerie said, adding a romantic flair and a lilting wave of a pretty hand.

"Yeah, I've always liked it, too," Andy said. "It's a family name every few generations, so I want to name my first son after him."

He met Wyeth's amused glance in the rear-view mirror. Then Wyeth eased the Thunderbird into the sandy parking area beside the Painter Chapel where strong evening shadows shaped like semi-tropical foliage splayed themselves flat against the stucco.

"Oh," breathed Chrissy. She aimed her camera and clicked photos of the setting.

Phillip parked and quickly went around to open Camellia's door. With car engines off, the island seemed to spring to life. Waves crashed in perpetual motion on the other side of the road at the beach. Palm leaves rustled, seagulls cried, and insects sent out buzzing mating calls as they rubbed their wings together. Songbirds floated unfinished melodies through the breezes.

Wyeth wandered to another vantage point and showed Chrissy a dramatic view of the chapel and the steeple under oak fingers that seemed to reach for the sky. Enthralled, she said, "The building may be the size of a chapel, but the effect of the setting is like an island cathedral."

She squatted in her jeans and tennis shoes to get more unusual perspectives in her photos, looking up with the sky, live oaks, and palms over various parts of the architecture. Wyeth gently pushed at her back and she tumbled over, laughing.

Camellia took photos of the open chapel doors while Phillip told her they remained unlocked most days in good weather so that visitors and guests on the island could come inside and pray. Andy showed Valerie a game with their hands he played with kids at church, and she giggled and told him she knew it. In unison, they formed a church and a steeple, then opened their hands to wiggle their interlocked fingers to show all the "people."

Wyeth took on the mantle of tour guide to the ladies as they all gathered at the front of the building. "My dad always tells visitors to the Painter Chapel that we don't think of it as a 'house of God' like the Temple in the Old Testament. You don't come here to meet Him, because if you're a Christian, Christ lives in your heart all the time. Dad reminds people that like the game Andy and Valerie were playing, Christians themselves are the church, gathering in a building dedicated to fellowship with other believers. He says they should be in fellowship with Christ and serving Him all the time, but often, people seem drawn to chapels and churches to pray."

They mounted the stone masonry of timeworn steps up to the doors. "Do you feel closer to Christ here?" Chrissy asked.

Wyeth gazed around the interior of the chapel. The rays of the setting sun splashed soft colors across the room through the stained-glass windows. "I don't think it's so much that I feel closer to Him here, but more that I'm reminded of His faithfulness because of the landmarks, as my dad calls them. This pew was smuggled here from a previous chapel on land the Painters owned in England. The windows, like the dome over the mansion, were also smuggled out."

He wandered over to the center aisle to squat down and point out the side of the wooden pew, carved with a crest and a regal letter P. "Dad thinks the carving of the family crest is pretentious here. Someday, he'll restore it again and put it in the library or the studios. I know my prayers have as much power in my room or on the beach as they do in church, but I still come here. The legacy and the leadership that will be expected of me is unsettling, and Dad says every Painter feels the same way."

He reached out to touch the carved Painter family crest. "That's why it's so vital to pass the landmarks along. They stand as testimonies. And it's a powerful experience for me to sit in the old pews, knowin' that my dad and all my Carolina ancestors have poured out their hearts and made lifelong marriage vows in this chapel."

Chrissy let her camera rest against her periwinkle blue sweater as it dangled from a strap around her neck. She traced her fingers through pools of stained-glass colors on the priceless pew and said dreamily, "I can see why worshiping and praying here would have so much impact. It would be such a reverent place for a wedding. Vows made here would not easily be forgotten."

"Oh, yes," breathed Valerie, taking a few steps down the aisle as if under a spell. "Are most Painter weddings held here?"

Wyeth rose and answered, "Yes, and Gregory weddings, too. But it's only big enough for private family events. If the bride has a lot of social expectations, she returns to her home church sometime afterwards and hosts a reception. Former guests to the island sometimes ask to come back to marry here in the chapel."

Camellia had taken a few steps down the aisle, surveying the room and the cross on the wall behind the altar. "Yes. It's such an intimate setting for a private wedding." Then she sniffed and wiped away a silent tear.

Phillip went to put an arm around her. "Are you thinkin' of Jacqueline and Tom?"

She nodded. "They seemed perfect together. I was so certain they'd marry someday. Now, I don't know. Anyway, I'm sure the Painters have rules about situations like that. I wouldn't want it to seem that they'd endorse what happened."

Phillip glanced back at Wyeth, who said, "From what I've heard, your friends are believers who made a mistake, and they've gotten things right in their personal relationships with the Lord. Now, they want Him to guide them to what comes next. I can't speak for my dad, but I think he would let them get married here."

Valerie gazed up at a satin sky, then scrutinized the shape of the shoreline on the tidal marsh side of the island. "So, from the air, this looks like the shape of a dog's head? I thought it was named for the legend about the golden retriever."

Andy picked up a limb that had fallen from a massive oak that dripped with Spanish moss. He tossed it into a pile of other limbs nearby and slapped the bark off of his palms, then he picked up his flashlight from the sand. "I'm not sure which came first—the people who walked the beach and knew it was the shape of a dog's head, or the legend. There's an island down the coast, below Charleston, and it has a shape like a dog's head, too."

"Are you referring to Hilton Head?" asked Camellia. She drew her new shawl closer and watched Phillip examine something on the ground. Wyeth stood over him, shining the beam of his flashlight.

"Yeah, you know about that?"

"Oh, sure, I have a relative who lives there. We visit sometimes. I like it." She squinted and bent over at the waist to get a better look at what Phillip had in his hand. "Is that a pocketknife?"

"It is," Phillip said, rising. "Someone must've dropped it last weekend when a group from a local church camped out here. See, someone's initials are engraved into the handle. We have a lost and found for the campsite, so I'll have my dad call the leader."

Looking across the waterway, he pointed. "Over there, the brightest lights, that's Gregory Global. A second shift crew is working."

Camellia peered over. "Oh, I didn't think about looking for your family's offices today when we were in town. Can you see it from your house, too?"

Phillip laughed and glanced sidelong at Wyeth. "Of course. And we see Painter Place from over there, through lots of picture windows. We never let either place out of our sight."

Wyeth chuckled and bumped his shoulder into Phillip's. "The meaning of Phillip's last name is 'watchman' and 'alert,' and they live up to it. Painter Place probably wouldn't exist today without them."

"And the Painters gave my ancestor a fresh start here on the island when he was penniless. We've had one another's backs ever since."

Camellia stared at Wyeth and Phillip as they stood side by side. "Finally, I think I understand. Nothing outside this island can separate what God built here, between your families. Only a Painter or a Gregory can end their history together. The bond is dissolved from within."

Andy went to stand with his brother and Phillip. "That won't happen this time around, not with this generation. But like my dad says, we don't know what the future holds."

"I wouldn't camp here. It's spooky!" Valerie shivered and tugged the polka-dot sleeves of her pink cotton sweater down, glancing around at the deep black of the tree shadows. "Some of the trees look like gruesome monsters."

She yelped when Andy grabbed her from behind to startle her. "Come on, now, you don't believe in monsters, do you?" he teased.

"Only the human ones. And don't start your preachin'! I know the Bible teaches that there aren't any ghosts, but I still think somethin' is goin' on in places that seem haunted. Have you ever been to one?"

"That's a spirit, but like you say, not a person's ghost. Demons have territory, according to scripture, and some people are more sensitive to evil than others. But you shouldn't fear that on this island. Haven't you heard the stories about the 'white spirits' around here?"

"Sure, but I also heard the stories about the ghost of a sea captain callin' for his drowned dog on stormy nights."

"Okay, that shipwreck of the Aquarius really happened, and it probably went down somewhere off our island. But the story about the ghosts is told by camp leaders around the fire to keep kids from sneakin' off from the group and gettin' hurt. Stick around for the next storm and I'll prove it to you."

As they reached the dark, looming structure of the boathouse, Wyeth pointed his flashlight toward a sturdy pole and walked up to flip a switch. Lights along the overhang of the roof popped on, revealing the outline of the building. But the sight wasn't comforting. Deep shadows jutted out at sharp angles.

The plopping and splashing of water betrayed whatever animals had run from them, and Camellia made a little whimper as she drew her shawl closer. "Don't worry, we aren't goin' inside, not at night," Wyeth assured her. "Too many things to get hurt on. But now you know where the boathouse is. We don't use it much anymore since the big bridge was built. Maggie Jane's dad, Big Jim Simmons, used to work out here and she has stories she tells sometimes."

"Where's her dad now?" Valerie asked. "I don't think I've met him yet."

"You'll meet him in heaven," Wyeth answered. "He was in a boating accident further up the coast, tryin' to help a friend. But he loved this boathouse and kept it in top shape. Andy's out here more than anybody now."

"It's harmless enough in the daytime," Andy pointed out. "You just have to be wary of water snakes."

"And small alligators," Phillip added. "Sometimes, they find their way here."

The girls backed away and Chrissy squeaked, "Alligators?"

"We have wildlife control come and pick them up," Wyeth assured her, and he reached his arm around her to pull her closer. "Phillip just wants you two to be wary, like we've learned to be. You can walk alone on the beach and the well-traveled areas, but not the marsh or around the boathouse. This is a natural habitat. That's why we let science groups and agencies come study here."

Chrissy leaned into his side but crinkled her nose. "I meant to ask, does pluff mud smell like rotten eggs?"

Wyeth chuckled. "Yeah, and it might take gettin' used to. We don't notice, but I've heard it described as organic and earthy. The moon controls the tide every day, and high tide brings sea life like the southern flounder into the marsh for food. Low tide leaves behind a meal for sea birds."

Phillip pointed down the shoreline. "Past the marsh, you can see some distant lights. That's the Big House and the studios."

"Is that the same marsh mentioned in the story of the wind songs?" Valerie asked. "Can we hear them?"

"I'm not sure." Phillip gestured for everyone to draw closer. "The marsh pattern has changed too much since then for the sound to be the same as in the legend. But we hear what we call songs, at the mansion, just south of the marsh. We're on the north side tonight and the breeze may not be in the right direction."

"What else is on the south side?" Camellia asked. "Phillip, isn't that where you live?"

"Yes, but our house is too far from the marsh to catch the wind songs. Andy's land is even further, down at the extreme south end."

Andy leaned against the raggedy bark of the tree he stood under. "Once I'm married, I'll build a house and pier at Brush Point. You can't listen to the wind songs in the legend, but the lot has huge live oaks. Maybe once I build the house the arrangement of the trees will create their own wind songs."

He reached out to grasp Valerie's hand. "Has anyone ever described the sound to you?"

She shook her head, wide-eyed in the shadows. "They can't really be like music, as we think of it. Maybe the sound is like when the wind sighs, whistles and moans around buildings in a storm?"

He turned to stare out at the marsh, where creeping dark fingers revealed the shallow creeks through the pluff mud and the marsh grasses. "People have different accounts of what they've heard on breezy days. It may be all about their expectations, or their imaginations, or what they bring with them to the island. But folks at the Big House, we all describe somethin' similar."

They waited silently. The trees creaked and rustled overhead. Water lapped against the pilings of the small dock at the boathouse. A dog barked in the distance across the water in Whitehaven. And the island seemed to stir with a thousand timeless whispers.

Just when Wyeth was about to gather them to the path to walk back to the chapel, their heads came up, alert. Camellia's hand flew to her heart, and Chrissy tucked her arm around Wyeth's waist. Andy pulled Valerie closer.

A drawn-out, low, breathy note like a wooden flute faded off into the air it flew on. When all traces of it had gone, a higher, shorter tone chased playfully after it. And the resonance of the third note sent tears rolling down Chrissy's face.

Chapter Nineteen

On Saturday morning, Chrissy sat with Wyeth and his parents on the veranda to linger over coffee and tea after breakfast. She told them about an offer to purchase her house, and she asked if Noble had time to look at the details and give her his opinion. "I have a reputable real estate agent and a financial manager that has handled our family accounts for years. But looking at this contract makes me feel so young and inadequate. You've only known me for a week, but I can't think of anyone I trust more."

Noble's smile was gentle as he studied her with the blue eyes that made her think of the Atlantic Ocean on a clear day. "You are young, Chrissy, though you've had to grow up quickly. When I was eighteen, like you, I faced a daunting future when my father and older brother Richard disappeared at sea. Uncle James died in the Great War back in 1917 before he could marry and have any kids. The Painters were never blessed with many babies, so my only living relative was my mother, Revanna. She wore black and sat in a rocker much of the time, starin' out at the ocean, as if some miracle would bring her husband and son home. When the war broke out, she'd smile and say she was guardin' the island from German U-boats. She died when my boys were small. Phil Gregory and his dad, Alton, were the only ones around to help me keep from losin' everything."

He sighed and turned to look at Savanna, then he reached for her hand. "Those were rough times, weren't they? But lookin' back, they were some of my best times, too. I married the woman of my dreams and had two sons, right here on the ground my dad left for me."

Savanna wore the special look she always had when her eyes met her husband's. Noble seemed to bask in it, and Chrissy glanced over at Wyeth, who winked and picked up his teacup.

With his wife's hand still in his, Noble turned back to Chrissy. "I'll be glad to look at the contract, and I'll call Phil to stop by and see what he thinks. Where will you go after you close on the house?"

She kneaded the seashells painted on her teacup with both hands. "I could use advice about that, too. I want to buy a cottage in a safe neighborhood near Whitehaven. It's been a long-time dream of mine to live in a small town on the coast. When Wyeth painted my portrait with the scarf and told me it reminded him of home, I felt this was where I was meant to be. Once Lucinda described the island, I couldn't get it out of my mind."

Now, she blushed and rushed to say, "I mean, this area, of course. It feels like home to me."

Noble raised his brows and looked at Wyeth. "She can stay here while she looks for something."

"Of course, she'll stay here," said Savanna with an elegant wave of her hand. "Eighteen is too young to be out renting something while she looks around. I'll keep the Sunflower Room set aside for the family this summer."

"I don't want to wear out my welcome," Chrissy said anxiously. "You've already been such gracious hosts. I'll be spending a week modeling in Atlanta soon. I have other job offers, but I didn't accept yet because I need to be available to sign the paperwork on the house."

Savanna leaned forward. "Chrissy, I have many friends in Atlanta, and it's no place for a single young lady to travel alone. Will you have a chaperone?"

"Yes, I will be with a group and have safe accommodations while I'm working, but I must take a commuter flight out of Whitehaven to get to the airport. It would be convenient if I left my car here in town."

Noble cleared his throat. "Do you need the income from this job, or do you enjoy modeling?"

"Oh, well," she began, tilting her head. "It's challenging, with long hours and travel. But it pays well. Sometimes it feels a little deceptive because I know how much a seamstress is adjusting a dress to look great on me. When I'm modeling designer styles which women will alter anyway, that's fine, but with a store line, the dress won't look the same on a typical woman. Right now, I don't need the income, but I was raised to be financially responsible. My mother kept me on a track for this career in case I never married. My time would be better spent in something other than modeling, but I don't know my next step."

"I see," replied Noble. "You're workin' until another path is clearly in front of you."

Wyeth had been quiet, but now he set his empty teacup down into the saucer. "What if you tell your agent to find smaller jobs for you, closer to Whitehaven, until you get your affairs settled?"

"I can, but I don't expect there to be many opportunities. The best jobs are in larger cities, like London, though that one landed in my lap unexpectedly. Right now, I'm on my own."

Juliette burst through the door, followed by Andy and Valerie. "Chrissy, Valerie says she'll help me do my hair for the dance tonight! I get to stand with Mama and Daddy when they welcome everyone to the island. Will you help me put nail polish on?"

Chrissy looked over at Savanna, who nodded and smiled. "Okay," Chrissy agreed as Juliette hugged her neck from around the back of her chair. "I have a pretty princess pink, the color of cotton candy. But the foundation of every manicure is to shape up our nails and then put them in a luxurious soak while we listen to our favorite song or tell a secret about ourselves. Can Valerie join us for that?"

"Yes!" Juliette exclaimed. "I want to hear secrets!"

"But you have to tell one, too," Valerie reminded her. "That's the deal. Maybe you could tell us something about your brothers."

Andy squinted and looked at Wyeth. "I'll take first watch outside the Sunflower Room door. My own secrets are rare in fact, numerous in fiction."

Wyeth screwed up his face and inspected his hands. "I have a better idea. Girls, I need a manicure before the dance."

Juliette giggled and plopped into his lap. She planted a quick kiss on his cheek and announced that she already knew all his secrets. Then she pointed at Andy.

"And I'm not tellin' him any! He teases."

What was it about strings of colorful paper lanterns glowing in the last light of a day that created magic? Wyeth wasn't certain, but that's how everyone always described the lights on the island. Year after year, his parents used as many colors as they could find, and their reward was watching attendees point out which one was their favorite. The luminous paper colors hung from the ceiling of the pavilion, along the railing, and between palms on the beach.

They continued the tradition of delighting guests at Painter Place. Tonight's Island Summer Dance was not for the Painters, as people sometimes assumed. It was a celebration of the family's many friendships.

Chrissy stood at his side, anticipating the warm welcome his parents would present from the pavilion gazebo. His baby sister stood with them, a natural at being center stage. She daydreamed of being an actress and postured behavior beyond her years. Now, her blue eyes were shining as she shared her smile with everyone. But his parents said ten years old was too young to remain at the dance for long, so she'd be going back up to the house soon with two of her best friends for a sleepover.

Wyeth surveyed the crowd and told Chrissy, "There's a limit to how many guests will fit on the pavilion dance floor, so attendance is by invitation only. Some will walk on the beach and pier, and the younger guests like to dance in the sand, then go off together to talk. The rules are, they must stay within the lights of the lanterns and torches."

Chrissy looked up with a mischievous half-smile. "Let me guess—for their own safety?"

"Certainly. And that covers a lot of other territory."

"You're blushing," Chrissy teased, nuzzling her shoulder into his and throwing him off balance. "I hope you've explored none of that shadowy territory over the years."

He regained his footing in the sand and opened his mouth to deny everything, but his dad spoke into a microphone to get the attention of the guests. Someday, he'd be in his dad's role, telling everyone who crowded around the pavilion about what a blessing it was to call them friends. He'd be the one telling them that the Painters hoped this would be an evening to count among their favorite memories.

Chrissy's sigh was brimming over with happiness and contentment. Hope and longing welled up in his heart as he watched her smile up at his parents and sister. If he was in his dad's role someday, could she be in his mother's? With her by his side through the years, it would be bearable to keep Painter Place for a generation that didn't include any children of his own.

Impulsively, he squeezed her hand, and she turned those lovely eyes to his. For an instant, he saw her posing in the sophisticated gown and wrap she'd modeled in London. That day, he assumed she was out of his league, and never would have dreamed she'd even look at a guy like him. How could the same woman be standing at his side, holding his hand, at Painter Place?

He felt swept into the familiar yet unsettling sensation of being in a timeless place, like a painting he was composing in his mind. Then Chrissy pulled her hand away and clapped, and he snapped back to reality to join the applause. The smooth sound of a song about the moon being out was the first dance of the evening.

Wyeth seized her arm and joined the throng of guests who wanted to begin the dance on the plank floors of the pavilion. She was beaming at people who waved and greeted them. And as he found a space for them to dance, she looked around in wonder.

"The lights! They splash colors across everyone's faces, like the stained glass in the chapel last night. What color is mine?"

Wyeth created a respectable distance between them and moved her to the music. "Yellow," he answered. "The color of hope."

"And the color of sunflowers, like the ones on the music box that our song lives in," she said.

He marveled at what the intimate look in her eyes did to him. Surrounded by romantic music, the twilight, the lights, and an island breeze laden thickly with romance, it all added up to one thing—promise.

"Have you finished the song you said you were writing to go along with the music for our song?"

"Not yet. I have the words in my journal, but I'm painting them into poetry."

He smiled at the imagery of Chrissy painting with words. Holding her to dance in the Painter Place pavilion felt as right to him as walking around his island or picking up his paintbrush. As he looked down at her, she seemed to read his thoughts. Then she made a soft cooing sound like a dove when theme song to the musical *South Pacific* began. "Some enchanted evening," she whispered. "What a perfect description for tonight. Perhaps I should use them in our song."

Wyeth let himself sail away with her in the music. "The sound of her laughter will sing in your dreams," sang Sinatra with an impeccable breath control. Chrissy wasn't the only one under the spell of the Island Summer Dance, and as the song lyrics claimed, wise men never tried to explain love.

Andy Painter doubted he would admit that watching his parents and baby sister kick off the Island Summer Dance moved him. But seeing Valerie's rapt attention on them, he knew she would be the one he might share the secret with. Since coming to the island, she watched his parents' relationship the same way he admired a shiny new fishing yacht. If she was that hungry for the love his parents had for one another, well—he was always trying to one-up his dad.

He had high hopes for his date tonight. His dad had been reluctant when Andy asked if he could honor the invitation he'd extended before he knew who she was. He prepared his parents for gossip about him being seen around town with the daughter of Dr. Anthony Rush. But after the confrontation at the marina on Wednesday, his dad had warmed to Andy spending time with her.

She was expectant and beautiful tonight as they went to the pavilion for the first dance. Then one guest seized Valerie's arm to exchange greetings. Valerie introduced Andy by his first name only, and her friend introduced her to a date, who turned out to be one of the Gregory family's acquaintances.

"It's a pleasure to meet you," the young lady said cordially to Andy. He told her the pleasure was his and shook hands with her date. Valerie's friend surveyed the crowd and asked, "Where is Eric? I haven't seen him in ages! We really need to catch up soon."

"I haven't seen him in ages, either," Valerie said, and she took Andy's hand with both of hers. "Andy is my date tonight."

The other young lady stammered, "You mean, you aren't—he said you two were practically engaged!"

"Can we chat later?" Valerie asked her friend, then she turned her dazzling smile up to Andy. "Andy's family is hosting this dance, and we should be up there with them right now. Hope you have a good time here tonight! Be sure to check out the refreshments and walk out onto the pier."

Reading all the clues, Andy smiled stiffly and told the couple he hoped they would have a wonderful evening. Then he let Valerie tug his arm toward the pavilion.

With a quick smile, she settled into his arms to dance. But they moved in silence, and he grew angrier with each step. Her friend stared at him and whispered something to her date, and he felt like a fool. How had he fared when compared to Eric?

Over the years, he'd danced a million times to as many songs, so his movements were automatic. He was stuck with Valerie as his date tonight, but he could pass her off to Wyeth and Phillip for a few of the songs soon and dance with their dates.

He could get through tonight. She would leave tomorrow.

The vocal harmony of the Everly Brothers soothed his nerves. Ordinarily, he would turn this song up on his car radio and sing along with them. But lyrics about the heartsick dreaming of someone who was left behind did not help Andy's mood.

With a turn that was more aggressive than he meant to swing her, he took a ragged breath and tried to relax. She danced well, and he felt a stab of jealousy that she may have had plenty of practice—with the last guy.

Suddenly, Valerie pulled him near, and he gingerly put his hands on her shoulder blades. Following her cue, he altered the pace of the slow, swaying movements and stopped using any turns or dips. He growled, "Don't cry on my shoulder for someone else when you're dancin' with me."

She drew back sharply to look up at him, then blinked. "What?"

"If you're missin' your old fiancé, go down by the water and walk the beach. People say it's a great place for memories of what might have been."

Valerie's eyes flashed in anger and she pulled back. The mournful words of a song floated on the warm summer breeze. "How dare you!" she hissed through clenched teeth.

"No, Valerie, how dare *you*! Was I goin' to be the last one to know about him?"

She glanced around to see if anyone was close enough to hear. "You never asked, Andy. The first night we met, you simply apologized on behalf of anyone who'd given me such a low opinion of men, remember? And you said I had issues with relationships. But never once did you act like you cared who caused my problem. You just started tryin' to fix it."

Andy glowered. The next song filled the pavilion, and he almost laughed out loud. Floyd Cramer's piano played the popular, haunting notes of "Last Date" while the tension grew.

"My mistake. I assumed when I asked about your low opinion of men, you'd have been up front about your broken heart and infamous father."

He wasn't sure which was colder, her tone or the look of steel in her eyes. "After this dance, I'll take care of myself. There are some handsome single guys here who will act more like gentlemen." She tossed her head and looked around for those single men, pulling back enough from Andy to create an awkward distance between them.

His mind raced to the guest list and his jealousy flared. But hadn't he been thinking about how to get rid of her, anyway? Here was his chance.

As she scanned the crowd and smiled sweetly at someone, he felt left behind, used. Smoothly, he led her near the railing on the pavilion for more privacy. In another song change, a tenor sang, "They all disappear from view, and I only have eyes for you."

"Are you on the rebound?" Andy asked through clenched teeth. "You go lookin' for other men as easily as your dad scouts out women. How many have there been, and how serious?"

Valerie narrowed her eyes. "I have a lot of friends in a small town, like you do. I went on dates to dances and group dates with friends. But there's only been one guy I ever got serious about, and I met him through a friend at the tech school last year. He started talkin' about marriage on Christmas break from his college and came to Georgetown to visit me a lot, but he didn't propose. He's a politician's son who's learned how to play all the angles to his advantage. Like you, he made the mistake of comparing me to my father, only he assumed I'd be warmer if I thought we were gettin' married. Then, I called him last spring to reschedule a date. Another woman answered the phone. When he grabbed it away, she yelled at him to stop playin' games and tell me the truth, that she was stayin' with him most nights, and he had to choose between us."

Her face was impassive, unreadable. She looked out at the couples laughing together as they stood in the sand beside the pavilion. "You're not the one who's a fool, Andy. I am. I told him never to call me again. Turns out, I shouldn't have given him my first kiss last Christmas, thinkin' he'd be the only one for the rest of my life. I wasted it on a man who didn't deserve it, and now, I can't even remember what that kiss felt like."

Chapter Twenty

"I've never met someone who's accomplished at everything he does at such a young age, like you are. I'm intimidated."

Startled, Phillip looked down to see if Camellia was serious. A paper lantern nearby splashed a soft pink across her heart-shaped face and the straight line of her nose. Her expression became bemused under his stare, and he tried to remember what she'd asked him.

Romantic music affected couples all over the pavilion as they pulled closer to slow dance. A group that called themselves The Flamingos sang about not knowing if the stars were out because they only had eyes for the woman they were with. Phillip preferred the thick mood instead of talking about himself.

"I spend my time at things I like and skills I need to have. They say practice makes perfect."

He should have known she was too smart for the short answer. "Did you practice singin' the song from *Kismet* for a girl in your future? Because guys don't do that, you know. And you worked it in beautifully during our first dance, right there around the gazebo. If I didn't know better, I'd say you'd paid the band to play that song."

"Oh. Point taken. Well, sure, I sing, mostly in the shower or to songs on the radio, or at church. 'Stranger in Paradise' was stuck in my head for days before the concert, so yeah, I confess to practicing beforehand, but—you're like the words to all my favorite songs."

With a hopeful smile, he looked down into her face. She smiled, too, but a raised brow told him his answer didn't satisfy her. "Then explain this: you didn't have practice in dating, and you maneuvered like an expert the night we met. You knew just how to sweep me off my feet and keep Brian at arm's length."

"Oh," he said as they glided through a turn. "Well, you picked me. Out of all the guys in the park that night, you sent me the signal to figure out how to make us happen. And I did. I couldn't fail, so I faked it."

His grin slowly faded as he looked into her eyes. She shook her head. "No, Phillip, you didn't fake it. You have a secret. A secret that forced me to notice you and makes people call you nicknames like 'The Dominator.'"

He winced and tore his eyes from hers. "Please, Camellia, don't think of me that way. It can sound heartless, and you know I'm not like that. People comment on how I handle myself, but I give the credit for that to my parents. At Painter Place, we grow up hearing how important it is to keep a good reputation and make wise decisions. Sometimes, our dads camped out with us up at Dog's Head to get us to talk about things going on in our lives, and they helped us brainstorm reactions to all kinds of situations so we wouldn't be surprised."

With a glance at his parents dancing nearby, he said, "My dad had most of the King's Road deal done when we went to London, but he was strategic in settin' me up to seal it. He wanted me to take the praise to help with credibility if something happens to him. He has health concerns. There's a certain genetic Gregory trait that came super-sized in me, according to my dad and Noble Painter, but only time will tell. I surrendered everything to Christ, long ago, so He equips me for a calling. If I have a secret beyond those things, it might be my hobby. I've always studied the wisdom and quotes of leaders I admire from history. Many people left us the best lessons they'd learned in life as quotes in journals, speeches, and books. I internalize traits I admire."

"Ah, I can see it now," she murmured. "Most people think new times make the past irrelevant. But the Bible says there's nothing new under the sun, and some lessons are universal."

"Then, you don't think my hobby is boring?"

"Phillip Gregory, you're the second most fascinating person I've ever met, after my daddy." As she laughed softly, the theme music to a popular movie transitioned to continue the romantic music set at the dance. "Speaking of my daddy, he likes to change the name Tammy in this song to Cami. He teases me and asks when this will happen."

Startled, Phillip looked into her face again. "You mean, is Cami in love?"

But she was looking over to her parents, who danced nearby. He turned to see them smile back at her, and her dad winked.

Camellia beamed back at Phillip. He almost forgot to keep dancing when he saw the look in her eyes. "Yes, and now he knows it finally happened."

Wyeth wasn't sure why he felt anxious about his brother, but he looked over Chrissy's shoulder to see if he was in the pavilion. "Chrissy, somethin's goin' on with Andy and Valerie. Can we get closer?"

"Of course. Is everything okay?"

"No," Wyeth blurted as Andy walked over to the stairs to leave. "Can you help? Ask him to dance. See if you can talk to him."

He intercepted Valerie and grasped her arm. She hesitated when he asked her to dance, but then she nodded. He led her to an open space on the crowded floor while he checked to see where Andy and Chrissy were.

Andy's eyes smoldered, and he was stiff as he let Chrissy pull him to a space near the railing. But she was elegant, vivacious, and irresistible. Wyeth saw him relax under her smile.

He turned his attention to Valerie, who seemed detached as she followed his lead. The warm, melancholic twangs of "Sleep Walk" were too leisurely for anything other than a slow dance, so he lightly set his hand on her waist and took her hand with his other one.

He glanced over at Chrissy again and noted Andy's hand on the waist of her satiny white bodice, just above the softly swishing lavender skirt. Chrissy tilted her head to hear Andy as he spoke near her ear, and her blonde hair swayed gently in the breeze.

With an effort, Wyeth looked away from her and down at Valerie. "What do you think of your first Island Summer Dance?"

"It's wonderful, Wyeth. It's been such a pleasure to visit Painter Place."

Wyeth raised his brows and tried to read her expression. She was evasive but composed. Had he imagined a quiver around her pink lipstick?

"I hope you'll spend a lot more time here, and I know Chrissy and Juliette do, too. Our adventure last night was a lot of fun!"

There—he saw it again. He hadn't imagined the tremble around her mouth. Yet, she seemed outwardly calm as she looked up. Not for the first time, he couldn't help noticing the anticipation she created with her smile. It lit up her eyes as if she was getting ready to say something interesting or make something fun happen.

"Yes, it's one of my best memories," she said. "I love this place, Wyeth. But I don't think I'll be invited back."

"Why not?"

"Because a guest tonight knew I had a serious boyfriend a few months before Andy came along, and she asked where he was. Previous relationships had never come up between me and Andy. When he made an issue about it because he thought I might be on the rebound, I told him the unfortunate circumstances. I was naïve and kissed a handsome jerk who talked about marriage and swept me off my feet. Then I caught him with a girl who was stayin' with him most of the time. I knew I would tell Andy eventually, but I wish I could've lived my dream here tonight at the Island Summer Dance."

Wyeth winced and drew a ragged breath. "Oh, I see," he said lamely. "He's upset?"

"It's a risk I took, Wyeth. I almost didn't see him again after the night he was with you and I found out who he was. Hardly anyone else would have minded about my past, though I admit, part of Andy's appeal for me is that I know he hasn't been romantic with anyone. He would never play games about a relationship. I respect his commitments, and more than anything I want to be his only one. I want his first real kiss."

She faltered. He saw tears well up in her eyes, and she rapidly mastered them as she blinked. "Andy's lookin' for a girl who's like him. I'm nothin' special."

Wyeth felt her shoulders quiver. His quick search for a comforting thing to say to her came up empty, and he hated trying to think on his feet.

Valerie glanced over at Chrissy and Andy and added, "I told him not to feel obligated to entertain me tonight. There are single guys here that I can dance with, and one's been lookin' at me. But that might make things worse. For the sake of our families, I may call it an early night and go back to my room."

"Will you give me a chance to talk to him? Maybe he and Chrissy can walk down to the pier with us. Andy acts like he's cool and smooth, but he—he feels things deeply, Valerie. The reason this matters so much to him is that you matter. You may not see yourself as special, but he does."

The song ended. Wyeth did not wait for her answer before leading her toward the stairs. Chrissy was watching him and tugged Andy's arm.

"Andy, the rules are about us. Our conduct, with women. Not necessarily about the women we date. If we meet the young lady we've prayed for, then we have to decide whether we can live with her past."

His brother leaned against the pier railing, looking out to the inky waves. "No, Wyeth, it's not that simple. A woman's convictions can't conflict with ours, because if we marry, we'll become the spiritual head of the family. We must be united in what we teach our children. Lots of other people probably compromise on that kind of thing, but not here. A woman would have to change her position to fit in at Painter Place."

Wyeth scowled at the dark water below. He rested his elbows on the railing.

With a shrug, his brother addressed the Atlantic Ocean. "I just expected—something different. I hoped I'd find someone who'd understand—someone who'd made the same commitment. It cost me a lot."

"But she made some of your commitments and kept the most important one. All she's given up was kissing before she was married, and you used to tell Dad he was overboard about that. You said a kiss was nothin' special, but she thought hers was. She thought her boyfriend would treasure it, and that they were on the road to a future together. She trusted where she shouldn't have, and someone betrayed her. If she could get that kiss back, you know she would."

He glanced over at the shadowy figures of Chrissy and Valerie as they talked on the opposite side of the pier. "She respected you enough to be honest. Can you start over again, from tonight? She's crushed that she's ruined her chance to be good enough for you. Remember the night she told you it might matter a lot that you're a Painter? She's pretty courageous to have weighed the risk of your rejection and decided that you were worth the pain."

He turned to study his brother's profile. "We've had a lot of fun this week, Andy. She's got such an irresistible smile, and she always looks like she's ready for adventure. She's a good sport about all the teasin' you dish out. Valerie's crazy about you, and to prove it, she's givin' you the dignity of walkin' away without drama. Just don't do that here, not tonight."

Andy stared out at the water, and Wyeth wondered what else he could say to help. He glanced around at other guests who lined the sides of the pier, and he prayed silently.

Then his brother stood straight. "I'll go talk to her."

Chrissy saw the two brothers approaching and stopped her conversation with Valerie. Andy said, "I'm sorry for the way I handled things tonight."

He put out his hand to Valerie. "Will you take a walk on the beach?"

Wyeth and Chrissy turned to the view of a rising moon that was cut short by the horizon. Strands of Chrissy's hair blew into her face and became trapped in her lipstick, and they both reached at the same time to set them free. Their hands bumped. They laughed and he lightly stroked her cheekbone.

"You have an artist's hands, Wyeth Painter."

"And you have a face that inspires a painting. What's a beauty like you doin' here with me?"

She parted her lips to tease back, but then paused at the look in his eyes. "You're serious."

He could only nod. He'd blurted what was in his heart. What had made him say something stupid and self-effacing like that?

"I have a long list of reasons for being here with you, but only one matters. Are you going to make me be the one to say it first?"

He caught the moonlight in her eyes and saw how it caressed her face with a subtle glow. It slowly dawned on him what she meant, and he swallowed a spike of panic.

She waited on him a few more moments. Then she sighed and pulled his face toward hers, and he froze. With a knowing smile, she tiptoed up to put her lips to his ear for an indescribably soft kiss.

Instantly, he wrapped both arms tightly around her and pressed his cheek to hers. "I'm in love with you, Chrissy Carnet."

"I know," she whispered, and lightly kissed his ear again. "You told me so in a painting."

Andy's grip on Valerie's hand was light as they skirted the foamy edges of surf that scalloped the beach. He'd been silent for so long she let go of hope and sorted through her rehearsals of how she'd remain dignified when he ended their relationship.

But she would not jump in and carry the conversation. He would own up to every word, every consequence of sending her away.

Another group of couples passed them and started banter with Andy, but they picked up on his subdued demeanor and hurried on. He slowed so they'd gain more distance as they moved ahead down the beach.

"Ow!" Valerie yelped, and she hopped on one bare foot.

Andy steadied her with a strong arm, then he looked down to find what she stepped on. "Let me see. Can you stand up now?"

Gingerly, she tested her weight on the injured foot and nodded. "Yes, I think it surprised me more than anything. I should look where I'm goin' but the sky is so splendid tonight. It's like—it's like an entire realm of splendor, you know? The kind in a fairytale. It goes deep upon deep, in layers of sparkling stars to wish upon, out into infinity, and the thought of it makes me feel gushy."

Andy burst out in a lusty laugh and she joined him. Then they couldn't stop, and while he was almost bent over holding his stomach, she had tears standing in her eyes and struggled to catch her breath.

When he could manage a few words, Andy said, "That's one reason I love you—you laugh so easily at yourself. You view the sky through a spirit of wonder, like Juliette, and you're not afraid to sound silly when you describe it. You don't take yourself seriously, so you're not easily offended. Here, let me make sure you're okay."

Still chuckling, he squatted down and reached for her foot, then brushed off sand as he squinted in the dim light. "I see a pink spot, but it's not cut. It could mean no more dancing tonight, but we'll make that call after you put your sandal back on."

Still holding her foot, he reached for a shell. Sand rained from it when he banged it against his thigh. "Ah-ha. A small whelk. That'll do it."

She missed the warmth of his hand after he put her foot down and stood up to show her the shell. "See here, it's broken, and it already had sharp edges and knobs, anyway."

Valerie put out a timid finger to explore the common shell. "Is the animal still in it? Maybe we should throw it back."

"No, this one is empty."

She sighed sympathetically for the creature. "I wonder if it died from having a broken home, or if the beautiful shell had no more value after the life in it had gone."

The surf swished and swirled. Waves curled and plunged back into an endless ocean. Music floated from the pavilion. And finally, Andy took her hand and placed the whelk into her palm.

"Valerie, I'll never be able to relate to what you've missed as you grew up in a broken home. I'll never know rejection from my father, or how much that might make me vulnerable to being misled by empty promises in a romantic relationship. But I can relate to wantin' to get physically closer to someone you care about. Remember, many men think of a kiss as consent to go further."

She searched his eyes in the shadow planes of his face under the moonlight, then she nodded. She looked down at the broken shell in her palm.

"Can I have it?" he asked, and she rolled it into his hand. With a swift movement, he threw it out to the waves.

"Don't hold onto the brokenness of your past, Valerie. My mom says brokenness is a blessing though it may take a lifetime to see it. We move forward if we're goin' to be of any value in the world. I won't ask about Eric, but if you ever want to talk about him, I'll listen. If you need someone to sound off to about your dad, I'll be there. If you want to leave your past behind and spend time with me to see if we have somethin' to build a future on, then I'm right here. But I don't want to waste any more time tonight talkin' about things we need to settle."

She looked up and smiled. "Does that mean we can still do our shag turn?"

"Only if your foot isn't hurting. Don't embarrass me."

"Okay. Andy, did you say you loved me?"

He sighed and reached out to take her hand. "Yes, I did."

Near the stairs to the dance floor, Chrissy grasped Wyeth's shoulder to empty sand from her sandals. He reached out his arm to steady her while she slid her shoe back on.

Then she turned at a light tap on her arm. Behind her, Valerie was also putting her sandals back on, and she gave Andy a nod. "I stepped on a broken whelk shell, but it's not botherin' me now," she told Chrissy. "Thank goodness, because it would be awful not to get to dance!"

While they chatted, Wyeth searched his younger brother's face. He felt a pang in his heart when he didn't see the teasing, happy-go-lucky guy he knew.

"The beach is so beautiful tonight!" Chrissy exclaimed as she and Valerie went side by side to the stairs. "But Wyeth says beach music will be next, and then some group dances like the Stroll. We need to mingle with guests. Walking in the surf alone with him is more fun and takes less skill."

"I know! I can stroll, but I don't do the shag turns well. Andy's a great dancer, so he knew how to adjust his move, and it works for us."

A young man strode up to Valerie's side and introduced himself. "I couldn't help noticing you when I arrived. Weren't you in town two weekends ago? If you're not with a date, will you dance with me?"

"Oh," Valerie uttered, taken aback as she looked up. "Well—I have a date, and he's the only one who can help me with the shag turns. I'm no good at those. But I'm flattered that you asked."

Her polite smile charmed him. He told her he hoped they'd meet again later, and he'd like to have her phone number.

Behind them, Wyeth and Andy paused, waiting on Valerie's admirer to finish. Wyeth raised a brow at Andy, but his brother calmly followed Valerie and Chrissy up to the floor.

The music changed to a rhythm and blues kind of beat and Chrissy looked up anxiously. Wyeth said, "Don't worry, it will be just like we practiced this week in the ballroom. Carolina Shag, remember?"

She furrowed her brows in concentration, following his lead. "Yes. Carolina Shag," she said uncertainly. "A six-count, eight-step pattern. We dance in a slot. Triple step, triple step, rock step. One-and-two, three and four, five-six. But Wyeth, the turns are tricky. You're so good at this, and I'm—" She followed him in a turn, and when they faced one another again, she looked astonished that she'd done it perfectly.

Side by side, Andy and Valerie passed their arms lightly over one another's waists in a shag step. Andy said coolly, "The stranger who wants to dance with you is paying more attention to us than to his partner. She's startin' to get annoyed."

Valerie pulled him closer than the next move called for and looked into his eyes. "I love you, Andy Painter. We're on the same page, and I'm not seein' anyone else unless you break us up."

He led her through their signature turn. Then he pulled her closer than the next move required. "Okay. You're my girl, I'm your guy. It's our time."

The cooing words about wanting to marry a girl and take her home filled the pavilion and thrilled shagging couples. The mayor and his wife danced close to Andy and Valerie. With a good-natured grin, the mayor quipped, "You young fellas are always tryin' to out-do your elders. You should have more respect. Where did you learn that new move?"

Andy played along. "Oh, you mean, that show-stoppin' turn? Yeah, that's somethin' new I learned recently. It's got some Georgetown attitude, and I'll be glad to show you how it's done in case you ever meet the mayor down there. This is Valerie."

"Hello, Valerie!" the mayor's wife said warmly, and they introduced themselves. "You must be from Georgetown. Welcome to Whitehaven and the Island Summer Dance! Hope you don't find us too backwards around here. You know how small towns are."

Phillip and Camellia made their way up to dance beside Andy and Wyeth and their dates. "Where have you two been? Everything okay?" Phillip asked. "Andy, I've never seen that turn before. Is it somethin' new, or did you make it up?"

Valerie burst out laughing and Andy grinned. "It's our signature turn. I call it 'Georgetown Attitude.'"

Chapter Twenty-One

It was a sultry afternoon in late August at Painter Place. Chrissy parked her Thunderbird under the oak that must have been ancient before the Painter mansion was built beside it three hundred years ago. Thick Spanish moss trailed from the branches like tears, and her heart felt as melancholy as the sight of the resilient old tree.

She sat for a moment in the shade. It was one of the few times Wyeth wasn't here to open her door as if nothing in the world mattered to him except that she'd arrived.

But he was in Charleston with Andy today, on some mysterious estate business. If they made it home tonight, it would be late.

She sighed wearily, pulled off her sunglasses, and turned to get her purse from the passenger seat. Juliette came bouncing out of the house and ran up to the driver's side door.

"Hello, sunbeam," Chrissy said brightly. "I missed you. Do you think you can help me with some luggage?"

"Sure, I can! Here, give me the keys. I missed you so much!"

She ran to unlock the trunk, chattering prettily about school beginning in a few days. They took Chrissy's things to the back door and into the sumptuous scents of the air-conditioned kitchen, where Maggie Jane promptly ordered them to put the bags down.

"I'll get someone to handle those. Ain't no job for a lady," Ida Mae said. Then she looked at Juliette. "Missy, you run along now. You have things to do for me, remember? And Miss Chrissy looks tired."

Juliette stopped short of pouting. Instead, she answered, "Yes, ma'am," which earned her one of Ida Mae's generous-sized cookies, fresh from the oven and wrapped in a napkin.

Ida Mae gently shooed Juliette away and turned to Chrissy. "You sit down here, now, and tell us how things went," she commanded, pointing to a kitchen stool near the massive worktable. Chrissy mutely obeyed. Ida Mae whisked a china dessert plate with two warm cookies and crystal goblet of lemonade in front of her.

"I shouldn't eat those," Chrissy lamented without conviction.

"Nonsense, they're calorie-free," quipped Maggie Jane. When her mother clucked under her breath and shook her head, she added, "Well, not exactly. But they aren't empty calories. You won't miss the ones we left out, and you won't guess what we used as flour."

Chrissy sighed and picked up a cookie. "I trust you to watch my figure."

Ida Mae snorted as she loaded up another baking sheet for the oven, and Maggie Jane smirked. "We ain't the only ones watchin' your figure, darlin', but Wyeth now, he ain't worried none about your weight."

The thought of Wyeth watching her figure brought an irrepressible grin to Chrissy's face. She picked up her napkin to wipe dewy condensation off the sides of her glass so she could sip the cold lemonade. "Well, you haven't gotten me fat yet. But after the stress of the job this week, gaining weight would be an excuse not to model anymore."

"What about the papers you went up to sign concerning your mama's affairs, at the lawyer's office?"

With a mournful look down at her dessert plate, Chrissy replied, "I know it's been a year since my world turned upside down at losing her. But settling everything was harder than I expected. It felt so—final. I know, it already was final, but—"

In an instant, her hands covered her mouth, and she squeezed her eyes closed. But with a sniff, she put them back into her lap. "And today, I took a cab by the house before I caught my plane. It was strange to see new draperies in the windows, and new plants by the front steps. That part of my life is over."

Wyeth leaned with his jean pockets against the weathered gray pier railing, one tennis shoe crossed over the other. Chrissy had fallen asleep on a blanket at the end of the pier. A rolled-up beach towel was under her head, and near one hand lay a fountain pen, a closed journal with a pretty ribbon marking her place, and a crumpled handkerchief.

When he'd arrived home, Maggie Jane stopped him and Andy at the door. She took the bouquet of sunflowers and daisies from his hands and put a plate in front of him. As she busied herself finding a vase, she assured him there was no hurry to run upstairs because Chrissy had gone to sit alone by the water after dinner.

With a quick blessing for the meal so Andy could eat, Wyeth remained standing at the table and asked Maggie Jane for her version of how Chrissy's week had been. He polished off a chicken biscuit while she gave him her observations in a nutshell. Chrissy was in a pensive mood and relieved to be back at Painter Place.

With a swipe at his mouth with a napkin, he turned to run upstairs to wash his face and change. Maggie Jane's voice behind him predicted he would be ravenous in an hour, and not to cry to her when he broke his neck running on the staircase like that.

There was time to finish dinner, after all. There was no need to risk breaking his neck. But if he had not rushed down to the pier, he would have missed watching Chrissy as she slept under the stars over his island. He wondered again if she was the answer to his prayers or just a dream.

The moon painted everything with silver and gave her blonde hair an aura of glowing light. The same breeze that gave him a slight chill made her stir on the blanket, and soon, she opened her eyes to meet his. A slow, luxurious smile spread over her face. "Hi," she whispered.

"Hi," he replied. "Tired?"

She shook her head, and he saw the cobwebs of dreams evaporate. "No. Not anymore. I could stay up all night, watching the sea and the sky. This is one of my favorite places."

"Want some company?"

"Only if it's you."

Wyeth grinned and settled himself beside her on the blanket. She propped up on her elbow, brushing her hair back with her hand. Then she reached for a light cotton sweater and sat up to pull it on. "Did you finish your business in Charleston?"

He helped her with her sweater and reached for her hand as it poked through the end of her sleeve. "Yes, and I rushed home in case you got here tonight. Rough week?"

She nodded, looking moodily out to the sea. "Grueling. But it's over now. I'm ready for a fresh start." Then she brightened and turned to him. "I missed seeing your new car in the driveway, and really missed having you welcome me when I parked mine."

"I truly hate it when you travel. Maggie Jane pronounced me a lost puppy and threatened to call animal control to come get me. I wish I could have been there with you for the lawyer's appointment."

"I wish you'd been able to travel with me, too. But remember, the agency had me in a room with two other models, and besides, we can't bring any distractions with us to a job."

"Distractions?" Wyeth tapped his palm to his heart, faking a traitorous wound. "After four months together, is that all I am?"

She bumped her shoulder against his, then she yelped as he snatched her into his arms. He nuzzled his nose into the soft place he loved under her ear.

With a breathy whisper that made her quiver as it tickled, he asked her to stand up. He rose and pulled her by both hands, then he let her go while he turned to pick something up from the corner of the blanket. She steadied herself and tidied her top and pants from the crumples they'd suffered during her nap.

Just as she was looking back up, Wyeth went down onto one knee in front of her. In his hands was a small open box, and a ring winked and shimmered like the starlight. "Chrissy, every day of my life is brighter since you came into it. I never dreamed love was like this, and I'll never get over you. Please spend the rest of your life with me, here, at Painter Place."

She could only gasp. "Wyeth!"

Pulling the ring from the box, he stood up again. He reached for her left hand, then held his breath as he tried it for size. It slid onto her finger, and he sighed with relief.

She stared at her hand. "I've never seen such a beautiful ring!"

"There's a matching wedding band. I'm terrified of losing it and you're much more responsible than I am. Will you marry me, so we can put them all on the same finger?"

With a cry of joy, she threw her arms around him. To hide his own stinging tears, he picked her up off the weathered board floor enough to twirl her around, as if they were dancing.

"This is my dream come true, and you are the love of my life!" she exclaimed as he set her back on her feet. "Of course, I'll marry you. I thought you'd never ask! I can't wait to be your wife."

"I wanted to see if you still felt the same way about me and Painter Place after the dust settled on your old life. It's better not to rush things, but ever since I decided to do this, it's been hard to hold on. A month ago, a jeweler helped me design this from some family heirloom engagement rings. It was ready for me to pick up today and I can't wait any longer."

She held her hand to the moonlight. "You designed it yourself?"

He put her hand against his, admiring the gleam of the diamonds. "Yes. My family often uses emerald cut diamonds for the main stone on engagement rings. They look like an artist's canvas that goes on forever into infinity. But I wanted to give you one made only for you."

"And the matched diamonds surrounding it look like a fabulous frame. Is there anything important about the three rows of diamonds for the band?"

"That's supposed to be the cord not easily broken, from scripture. One is the bride, one is the groom, and the middle one is Christ. The heirs to the mansion seem to choose that configuration, so I went with tradition."

She wrapped her arms around his waist and pressed her face against his shoulder. "Wyeth, it's perfect, and we're perfect together. I don't know why God has given me my dream, while others never get theirs. But I'll spend my life showing Him how grateful I am."

Wyeth squeezed her tight when he heard her voice catch. "Then you know how I feel. Have you finished the words to our song yet?"

She sniffed and pulled back to look up at him. "Yes, I think so. I'm saving them for a special occasion."

He laughed. "A proposal isn't a special enough occasion? I'm cut to the heart!"

Her eyes teased him. "It's special, but not enough. I'll sing our song to you on our wedding day."

He sobered. "Then let's set a date soon. The song is ready, and so am I."

A breeze sent their hair across their faces, and they turned toward the ocean to let it push those strands back in place. Wyeth followed her gaze up to the moon. "You still want to stay up and watch the sky over our island, or do you want to go to the Big House and share our news?"

Chrissy sighed contentedly. "I want to savor this night, right here, just me and you. Let's dream of a million moonlights together at Painter Place."

Andy's deck shoes tramped the new boards of the pier he'd built near the southern tip of the island, below the Gregory estate. It was finished last week, before the long Labor Day Weekend, and he had invited Valerie out to celebrate.

"It's impressive," she said. "Is it larger than the one at the Gregory's?"

"Yep, by a lot, for now. Mine's built under the latest hurricane codes, but a strong storm will take theirs out. I'm sure they'll rebuild larger after that, to the new materials and codes. They don't have time to mess with boats, so it's mostly there for entertaining. Someday, Wyeth wants to get a boat for all of us at Painter Place to use on weekends. He could dock it here."

"Will he name it after Chrissy?"

Andy turned a startled look her way. "Would you want me to buy a boat and name it after you?"

She laughed. "No! Boats are way too much work. I like to think I take no effort at all. Besides, the *Fair Weather* didn't live up to her promises."

They'd reached the end of the pier, where built-in benches lined the railing. "I'm sorry to disappoint you, my dear, but you take a lot of effort. I used to do anything I wanted with my extra time. Now, all I do is brainstorm how I can impress you."

He grabbed her waist and pretended to be throwing her over the side. "Let's see if you float!"

With a half-hearted scream, Valerie surprised him by clinging instead of resisting or trying to brace herself against the new railing. He stopped short before tumbling them both into the water below, then set her back on her feet. They stared at one another, panting from their struggle in the afternoon's heat. "Why didn't you try to stop me?"

"As long as I'm with you, I'll be okay," she gasped. "I'd rather go into danger with you than be safe by myself."

She let go of the back of his shirt so she could wipe sweat off her forehead, where it threatened to roll into her brows. "You're my life ring. If I hold on to you, I'll float."

Andy let her go, then used his arms to wipe sweat from his forehead and upper lip. "But if you'd pulled me in with you, I might have lost this in the current, and you can't imagine how upset my parents would be. The stones have been in the family for over two hundred years."

He reached into a pocket of his khaki shorts and brought out a sapphire blue velour bag. The silk drawstring was tied in a bow, which he nervously pulled open. When he'd shaken the item out onto his palm, he reached with the other to take her hand. "It's a life ring," he said solemnly. "Will you spend your life holdin' on to me?"

From the moment she'd seen Andy take the jeweler's bag from his pocket, Valerie stood motionless. Now, her eyes darted all over his face. "Andy—this is real? Not one of your jokes?"

He laughed. "Valerie, please tell me this doesn't look like a ring from a bubble gum machine. My dad has warned me for years that all my teasin' would catch up with me one day."

She tore her eyes from his face and stared down at the ring. He pushed it gently over her knuckle onto her finger, and she used her free hand to stifle a soft cry.

He wiped his brow again and got down on one knee in front of her. "Valerie Rush, please marry me. It's only been three months since we officially became a couple at the Island Summer Dance, but I can't imagine life without you. There's no reason to keep waiting. I love you, and I want to build you a house right over there, under the live oaks. Let's raise babies who take after you instead of payin' me back for all the ridiculous things I've ever done. If you'll just say yes, I promise, I'll try to spend my life makin' you glad you did."

A boat out in the waterway slowly glided past. A group of people started waving at them, then realized Andy was on his knee. With a round of cheers, they yelled, "Say yes!"

Andy stood up, looking expectantly at Valerie. "Yes," she whispered.

With a whoop, he held up her hand to the group on the boat, and it flashed in the sunshine. "She said yes!" he shouted.

More cheers and whoops erupted from the boat, and Andy grabbed Valerie up in an exultant hug. "Should the wedding be here?" he asked.

"No, every boat in town will show up! I want to get married in the chapel."

Phillip drove into Charleston with the top down on his Maserati on a Friday in mid-September. It was only about eighty degrees, but the humidity made him feel like it was one hundred. Still, it was better than the gales from Hurricane Donna a few days before. That storm spawned a tornado in the city and then barreled up to destroy fifty percent of Topsail Beach.

A news update came on about the murder investigation of Ad Coors, the beer company heir, whose body was found on September 11. Phillip parked his car but kept the radio on. Then he switched off the engine, rubbed his temples, and said a quick prayer for the family.

When he looked back up, there was so much on his mind. Would he be the next heir in the news updates? Would it be his sons? Did he need to live under security guards or trust the Lord for protection—or was a life with bodyguards the Lord's protection?

Two ladies walked by, fanning themselves in the heat and admiring his car. Even this weather wasn't preventing the mainstay of commerce on King Street, and he was getting ready to make a significant contribution.

Shoppers rushed into stores for the reprieve of fans and air conditioning, their minds on today's wants and needs. Life was going on for those whose time was not up yet, oblivious to daily dangers, lives and property lost in last week's hurricane, and murdered heirs. They didn't yet care how much Charleston would change with the construction of the new interstate into the city.

Life was short. No one knew what tomorrow would bring. He straightened his shoulders and stepped up the curb to the sidewalk. With sudden clarity and a renewed purpose, he marched quickly toward his air-conditioned destination.

On his way to the Heyward's mansion on Murray, Phillip passed the homes of many residents seeking the stir of a breeze on sprawling southern porches with "haint blue" ceilings. Camellia led him out to do the same, swaying on a porch swing overlooking the Ashley River, where they waited on dinner and listened to a transistor radio.

The scent of poet's jasmine and hydrangeas wafted through the air. The uplifting, dependable melody of church bells rang out around the "holy city." Phillip and Camellia leaned into soft cushions in the swing and shared the events of their week.

When the song "Misty" came on the small radio, they paused to listen. Camellia beamed when he squeezed her hand, and he joined her when she sang along. "Walk my way, and a thousand violins begin to play, or it might be the sound of your hello."

After dinner, Phillip asked her to walk with him down to White Point Gardens to watch the sunset. Along the way, she told him about her last letter from Jacqueline. Since getting married in a private ceremony at the Painter Chapel, she and Tom had settled into a small apartment near his campus and part time job. She'd found work as a receptionist at a doctor's office, the same one that would deliver their baby.

"Can you tell if she's content now, all things considered? Or is that a secret between girlfriends?" Phillip asked.

Camellia squeezed his arm. "It's not a secret. She's content and accepts the direction her life has gone. She sees Tom for what he is—just a guy tryin' to do the best he can after makin' mistakes. He couldn't live up to his reputation as the youth group hero, and she wasn't the perfect girlfriend. But they've been together a long time. Their love has endured, and they're excited about their baby."

Phillip led her slowly up the steps of the gazebo across from the guest house on the corner of Meeting and South Battery Streets. Few tourists or residents strolled the park tonight. They were getting children ready for early bedtimes and school days.

"Camellia," Phillip said softly, and she turned from the view of sails glowing in last light. "The only thing better than bein' with you here is bein' with you at Painter Place. The sooner you come and live there with me, the happier I'll be."

He took her left hand. "I'm like Tom. I'm just a guy, doin' the best I can. I can't promise you I won't make a mess of things sometimes. I can't promise that our lives will be perfect together, or that I won't lose everything. But if you'll love me enough to forgive me, respect me, and help me get back on track, I'll spend my life makin' you glad you did."

Wide-eyed, she breathed, "Phillip—"

"You're too good to be true, too beautiful to be real. And yet, you're strong, the kind of woman who knows life's not a bed of roses."

Still holding her left hand in his, he put his right hand into his pocket. In an instant, he fished out a ring that sparkled under the lanterns in the park. "Camellia Melody Heyward, I've loved you from the moment we met and danced here by this gazebo. I was a stranger in paradise that night, but not any longer. Like you said then, we don't believe in kismet, or fate. We believe in God's power to answer our prayers. I believe He answered mine when I met you, so there's no reason to keep waiting to see if this is right. Will you be my wife?"

Gulping, she could only nod while he slid the ring on her finger. "It's scandalous," she croaked.

He laughed. "That's what your friend Loretta in the jewelry store told me you'd say. But she said you'd love it."

"I do," she cried. "And I love you. Do you have a handkerchief?"

"She told me you'd need one of those, too," he said, reaching back into his pocket. "Besides, I couldn't conceal the ring box on me, so I wrapped the ring in the handkerchief."

"Why three diamonds?" she asked as she mopped up her eyes.

"For the three of us in our marriage. The center stone, which they call a radiant cut, is symbolic of Christ. The smaller single diamond on each side, surrounded by the loops of tiny matched diamonds, are each of us."

"Maybe the tiny diamonds are our children?"

He groaned and pulled her into a hug. "Does that mean you will?"

"Have that many children? Not likely. I can't count these diamonds."

He pulled back, grinning. "Will you wear this as a promise to marry me?"

"Only if you'll marry me in the Painter family chapel."

Chapter Twenty-Two

"We made it through Autumn without a hurricane to ruin the chapel or the island," murmured Phil Gregory as he leaned toward Noble Painter. "Now, if we can pull off that reception for a triple wedding at the pavilion, we can rest before we plan the holiday guest list and New Year's Eve dance."

"Where did the time go, Phil?" Noble's voice was nostalgic as he watched his sons having wedding portraits done outside the chapel doors. "And who'd have dreamed three of the boys would marry here on the same day?"

Phil sighed. "You know none of the boys would let the other be first. Now they need to have kids who grow up together."

"Phil?"

"Yeah?"

"You haven't forgotten my dream, right? If I'm not around to see it come true, you keep prayin."

Phil lightly slapped his friend on the back of his tuxedo. "I have your back. You have mine. If I have a grandchild who's the match for yours, we'll weld Painter Place together for good. Times will change, but if God's in this, it will happen."

They watched Wyeth and Chrissy take their place by a stained-glass window that framed Chrissy's simple, sleek white dress. Beside her, Wyeth was the perfect partner.

"They look like those newlyweds on the top of a wedding cake. Can you feel it, Phil? They're all happy. It's the best day of their lives. But my Wyeth, now—he's moved more deeply by his wedding. Before this summer, he didn't think this day would happen for him."

Phil waved at his wife, who gestured for them to join her. "Yes, I can see it. You always told him never to give up. Come on, Noble, we need to grin and bear it for the cameras."

"Yeah, I'm on my way," Noble said. He took one step, then paused. He felt it again, the same presence he'd felt when the pastor told Wyeth he could kiss his bride. But he didn't turn around to look at the open doors to the chapel until after he'd witnessed his oldest son's first kiss.

There was nothing unusual behind him then, but just the same, he found he couldn't shake it off. His eyes scanned the gardens around the chapel and then stopped.

The palm fronds and foliage hiding Weaver weren't so different from the Amazon jungle setting where Noble had first met him face to face. When he finished painting the *Jaguar*, they talked about this day. As long as Weaver lived, Noble knew he would never forget his promise.

No one else would know he had been here, and Noble couldn't mention it. But the face full of stories was there for Noble to read as his son had in London.

Noble nodded almost imperceptibly. The Weaver did the same. And just before he melted into a fountain spray of palm fronds, he mouthed two words.

"Thank you."

Epilogue

The Big House, February 1965

Two-year old Chad Gregory gingerly touched the hand of the newborn granddaughter in Noble Painter's arms. The baby opened eyes that were the same sea blue as Noble's, then her tiny fingers clenched his forefinger. He resisted jerking away in surprise and gazed into her eyes instead. She made quirky movements at the corners of her heart-shaped pink mouth, as if trying to smile, and the toddler was enchanted.

Noble said, "Chad Gregory, meet Caroline Amanda Painter. I think she likes you."

Chad giggled and leaned closer to the baby, who had a strong grip on his finger. "Her hair is light, like mine."

"And mine," piped in Patrick as he came to stand beside them. "Chad has a big sister. I have a little sister. Right, Poppy Noble?"

"That's right, Patrick," agreed his grandfather. The baby looked at Patrick, then yawned and closed her eyes. She released Chad's finger and sent a fist into the air before she rested her hand on the lacy white blanket that wrapped her like a cocoon.

Chad's eyes lingered on the sleeping baby. Patrick pulled his arm and said, "Come on, let's go play!"

But Chad looked back at the little girl, then up to meet Noble's smile. He turned when Patrick put a toy in his hands and urged him along.

Noble stood up and rocked the precious bundle in his arms while he walked to the library window. He turned his granddaughter toward a view of the Atlantic Ocean, then whispered her name. "Caroline. Caroline Amanda, look out the window. You are home."

She stirred. Her eyes dreamily glanced up to him, trying to focus, then went to the window. She stared for a few moments before meeting his eyes, and he was certain something passed between them.

Noble felt like he'd burst with love. And that wasn't all. He had that unsettling sense of certainty, of knowing. He looked around to be sure no one could hear when he whispered, "I think Jesus just gave me a promise about the future. Are you the one? Will you be the artist who bonds the Painters to the Gregory family?"

But Caroline had wandered back into whatever dreams babies had. He glanced over at the boys as they played and found little Chad watching them.

Noble smiled at him and then down at his granddaughter. He kissed the lock of white-blonde hair on her forehead. "That's right, baby girl. You sleep now. All will be well."

To Readers

Did you like this book? Please take a minute to write a rating or short review online with your favorite bookseller. The author really appreciates it!

Want more from the Painter Place Saga? Visit Southern Sky Publishing[1] to continue the story!

Be sure to check out the character list and the book club discussion questions. Also, feel free to visit the artist's website and social media links for updates, coloring pages, music, giveaways, and exciting newsletters!

<u>*YouTube Channel*</u>[2]

<u>*Southern Sky Publishing*</u>[3]

---

1.   *http://www.southernskypublishing.com*

2.   *https://d.docs.live.net/8e73d9acf85913cd/*

  Pamela%20Poole,%20Artist%20and%20Author

3.   *http://www.southernskypublishing.com*

Main Characters in Landmark, Painter Place Saga Book 4

Noble Painter – Noble is an artist and the patriarch of the Painter family. He is married to Savanna and has three children: Wyeth, Andrew, and Juliette. His parents and older brother are deceased: Samuel, Revanna, and his brother Richard.

Savanna Painter – Noble's wife. She is an author and speaker, and mother to Wyeth, Andrew, and Juliette.

Wyeth Painter – Artist and next heir to Painter Place. He is 22 years old and fresh out of college in Landmark. Due to a serious illness that almost took his life as an adolescent, Wyeth is not likely to have any children, and this is a blow to the lineage at Painter Place. The island and estate are inherited through the artists in each generation. Though he will be the heir that works to hold on to the legacy of the island, it will be his brother or sister who provide the next heir. Wyeth fears he will never marry.

Andy Painter – Wyeth's younger brother. He is 20 years old in Landmark. His dream is to live on the island, provide the next heir, and open his own marina someday in nearby Whitehaven.

Juliette Painter – Wyeth's little sister, a surprise addition to the family late in life for her parents. She is ten years old in 1960 and she aspires to be an actress someday.

Phil Gregory – Phil is the current patriarch of the Gregory Global financial empire, a family-owned business which is built upon with each generation. The Gregory family and the Painters have been bound together for almost 300 years by their escape from England and settlement on the island. Phil is married to Lucinda and has two sons, Phillip Jr. and Justin.

Lucinda Gregory – Phil Gregory's wife, mother to Phillip and Justin.

Montgomery Heyward – Charleston businessman married to Charlyn Heyward. He is father to Camellia, his only daughter.

Montgomery is the catalyst for the meeting between his daughter and a man he has picked out for her to marry, Phillip Gregory.

Charlyn Heyward – Montgomery Heyward's wife, mother to Camellia.

Camellia Heyward – A Charleston native, popular with a high society group in the city. She is 20 years old in Landmark and has a job as a junior interior decorator. Her parents want her to meet and marry Phillip Gregory.

Chrissy Carnet – (Pronounced car-nay) Young model and love interest of Wyeth Painter. She does not know her father, and her mother was assassinated by his enemies almost a year before she meets Wyeth. She is not aware that her father and Noble Painter arranged for her to meet the heir to Painter Place. Chrissy is 18 years old in Landmark. Her mother had a job in intelligence with the government and raised Chrissy to be mature for her age. She is trained in self-defense.

Valerie Rush – A church secretary in Georgetown, SC, between Painter Place and Charleston. Valerie is 20 years old and has a pottery studio. She meets Andy while visiting Whitehaven with friends, and neither of them knew one another's last names. It turns out to be important, since her eligibility to marry into the Painter family is threatened by her estranged father's notorious reputation as a womanizer.

Audrey Rush – Valerie's mother, estranged wife of Dr. Anthony Rush, a heart surgeon in Charleston, SC

Dante Kent – British artist and friend of Wyeth Painter. He is generational steward to Seamure, an estate with similarities to Painter Place and which has ancient castle ruins on the grounds. This is important in Painter Place and Hugo.

Maggie Jane Simmons – Young lady who grew up at Painter Place. She is the daughter of the chef and housekeeping manager on the island, Ida Mae. Her father was Big Jim Simmons, the deceased former handyman on the island. Maggie Jane's fiancé, Roy, was killed in Vietnam a few months before Landmark takes place.

Ida Mae Simmons – Head chef and housekeeping manager in the Big House at Painter Place. The family considers her to be in charge, and she considers them her responsibility. Her family has always worked at the island. She married Big Jim Simmons, a hobo/evangelist who came to the island seeking work and help when he was sick.

Beneath the Surface
Discussion Topics for Book Clubs

*White Island, known by the locals as Painter Place, is a fictional setting in South Carolina. It is between Myrtle Beach and Charleston. In the Painter Place Saga, the island represents faith and family in our lives and is connected by a bridge to the mainland. Have you considered the ideals and faith of your family, and are those things worth the extra personal cost as you struggle to uphold them "across the bridge," out in a world that doesn't like them?

*In the novel Landmark, the fourth story in the Painter Place Saga (but first chronologically), readers learn the origins of the first settler to the island and what motivates the generations who come after him. This theme is found in the pages of the Old Testament of the Holy Bible. History records that some biblical heroes used by the Lord for miraculous deliverance set up stones as a testimony to the awesome power and grace of God. Despite the charge to future generations to remember what these landmarks meant, the pages of scripture fill us with dismay as the next generations seemed oblivious to the testimony of their elders and the landmarks. Yet there is always a remnant who heeds the past. Are you setting up any "landmarks" of testimony for your children and grandchildren and praying for future generations?

*Do you have ancestors who passed along their testimonies, character, reputation, and faith to you? Have you been intentional about leaving a spiritual legacy for your children?

*The "Billy Graham Rule" was in the political news recently. The evangelist and his trusted team held one another accountable to never be alone with a woman other than their wives. This is such a common-sense way to behave and is a vital key in the lives of the men and women at Painter Place. Not only will this help the characters avoid temptation, it helps them avoid accusations and lawsuits. What are you doing to protect yourself and your children from attack and slander?

*There are inescapable consequences for our actions, for ourselves and everyone around us. In Landmark, Camellia reminds her friend Jacqueline that nothing we do is our own business. Have you considered the collateral damage that bad choices have on your family, friends, and career, or do you consider that to be your privilege?

   *Read the Author's Notes in the beginning of this book. The decade between 1950-1960 has become iconic to America's dating culture, when norms in morality and common sense were overturned in freedom that couples in no other country modeled. Few countries had dating practices. Influences like Hollywood, the privacy of cars and theaters, and new music styles dictated how American teenagers viewed life. Yet it was only the start for a cultural upheaval that followed in the next decade. Is sexual purity important to you, and why? What do you think dating practices should be? Do you try to influence your children, grandchildren, and friends to use wisdom and restraint in dating relationships, or are you afraid of sounding old-fashioned?

   *Do you know what you believe about who Jesus is? Are you prepared to express this to others if the opportunity arises?

Acknowledgements

Only those involved in creating a novel can appreciate the effort and teamwork that go into it. My faithful friends and beta readers have been a vital part of polishing this diamond in the rough. Their critiques gave me the confidence to be myself as an author, without regard to opinions about what modern readers like or how quickly they rush on to another book. Nothing I can do will create the "perfect" book for every reader's taste! Michelle Castro, Christin McCall, Diana O'Neal, Ann Felty, Karen Summey, and Amanda Doss, I hope you will consider this finished product as part of your own accomplishment.

My son Andy is ever an encourager for me to write the kind of books I want to read. My husband, Mark, makes loving sacrifices so I can pursue my calling as an artist and author. And my friends are faithful with their prayers, support, and encouragement. May the Lord multiply back to all of you the blessings you've given me!

Meet the Author

Pamela Poole writes inspirational mystery and suspense that explore the intersection of faith, history, and the unseen spiritual realm. Her stories are grounded in a clear Christian worldview and shaped by a deep respect for both historical preservation and biblical truth. Pamela writes inspirational stories that bring together Christian faith, historic places, and hidden truths. Her novels reveal how the past can press into the present, where faith becomes essential to discernment and courage. Her characters are ordinary people facing extraordinary challenges, learning to trust Jesus when darkness threatens and answers are not easily found.

Pamela is the author of the Strange Sands Suspense series and the Painter Place Saga, blending richly detailed settings with themes of calling, obedience, redemption, and spiritual warfare. Her fiction offers clean, thought-provoking suspense designed both to engage the imagination and to encourage the heart.

When she isn't writing, Pamela enjoys research, painting in her art studio and on location along the Southern coast and making memories with her family and friends.

Readers and art enthusiasts alike can enjoy her YouTube channel[4] for painting demos and art education presentations. To enjoy the latest content, sign up for her fun-filled newsletters and follow Pamela Poole Fine Art[5] and Southern Sky Publishing[6].

---

4. https://www.youtube.com/channel/UC9aV3zHRlASXUUBEF7xbT9Q

5. https://www.pamelapoole.com/

6. https://www.southernskypublishing.com/

Books in the Painter Place Saga
Novels
Painter Place, Painter Place Saga 1
Hugo, Painter Place Saga 2
Jaguar, Painter Place Saga 3
Landmark, Painter Place Saga 4

Legends (Short Stories)
Wind Songs of the Marsh, Painter Place Saga Legend 1
King's Ransom, Painter Place Saga Legend 2
The Castaway and the Mermaid, Painter Place Saga Legend 3

Devotional
Inspired Artistry – Embracing the Creative Calling

The Strange Sands Suspense Novella Series

The *Strange Sands Suspense* series follows architectural historian Mercedes Annalee Ellison as she investigates historic properties along the South Carolina coast—only to discover that the past often carries spiritual consequences into the present. Routine preservation projects quickly become encounters with hidden passages, ancient vendettas, and unsettling artifacts tied to the unseen realm.

Rooted in a clear Christian worldview, each faith-filled novella blends mystery, suspense, and spiritual warfare with themes of obedience, calling, and trust in God. Clean, gripping, and thought-provoking, *Strange Sands Suspense* is perfect for readers who enjoy inspirational suspense where light confronts darkness and faith makes the difference.

The Old Cedar Chest, Strange Sands Suspense 1, Hilton Head, SC
The Hidden Hallway, Strange Sands Suspense 2, Savannah, GA
The Freedom Staircase, Strange Sands Suspense 3, Charleston, SC
The Dark Passage, Strange Sands Suspense 4, Bluffton, SC
The Devil's Drawer, Strange Sands Suspense 5, Beaufort, SC
Book 6 is coming in 2026! St. Augustine, FL

Accolades for the *Painter Place Saga*

Painter Place, Painter Place Saga 1
"If you are looking for a well written, CLEAN, sweet romance with a good story-line included this is for you! Would I recommend this book? ABSOLUTELY!"
-Liz, Top 100 Reviewer

Hugo, Painter Place Saga 2
"Another tremendous read by this author Pamela Poole. Book 2 in the Painter Place Saga doesn't disappoint as we remember the category 4 hurricane that came in with a vengeance in South Carolina. Continuing with family drama we are captured with the lives of Painter and Gregory families. I highly recommend reading this saga. You'll never want it to end."
-Gingy, Reader Review

Jaguar, Painter Place Saga 3
"This is the first book I've read from Pamela and the first I've read in the Painter Place Saga. Whew, there were things in this book that just left me speechless they were SO good!!!"
-ASC Book Reviews